SHADES OF WRATH

"How did Wendy die?" Caprice asked.

"The work crew found her," Brett said. "The word's going to get out soon enough. That balustrade that looked down over the foyer gave way. She fell and broke her neck."

"Wendy warned me about that balustrade, and she was smart enough not to go anywhere near it herself. What aren't you telling me? Is there something else that makes you think this is more than an accident?"

Again he stopped, hesitated and cut her a probing glance. "It wasn't an accident. On preliminary examination, the coroner thinks someone hit Wendy Newcomb on the side of her head, possibly with one or more of those rolled-up window shades, and that's probably why she fell . . ."

Shades of
Wrath

Karen Rose
Smith

KENSINGTON PUBLISHING CORP.
http://www.kensingtonbooks.com

KENSINGTON BOOKS are published by

Kensington Publishing Corp.
119 West 40th Street
New York, NY 10018

ISBN-13: 978-1-61773-774-9
ISBN-10: 1-61773-774-7
First Kensington Mass Market Edition: December 2016

eISBN-13: 978-1-61773-775-6
eISBN-10: 1-61773-775-5
First Kensington Electronic Edition: December 2016

10 9 8 7 6 5 4 3 2 1

Printed in the United States of America

For women who have faced domestic violence.

In memory of Sunnybud, a stray yellow tabby
I cared for and loved deeply for three years.
He had an independent spirit
that wouldn't let him be confined.
But he gave me his trust and affection
and I cherish my memories with him.

Acknowledgments

I would like to thank Officer Greg Berry, my law enforcement consultant, who so patiently answers all my questions. His input is invaluable.

Chapter One

The mansion that stood before Caprice De Luca was a bit rundown but still magnificent. As an early September breeze tossed her long dark brown hair, as well as the leaves around her feet, Caprice remembered that the Tudor revival had hit America during the 1920s and 1930s when this edifice had been built. It was a monstrous home, yet charming, too, because of the steeply pitched roof with prominent cross gables. Those gables were embellished with half-timbering against stucco walls. Decorative chimney pots topped the thick brick chimney.

End-of-the-day light flickered against the tall windows arranged in groups of three. Each had diamond-shaped panes that reflected the sunlight. As a home stager, Caprice considered how light shone into a room. However, she wouldn't be looking at this house to stage it to sell. She'd be planning how to furnish and decorate it.

Caprice ascended the front steps, passing under the arched portico that supported a room above it. She couldn't wait to see the inside. Wendy Newcomb had said she'd be waiting for her.

This estate had been donated to Sunrise Tomorrow, a cause that had been a passion of Wendy Newcomb's since she'd established a foundation for the women's shelter in Kismet about a decade ago. She ate and slept her work, advocating for and caring for women who were victims of domestic violence. Caprice was here today to take a look at the mansion and propose ideas for decorating it so that it was suitable for a housing facility for women who were in need of transitional care. She was going to make their rooms feel like places they'd want to spend time.

The heavy, wood-paneled door stood slightly open. Before Caprice understood what was happening, a yellow tabby cat ran up the steps and slipped inside. Did the Wyatt estate have a resident feline?

Caprice pushed the door open wider, but it took an effort. Maybe the hinges were just warped . . . or maybe that door was meant to be a barricade. Instantly, she was in awe of the Carrara marble floor in the grand foyer and the spacious living room before her. She'd started across the foyer when she heard angry voices near the wide, curved stairway that led to the second floor. Since the mansion was practically empty, except for sawhorses, ladders, and building supplies, she could hear some of what was being said across the room.

A man's voice rose and carried all the way to the foyer. "Where is she?" he demanded.

Caprice recognized Wendy's voice, lower than his. She couldn't catch every word. From what she knew of Wendy, the director of Sunrise Tomorrow was trying to remain calm and serene in the face of an angry male.

Whatever explanation Wendy gave didn't seem to satisfy the man, and now Caprice recognized his voice too. It belonged to Warren Shaeffer, CEO of Kismet's Millennium Printing and the president of the town's Chamber of Commerce. He didn't fly off the handle easily. Stoic was usually his middle name. Apparently not today.

Moving closer to the stairway, Caprice saw Warren point his finger at Wendy. "You have no right to interfere."

Unsure exactly what to do, Caprice continued to approach them. She could see Wendy was red-faced. Oblivious to a third party, Wendy poked Warren Shaeffer in the chest and determined in a clipped voice. "I don't need to tell you anything. You'd better leave before I call the police. I don't think you'd want the general public to know that you can't hold your temper."

Suddenly Shaeffer shifted on his feet and spotted Caprice. He seemed to take a breath, rein in his anger, intentionally relax his shoulders, and act as if this interchange with Wendy was no big deal.

Caprice was almost at Wendy's side now as he made a nonchalantly composed remark that she didn't expect. "I'll look forward to seeing both of you at the next Chamber of Commerce meeting." With a forced smile at Caprice, he hurried to the front door and exited the house.

Wendy looked so relieved as he left. She pasted on a smile just as forced as his had been and pretended as if her conversation with him hadn't affected her at all. "That was an unexpected meeting," she apologized. "Come on, let me show you around. The workmen have left for the day."

It was obvious Wendy didn't want to talk about the encounter that had just happened. But as she walked beside Caprice and led her up the stairs, Caprice could see the woman's hands were shaking a little. A result of stress . . . her position . . . the legacy of the Wyatt estate? Or because of Warren Shaeffer?

Caprice had never seen him lose his temper. As head of the Chamber of Commerce, she had watched him remain cool over many a heated discussion. However, those discussions hadn't been personal. Today's discussion with Wendy had sounded very personal.

The stairs led to a second-floor hallway. As they reached the second-floor landing, Caprice could see a balustrade that stretched from one side of the hall to the other. It overlooked the spacious foyer.

She could smell the dust in the air, spotted sawhorses down the hall and drop cloths in the first bedroom. Roller window shades, perhaps collected from the upstairs rooms, lay in a stack near the balustrade. Sitting next to the pile of shades was a yellow tabby blinking at her with jewel-like green eyes.

Caprice started toward the wooden railing, intending to get closer to the cat.

Wendy caught her arm. "Oh, no! Don't go there. The balusters aren't stable. I told the contractor he should put a warning sawhorse there or something, but he hasn't. I'll remind him again tomorrow."

Caprice glanced down at the pile of shades, with their scalloped edge and fringes and wooden bar across the front for lowering and raising the window covering. They were yellowed and looked as old as the house. Then she again studied the feline.

"Are you friendly?" she asked him.

As if in answer, he stretched and came to her, rubbing against her retro plaid slacks with an insert side pleat that ran from knee to ankle. Retro fashion was one of her passions. Cats and dogs were another.

She crouched down and offered him her hand. He butted his head against it.

"He's very friendly," Wendy said. "I found him curled up in one of the bedrooms upstairs when nights began turning colder. I've been here almost every day to check on something, so I feed him wet food, then leave a bowl of dry in the bedroom upstairs. I've named him Sunnybud. I think he slips in through a broken basement window when the door isn't open. He doesn't seem to mind the workers who are in and out."

The tabby purred as Caprice petted him. Then suddenly he left her, crossing to sit once more beside the pile of window shades.

Wendy motioned to the rest of the upstairs and began walking. Caprice glanced over her shoulder at the tabby who seemed content where he was.

As they walked down the hall, she asked Wendy, "Is most of the work here cosmetic, or are there structural issues?"

"Fortunately, inside the house, most of the work is cosmetic—steaming off wallpaper, patch plastering, painting, modernizing a few of the bathrooms. We also have to add a new roof. I don't want any problems in the next few years with leakage. But all in all, the mansion is in amazingly good shape. Houses were built to last in the 1920s. This one had a grand past with good upkeep until the last dozen years or so. When Leona got sick, everything seemed to be a burden, even lifting the phone to call a plumber."

Leona Wyatt had faced a battle with cancer. Scuttlebutt had it she thought she'd won after her first bout with it. But eight years later it had come roaring back and had taken her.

"She had children, didn't she? Couldn't they help her?"

A look passed over Wendy's face that Caprice couldn't quite decipher. But then Caprice learned its meaning—disgust. Wendy said, "Her son and daughter didn't pay much attention to her, even when she was sick. They were no help at all."

Caprice wondered if that was why Leona Wyatt had left her son and daughter money in trust, yet left the mansion and the rest of her money to Sunrise Tomorrow. She'd heard the Wyatt siblings were squabbling over the fact they felt they should have received the legacy left to the Sunrise Tomorrow Foundation. However, there had been a stipulation in Leona's will that if they contested it, they would receive nothing. The Wyatt estate had been through probate and settled without incident. Apparently the brother and sister hadn't wanted to take a chance on contesting the will and losing . . . or spending years in court awaiting a decision.

Caprice followed Wendy from room to room, snapping photos on her phone, loving a peek into the house that had to be filled with memories of days gone by. They chatted about goings-on in Kismet as they walked. When they finished on the second floor, they descended the back stairs into the kitchen area where a brick fireplace stretched from floor to ceiling in the sitting area. A butler's pantry and maid's suite were located behind the kitchen. Caprice noted the utility room was almost as large as her living room.

Wendy explained, "I want to uphold the original grandeur of the house, yet I want it to be homey too. Does that make sense?"

"Perfect sense. You said this would be a transitional facility. Just what does that mean?"

An old-time deacon's bench still sat in one corner of the kitchen. Wendy motioned to it, and they both took a seat there.

"Most of the women who come to Sunrise Tomorrow need a port in a storm for a couple of nights until they find shelter with a friend or a family member," Wendy explained. "Once they've left their immediate situation, obtained a PFA—Protect from Abuse order—most are involved in programs such as counseling and job training."

She shifted a bit on the bench. "But some women need a haven for longer than a few nights. Before the Wyatt legacy came through, I'd encouraged the board of the foundation to consider buying some sort of apartment building to house women in those circumstances. Now the Wyatt estate will be perfect for that. Clients can stay a month or two or three, do job training onsite, pick up skills they need, as well as gain self-confidence and independence. Our main facility will be what it still is—an emergency haven with services for follow-up. But this place? This place can be so much more. I'm excited about it, Caprice, because we can help so many more women."

Caprice waited a beat, but then asked, "Do you want to talk about what happened earlier . . . when I first arrived?"

Wendy stared into the empty fireplace, soot-stained from years of use. "I can't talk about most of it, you know that. Although I'm not a therapist, the work I do is confidential. It has to be."

Wendy said that last with such vehemence Caprice studied the woman's face. There were lines around her eyes and around her mouth. Her nose looked as if it might have been broken. Strands of gray salted her medium brown hair. Caprice didn't know Wendy's story. Nobody did, as far as she knew. And that was a feat to keep background a secret in a town the size of Kismet. On the other hand, Wendy's present-day life seemed to be an open book. She lived with her significant other, Sebastian Thompson, and his two sons. But her past was a blank slate on the gossip mill.

"I know you have to keep confidences," Caprice agreed. "But that discussion I walked in on concerned you, too, didn't it?"

After hesitating, Wendy admitted, "It did. And I'll confess Warren Shaeffer scares me. He has one of those Jekyll-Hyde personalities. Only those closest to him see the Mr. Hyde side."

No, Wendy couldn't break any confidences, but what she was implying was that Warren's wife had probably sought services at the shelter. His question, *Where is she?* could mean that Wendy had helped his wife relocate somewhere else, at least for now.

Obviously wanting this discussion to be over, Wendy stood. "Let me show you the rest of the house. I have a meeting in half an hour, but we can finish touring the inside anyway. You can explore the grounds when you come to actually do the decorating. I'm going to trust you with the furnishings for most of it. I think you understand what I want. But after you turn your proposal in, I'd like to discuss updating our original quarters. Do you have time to fit that into your schedule too?"

Furnishing and decorating the Wyatt estate and updating the original Sunrise Tomorrow facility could bring in substantial income. She'd fit it into her schedule somehow.

"I'd be glad to talk about updating. When would you like to do that?"

"Why don't we keep that less formal? Why don't you come to dinner on Saturday with me and Sebastian and the boys?"

Caprice didn't know how long Wendy had been living with architect Sebastian Thompson and his sons, but it sounded as if they'd formed a family.

"I'd like that. Where do you live?"

"We live in the Poplar Grove Co-housing Development. Do you know where that is?"

Although Caprice wasn't exactly sure what co-housing meant, she'd passed the Poplar Grove development on occasion. It was located east of town.

"I've never visited the development itself, but I've gotten a glimpse of it when I visited Ace Richland's estate."

"That's right, you helped him out of a sticky situation not so long ago."

Last spring, Ace—a rock star legend—had found himself a suspect in a murder investigation, and Caprice had indeed helped clear his name. Treating that lightly, however, she responded, "Ace and I have gotten to know each other since he bought the house I staged."

"He's on tour now, isn't he?"

"He's zigzagging across the country. He returns every couple of weeks to spend time with his daughter."

"The way it should be," Wendy said. "Sebastian complains he wants to spend time with his boys, but they don't want to spend time with him anymore. You have to take advantage of bonding time while you can."

"I'd like to find out more about co-housing."

"Basically, it's cooperative living. We're not self-sustaining like many co-housing communities, but we help out each other when we can. I'm sure Sebastian can tell you all about it. He's the one who developed the mission statement."

"I look forward to it," Caprice said.

As Wendy walked Caprice out of the kitchen into a smaller dining room and then a much larger one, Caprice began envisioning the colors she would use to warm up the house as well as the groupings of furniture she'd select that would invite conversation. This project could easily consume her.

She smiled to herself. It was exactly the kind of project she liked best.

Caprice would have loved to have taken her dog, Lady, along to the Wyatt estate, but she hadn't known what she'd find there. She also hadn't known whether Wendy liked dogs or not. So she'd asked her neighbor Dulcina if she'd watch Lady while she took care of business. Now as she climbed the steps onto Dulcina's porch, she couldn't help thinking about Warren Shaeffer and his anger toward Wendy . . . and Wendy's obvious fear.

However, when Dulcina opened the door, Caprice forgot about her experience at the Wyatt estate. Halo, the tortoiseshell stray cat who'd been pregnant when Dulcina had adopted her in July, wound around her legs. Halo's seven-week-old tortie kitten, Miss Paddington, and Caprice's cocker, Lady, chased each other through the living room.

Caprice couldn't help but laugh. "How do you get any work done?"

"They were all napping until about fifteen minutes ago. Then Paddy decided she wanted crunchies and the gang all woke up."

Mason and Tia, Halo's other two kittens, now came racing into the living room too. Halo was a silver-haired tortie with tabby-like stripes and golden spots of coloring. Her firstborn was Miss Paddington, who had a unique tortoiseshell split-color face—tan and gold on one side and dark brown on the other. Her body was likewise defined. Mason, a gray-striped tabby with a white chest, was the boy in the bunch, and as rowdy as could be. Tia, third-born, had fur that displayed striking tortoiseshell colors and lots of white. A princess, she usually held herself above the fray. But not this evening. They were all joining in.

Caprice stepped inside, careful to watch the screen door so no fur babies escaped.

"Coffee?" Dulcina asked.

"Sure. I have time."

The kittens and Lady continued their chase, but Halo followed Caprice into the kitchen. She was becoming quite attached to humans. No one knew her whole story. Caprice's Uncle Dom had found her when he was pet-sitting for a client. Caprice had captured her and taken her to her veterinarian, who surmised Halo had been in an accident. She had a slight limp and he suspected a broken bone had healed. Dulcina had decided to take in Halo, even though she'd been pregnant. The birth of the kittens had been a joy to watch and experience. They were seven weeks old now, and Caprice had some good news for Dulcina.

As Dulcina set to brew two mugs of coffee in her single-cup brewer, Caprice asked, "So, do you think Tia and Mason are ready for their forever homes?"

"If I can find good ones," Dulcina answered, sounding worried. "A couple of people have asked me about them, but I just didn't feel they were right. Not real cat lovers, know what I mean? I almost feel like I have to do background checks and home studies."

Caprice laughed. "They've been your babies as well as Halo's since they were born. Of course you're invested in their welfare. But I might have a solution."

"You know two cat lovers?"

"I know one cat lover, and wouldn't it be good to keep Mason and Tia together?"

"It would! Who do you have in mind?"

"My Uncle Dom. He's living in his own place now, and he'd like to adopt the kittens. He does bookwork at home for a few clients, and when he pet-sits, the two of them could keep each other company."

"Doesn't he housesit too? What would happen during those times?"

"He's already thought of that. I told him I'd bring them to my place."

"Wouldn't that be a riot with your two cats and Lady? I suppose I could bring them back here too."

"I know he'd love Tia and Mason and care for them as if they were his kids. But it's your decision to make. Don't feel pressured because I suggested it."

"Before I make any decision, he should meet them. I'd like to see him interact with them. Do you think he'd come over for a visit?"

"I'm sure of it."

Dulcina and her uncle had met in the summer when they'd all attended an Ace Richland concert together. In fact, Dulcina had been dating then. But she'd broken up with Rod.

One of the mugs had finished brewing and Dulcina set it in front of Caprice at the table. "Pumpkin spice."

Caprice took a whiff and smiled. "Perfect for this time of year."

As Dulcina watched her mug of coffee brew, Caprice asked, "How are you doing?"

"Thank goodness I have the kittens," she said as the three balls of fur ran into the kitchen and tumbled over the cat bed Dulcina had tucked under the desk area of the counter. "Between work and them, I don't think about much."

"Have you talked to Rod since your breakup?"

"No, there's no point. His girls were having a hard time accepting me dating their dad, and he was doing nothing to make the transition easier. Yes, they come first. But if I was going to interact with them, and we would eventually try to make a family, he needed to include me in their family life. He wasn't doing that. He wouldn't even discuss it."

"The concert didn't help as it should have."

"No, it didn't. His older daughter, Leslie, had her mind closed to Ace's music even before we attended the concert. I think Vanna and I could have become friends, but Rod prevented us from trying. Even when they came over to visit the kittens, he wouldn't let Vanna stay a little bit longer even though she wanted to. He could have left her here while he took Leslie to her activity, but he wouldn't do it. That was the final straw for me. I understand his wife walked out on him, and he has trouble trusting women. But with that huge issue between us, we couldn't form a real relationship."

"Were you ready for one?"

"I thought I was. But my marriage to Johnny was unforgettably right. I'm just afraid I'll never have my expectations met again. How are you and Grant doing? I know you had a rough patch this summer when he saw his ex-wife."

"He needed to do that." Caprice was sure of it now,

even though at the time she hadn't been. "He and Naomi lost a child. That's something both of them will deal with for the rest of their lives. He's been sharing more with me about what they talked about and what he felt, and we're becoming closer every day. I love him, Dulcina. I'm all in."

She'd known Grant Weatherford, her brother's law partner, since he and her brother were college roommates. Divorce and tragedy had brought Grant to Kismet to find a new life and join her brother in his practice. She and Grant had had their ups and downs, but he was now the love of her life.

Dulcina nodded. "That's the way it should be if your relationship is going to last."

Mason chased Tia over to Caprice's chair; then he climbed up her pant leg and ended up on her knee, looking up at her.

"You're just too adorable and you know it," Caprice told him.

He meowed at her, a squeaky little meow that he was growing into.

Dulcina just shook her head. "They make me laugh and they fill me with joy. Just call me or text me when your uncle wants to visit. You know me. I'm flexible."

Caprice liked to think she was too. "I'll check with Uncle Dom and see when he's free. I know he's anxious to make his new place a home."

For some reason, Caprice's mind wandered once more to the Wyatt estate. Had that mansion ever really been a home? Her objective would be to turn it into one for women who sorely needed a place of warmth and stability.

* * *

On Thursday morning, Caprice stood at the door to Sunrise Tomorrow, the original facility. Wendy had received her proposal for decorating the Wyatt estate and had a few questions that she wanted to talk over in person. Caprice said her name through the intercom and waved at the camera. She recognized the security camera setup as one that accompanied her own alarm system. The shelter had to be careful whom they let through its door. Caprice did, too, when she was involved with solving a murder. Not so long ago, danger had come calling.

Wendy opened the door herself, wearing a smile. "Come on in. We can talk in my office."

The original facility for Sunrise Tomorrow was very different from what Wendy wanted to accomplish at the Wyatt estate. This building had once been an assisted living facility that had gone bankrupt. Wendy had rounded up a group of investors and taken on the challenge of turning it into a shelter with rooms where women could spend the night. An office area had been utilized for day-to-day administration. Caprice walked through a small reception area and around a large desk where a receptionist sat to monitor not only who came in and out, but what was going on inside too. The inside of the shelter could use a little polishing. The furniture was looking shabby. But she wasn't here to talk about that today.

She suddenly stopped as she spotted a woman who came from a back hall and walked through the reception area to the other wing. Caprice recognized her. Alicia Donnehy . . . and she was carrying a stack of what looked like just-washed laundry.

As if her high school classmate could feel Caprice's eyes on her, Alicia stopped and glanced over her shoulder. She didn't wave or say hello. A shuttered look came across her face and she turned toward the direction where she'd been headed and continued walking.

Alicia had been on the committee with Caprice to plan their high school reunion in July. What was she doing here? She was carrying laundry. Did that mean she was a volunteer? If so, why?

Caprice's curiosity had gotten her into a lot of trouble . . . from childhood to the present day. She'd always asked questions that had baffled her teachers, stumped her priest, and amused her parents. Now the implications behind seeing Alicia here were serious.

Caprice hurried to catch up with Wendy and noticed a woman rifling through Wendy's file cabinet. She turned when Caprice and Wendy stepped inside.

Wendy said, "Lizbeth, this is Caprice De Luca. Caprice, this is Lizbeth Diviney. She's my second-in-command and can answer questions when I'm not around. She's going to be the director of the new facility once it's up and running."

Lizbeth was a redhead with a pixie hairstyle. She was only five foot two and as slender as Caprice would like to be. In a quick movement, Lizbeth pulled a folder and shut the file drawer. Then she shook Caprice's hand. "It's great to meet you. I've heard good things about your work."

She waved the folder at Wendy. "I'll get right on this." In the next moment, she was gone from the office.

"She's high energy," Wendy said with a smile, and motioned Caprice to a chair.

Wendy's desk held stacks of papers, but otherwise the space looked feminine with its flowered chairs and pin-striped wallpaper. Wendy didn't waste any time.

"Your proposal makes a lot of sense to me and I agree with ninety percent of it. The other ten percent has to do with the grand salon at the mansion and your bunk bed idea for two of the rooms upstairs. I'm thinking of having a partition divide the grand salon into two rooms. Two workshops could be conducted at the same time that way."

"No problem there," Caprice agreed. "Do you want them decorated the same way, or do you want two different designs?"

"Even though I have the money with the legacy, I'm not going to splurge. Let's keep them both uniform. That's more economical, isn't it?"

"Yes, it is. And the reason you don't want the bunk beds?"

"I don't want these rooms to have a prison-cell feel. Bunk beds could suggest that, don't you think?"

"I proposed the bunk beds because it would give residents more room for a sitting area or double desks. Those rooms upstairs are anything but small or cell-like, and of course the decorating would make all the difference. Light, airy draperies and coordinating bedspreads would never give a jail atmosphere. But again, that's up to you."

"Let me think about it."

Wendy had pulled a list in front of her along with Caprice's proposal that she'd printed out. They went over several more items.

Wendy was an easy client to work with because she seemed to take Caprice's suggestions, and Caprice had no problem compromising to give Wendy exactly what she wanted.

"I suppose you'll have volunteers working at the transitional facility too," Caprice said finally.

"We count on our volunteers," Wendy agreed. "And

the women who've been helped by us want to give back."

"Are your volunteers all women who've needed to take refuge in the shelter?"

Wendy didn't hesitate to answer. "They usually are. The truth is, most people don't want to get involved, not with anything that has to do with domestic violence and protective orders."

"I can see that."

She again thought about Alicia and wondered if her best friend, Roz, knew Alicia better than she did. Roz had been on the reunion committee too.

Wendy glanced up at the clock hanging on the wallpapered wall. "I have another meeting in fifteen minutes. I think we've covered everything."

Caprice rose to go.

Wendy snapped her fingers. "I forgot to tell you that you're most welcome to bring along Grant Weatherford to dinner on Saturday. Rumor has it that the two of you are dating."

"We are," Caprice answered. "I'll ask him and see if he'd like to come along. He might be interested in the co-housing concept, too, and enjoy talking to Sebastian."

Wendy's phone rang. She held up her finger to Caprice and picked it up.

Caprice waited.

Even three feet from the phone, she could hear an angry voice on the other end and it sounded male. Wendy seemed to take a bolstering breath; then she slammed down the receiver without saying a word.

"Trouble?" Caprice asked.

"Trouble we often get here."

"An angry husband?"

Wendy just nodded. Then she said, "That's one of the reasons why a state-of-the-art alarm system as well as security cameras are a must for the new facility, no matter what the cost. I'd like to have a few inside, too, in the public areas. Do you think you can come up with inventive ways to disguise them?"

"My family insists I can be very inventive."

Wendy gave Caprice a weak smile. "It's coming together, Caprice—all of it. I'm determined to keep these women safe from anyone who intends to do them harm."

Wendy's vehemence came from more than a desire to do good, Caprice suspected. Maybe someday soon she'd find out what had driven Wendy into this life's work.

Chapter Two

"Co-housing is simple really," Sebastian Thompson told Caprice and Grant on Saturday evening as he took another bite of the vegan casserole Wendy had baked.

Caprice wasn't sure how the casserole was going over with Grant, who was pretty much a meat and potatoes man, and a dessert enthusiast too. But when they'd arrived at Sebastian's house, Wendy had given them a brief tour around the modest two-story Colonial and then informed them that supper would be all vegan but good vegan.

Caprice had laughed at Grant's expression, knowing he probably thought those two words together were an oxymoron. But he was being a champ about it, eating everything Wendy put in front of him. Or maybe he was really enjoying the couscous with cranberries and walnuts, the broccoli casserole with cheddar and garbanzo beans. But she doubted it.

Grant, who had been listening intently to Sebastian—a tall, thin man with a narrow nose and a receding hairline—responded, "I don't know if anything can be simple when a community has to agree on the decisions. I have enough problems with negotiations with two people."

This time Wendy chimed in. "The difference is, Grant, our community all wants the same thing. We have a wonderful mission statement that says it all."

"Just how does the co-housing work?" Caprice asked.

"Mainly, we keep in touch with each other. We have meetings once a month and rotate the houses where we have them. I don't know if you saw that pavilion in the middle of all the properties, but we use that in the spring, summer, and fall for barbecues once a month. The point is, we know what's going on with each other," Sebastian explained. "If, for instance, Mrs. Rawlins, who's sixty-five, moves in and needs someone to cut her grass, a neighbor does it for her. If someone is sick and goes into the hospital, neighbors pitch in with meals and child care. In fact, we do have day care in the neighborhood. One of our neighbors, Melissa Stonehouser, takes care of children in her house."

"So what you're saying is—you're one big family, sort of like families were a long time ago. You help each other out when you need it," Caprice concluded.

"Exactly," Wendy said with a nod. "There are additional perks, of course. We have holiday events, open houses, progressive dinners."

"What happens if someone doesn't want to participate?" Grant asked.

"Someone who doesn't want to participate wouldn't have moved into this neighborhood," Sebastian answered easily.

Sebastian's two boys, Kevin and Cody, who were fourteen and sixteen, hadn't said much during the meal. Now the older one, Cody, chimed in, "It's like we all have a pact here to help each other."

A pact, Caprice thought. A pact usually consisted of secrets as well as loyalty. What kind of secrets did this neighborhood hold?

The Rottweiler—black with brown patches—at Kevin's side rounded the table and came to sit by Caprice's chair. She patted him on the head and directed her attention to the younger son. "Is he allowed to have anything from the table?"

"Wendy doesn't like us to feed him from the table, but you can sneak him a carrot or a piece of broccoli."

Not standing on ceremony, or even good manners, Caprice took a broccoli floret from her plate and gave it to the dog. He gulped it down.

"He already had dinner," Cody explained. "He's just trying to get the extras now."

Caprice laughed. Leave it to animals to open up kids and adults.

"He's great," Caprice assured the teenager. "What's his name?"

"Dover," Cody answered with a grin. "He came from Dover, Delaware. He was a rescue. Wendy's dad found him. He said he would have kept him, but he worked too many hours. He said this kind of dog needed to run and play and jump."

Cody nodded and added, "We said we'd take care of that."

"I have a cocker spaniel and two cats. Grant has a cocker too. He's the brother to mine."

"Wow! Maybe they can all meet up and play sometime," Kevin suggested. "Do you ever take them to the dog park?"

"We do," Grant answered him. "We'll have to set up a time and they can play Frisbees together."

Just then the doorbell rang. Wendy and Sebastian exchanged a look. Wendy said, "I'll get it. Keep eating, everybody. Dessert's coming up."

As Wendy stood to go to the door, Caprice caught another look she exchanged with Sebastian. She seemed to suddenly look tense, her shoulders tighter, her body more rigid. Or maybe it was just Caprice's sixth sense on alert. Nana often told her she had a strong one.

After Wendy answered the door, Caprice saw a woman come in who looked to be in her late fifties. Thinking they needed some kind of explanation for the interruption, Sebastian nodded to her. "That's Cordelia. She's a neighbor."

Caprice studied the neighbor who had her head bent near Wendy's when she saw that Wendy had company. The two women were speaking in hushed tones. While Grant and the boys talked about sports teams, Caprice's innate curiosity had coaxed her to listen for conversation.

The neighbor said, "I'll make sure there's someone there to meet her." Then she lowered her voice even more. Caprice caught the word "Virginia."

The conversation didn't take more than five minutes; then the woman left and Wendy was back at the table. She put on a cheery face and asked, "Is everyone ready for some carob and peanut butter cookies? And how about hot apple cider. Homemade, of course."

With an eye roll, Kevin said, "Everything's homemade. And organic."

"You'll thank me when you win another track trophy," Wendy assured him.

"Maybe," Kevin agreed. "Knocking caffeine out of my diet did help."

Sebastian stood and helped Wendy get dessert ready. He brought over the tray of cookies to the table. "I still have coffee with caffeine in the morning. Wendy hasn't quite convinced me to cut that out of my diet yet, but I'm working on it. I might switch to decaf, but she'll never get me to drink that herbal tea."

The conversation turned to healthy food and cutting carbs. Caprice decided, by outward appearances, Wendy and Sebastian and the boys seemed to have a happy life, a normal life. Yet something about Wendy's work, and even the vibes about the neighborhood, made Caprice wonder just how normal it was.

She said as much to Grant when they'd returned to her house about an hour later and took Lady out for a walk.

It was a beautiful night with a half crescent moon. There was just the hint of smoke in the air as if someone had lit a fire pit or woodstove to ward off the evening chill.

Grant held Lady's leash and the cocker heeled as well for him as she did for Caprice. Caprice still trained her several mornings a week with the usual commands. A year old now, Lady loved praise and treats, so it was a fun time.

"What do you really think about the co-housing concept?" Caprice asked Grant as they walked.

"I think it's as you said—they act like one big family. I don't know if that's for everybody."

"You wouldn't like it?"

"I don't know. It would be nice to have neighbors you can depend upon. On the other hand, I don't really want people nosing into my business, my relationships, my activities. You know, like family does," he said with a sly smile.

He meant her family, of course, and he was right. But she was used to it. It was the way she'd grown up and the way she lived.

"Did you hear any of the conversation between Wendy's neighbor and Wendy?" she asked him.

"I wasn't listening. Kevin was telling me about his track meet."

She nodded. "I just heard a snippet, something about someone meeting someone, someone named Virginia. Or else they were talking about the state. It was hard to tell."

Grant stopped walking and she could see him study her under the streetlamp. "It's possible you're reading too much into a conversation between neighbors. I know what you're thinking."

"And that is?"

"You think Wendy helped someone relocate, either her name was Virginia or she went to Virginia."

"It's possible. If the neighbor was involved with it, maybe that's what they're co-housing neighborhood is about."

"What? Secreting away wives who were abused?"

"Possibly. Is it really so far-fetched? Maybe everyone in that neighborhood has known someone or experienced domestic abuse themselves. I've heard statistics that say, worldwide, one out of three women will have experienced abuse during their life span. That's mind-boggling."

Grant started walking again but remained silent. Caprice understood Grant's silences now. He was thinking about something, something he might eventually talk to her about. Finally, he said, "Speaking of family."

Her ears perked up, the same way Lady's would when treats were mentioned. They stopped at the corner and Grant motioned across the street. They crossed and then started back in the direction they'd come. Caprice waited.

"I spoke to my mom yesterday."

He was quiet for a few moments and then continued. "I asked her if she and Dad would like to come to Kismet for a visit."

Caprice couldn't contain her curiosity. "What did she say?"

"She wasn't sure Dad would agree to the trip, either to fly down or to drive. She admitted he does have a vacation coming."

"Do they usually take vacations?"

"No, they don't. When he takes days off, he uses them to work around the farm. He leases out the land, but they still have a few chickens."

"It would be nice if they'd come to Kismet. I'd like to meet them."

"And I'd like them to meet you. If they won't make the trip, would you drive or fly to Vermont with me? Simon said he'd be glad to take care of Patches."

Simon, Grant's neighbor, was retired and enjoyed watching Grant's cocker spaniel. Caprice hurriedly said, "I can hire Uncle Dom to stay at my house and pet-sit."

As they passed under another streetlight, she caught a glimpse of Grant's expression. He looked worried.

She stopped and took him by the arm. "What's wrong?"

"I want you to remember that my parents are nothing like yours."

He had talked about them a bit not so long ago for the first time. He'd mentioned his brother in passing too.

"I haven't led a sheltered life, Grant. I've been around parents other than mine. Roz's mom for one and clients I've taken on. I understand if your parents aren't . . . emotive."

"They can come off as cold," he warned her. "It isn't just a matter of not sharing emotions. It's a matter of not sharing much at all. Your parents talk to anyone and everyone, and find it easy to do that. Mine are solitary. They have each other and that's all they seem to need. But they don't talk to each other the way your parents talk to each other."

"You mean saying everything that's on their mind?" Caprice asked with a smile.

"They keep what's on their mind safely hidden."

She shrugged. "They're your parents, Grant. I want to meet them, however we have to do it."

They were between streetlights, hidden under the canopy of a maple and an elm. Grant commanded Lady, "Sit," and she did. During the next moment, he wrapped his arm around Caprice and kissed her.

Her heart beat madly, and she wondered how a cool September night could suddenly feel so hot.

When he broke away, he murmured, "You always seem to know what to say."

She countered with, "You always seem to know what to do."

He laughed. "You're saying we complement each other."

She took his free hand as they walked. "We do."

He squeezed her hand and she thought again about meeting his parents. If he was thinking that far ahead, maybe he was thinking about marriage too. She knew she certainly was. Maybe it was time she started searching for a vintage wedding gown online.

* * *

Caprice's Sunday open house was in full swing. Although she'd labeled the theme of this house Cozy Chalet, it wasn't what most people thought of as a chalet. At 5,000 square feet, with a double-car garage and three levels that included an elevator, it might be shaped like a chalet, but it was at the high end of the sales scale. Located on a hilly property with a view of forests and pine groves out the front dormer window and off the back deck, it could be an advertisement for a ski lodge. It had four bedrooms—one on the lower level, a master suite on the main level, and two more on the mezzanine level. She supposed it wouldn't suit a family with young children, but a family with teenagers could find it the perfect arrangement of rooms.

The sellers, a couple in their late forties, had put the house on the market because they were empty nesters and wanted something smaller. But most of their furniture had been more fitting for a Colonial home than a chalet. Caprice was striving for cozy, and it started with the grouping around the floor-to-ceiling massive stone fireplace. Anyone who walked in here would find it a comfy home but could also imagine themselves staying here as if it were a retreat.

She'd rented faux suede furniture in navy that anyone could sink into. The golden oak accent tables were thick and heavy. She'd used scatter rugs in navy and sunset colors. Whatever family lived here would be able to view the sunset from the French door windows or on that beautiful deck that ran around the living room and kitchen on the middle level. She'd decorated one of the bedrooms in primary colors with a simple oak bed, bookshelves, and desk. In the second mezzanine bedroom, she'd employed pastel hues and added whitewashed cupboards and a rolltop desk. The master bedroom on the main level was a retreat for the grown-ups in pale blue and rust with a king-sized brass bed, an antique armoire, and a cedar chest that could hold any prized possessions.

Nikki had come up with quite an array of food in the beautiful kitchen with its white cupboards and black granite counters. She'd readied Gruyère and turkey paninis, a crab fondue, as well as a turkey burger slider covered in cole slaw. She also served hearty soups that could warm a skier on a cold slope— butternut squash soup and a tangy taco soup. The entrées today were all about what would be filling, hot, and comfy.

And the desserts? Nikki served a brownie pie with a brownie as the bottom layer, peanut butter cream in the middle, and shaved chocolate on the top. Caprice guessed that would be the first to go. Her sister had also made fruit crepes for lighter fare and the filling had a splash of bourbon. She'd even come up with a gingerbread man cake accompanied by whipped cream topping. It was cute and Caprice suspected that would go fast too.

Since drinks on a day of schussing were as important as food fare, Nikki made sure they had the proper machinery that would spurt out the perfect lattes, cappuccinos, and even mocha freezes. There would be milkshakes too. As always, Nikki seemed to be on the mark with the food and she knew what she was doing in the kitchen. She and her business might have been in trouble a few months ago, but she was adding success after success to her life now. She was more organized than ever with capable assistants. At first she hadn't been sure she could schedule more than one event a night, but Caprice had convinced her to rely on others. To Nikki's surprise, everyone she hired did a fantastic job.

Caprice had tasted some of the food and was on her way down to the family room when she recognized the voice of one of the guests as he hailed her. It was her brother Vince. With his brown hair and dark brown eyes, his casual black slacks, and diamond-patterned sweater, he cut a dashing figure.

"What are you doing here?" she asked.

He pointed across the room at the pool table where her friend Roz, of all people, had picked up a pool cue and was talking to someone. He waved to her and she came over to them.

"Caprice wants to know what we're doing here," he said above the din of the other voices.

Roz was tall and willowy with a model's figure, shoulder-length natural blond hair, and green eyes. She and Caprice had been friends since high school. They were polar opposites in looks but kindred spirits otherwise. "You couldn't tell her why we're here?" Roz asked.

"I thought she might like to hear it coming from you. You know, that bonding girl thing."

Roz proceeded to punch Vince in the arm.

He held up his hands in surrender. "Kidding, really." Everyone laughed.

"So are you just checking up on me?" Caprice asked.

Vince shook his head. "I'm considering buying a house."

While Caprice was trying to absorb that news, Roz told her, "You did a fantastic job with this one. I like the blue-gray color of the siding and the cream-colored dormers, as well as the French doors. The decks look as if they've had a recent facelift."

"I like the two-car garage and the game room," Vince said. "I'd change that smaller bedroom on that middle level into a home office. It would be perfect for that."

"And keep the master bedroom on the first floor?" Roz inquired.

"Sure. It has a great en suite. I love that huge shower."

Caprice looked from one of them to the other. They'd been dating seriously for months. "Do you think you need a house this big, this pricey, and one with an elevator?" She was still surprised her brother was considering purchasing a property.

"I think Roz and I need enough room to pursue our different activities without stepping on each other. I don't want her to feel I'm checking on her."

"And I don't want him to feel as if I'm always looking over his shoulder," Roz admitted. "This house seems like a good size for that."

Another surprise—they were obviously considering buying this house together . . . or at least living together.

"Do you care that the utility room is in the basement?" Vince asked Roz. "You'd have to carry up the clothes."

"There's an elevator, Vince. What more could I want?"

"Let me get this straight," Caprice concluded. "You're looking at the house together?"

Roz and Vince exchanged a look; then Vince decided to be their spokesperson. "Our vacation together was successful, and so . . . we're thinking about living together."

"Vince is the one who's house hunting now."

"I'm going to take another look at that slanted

ceiling in the room I'd like to make into an office," he decided.

"Go ahead," Roz encouraged him.

After Vince headed toward the stairs, Caprice asked her friend, "You'd really move in here with him?"

"I'm seriously considering it. He's determined to buy a house on his own. He says if something goes wrong, then it won't be so messy for us to pull apart. I'm a little worried about that because I don't see it as a commitment. You know, if you leave yourself an out."

"Maybe he's worried that you need an out."

"When did life get so complicated?" Roz asked in frustration.

"Do you like the house?"

"I can see myself living here with Vince and being happy. But the truth is—we don't need anything this big. We had a wonderful vacation, Caprice. We got along, we laughed, we canoed, we tasted wine. It was great. I'd just like to see what normal life would be like with Vince. But I think he believes he has to compete with my past, what I can afford, what Ted gave me. He doesn't."

Roz's husband, who had been murdered, had been rich and powerful. But he hadn't loved her as a husband should either.

"Vince will figure it out. Trust him." Then Caprice lowered her voice. "I have a question for you. Do you know anything about Alicia Donnehy's marriage?"

An expression crossed Roz's face that said she did. She hesitated a second, but then she admitted, "I saw Alicia one day last winter at Grocery Fresh. She looked as if she had a black eye under her makeup.

"What was her explanation?" Caprice asked.

"She used the old 'I walked into the door in the

middle of the night' excuse. But I wondered about it. And when we were at the reunion meeting one month, I saw bruises on her wrist. I didn't say anything that time."

Caprice bent closer to Roz and lowered her voice further. "You can't tell anyone what I'm going to tell you."

"You know I won't."

Yes, Caprice did know Roz wouldn't. After their high school days, they hadn't kept in touch much, but when Roz was suspected of murder, Caprice had jumped in and they'd become fast friends again. Roz had stayed with Caprice for a while and even ended up adopting the dog that Caprice had taken in. Dylan was now Roz's best buddy, just as Lady was Caprice's best buddy.

"So tell me," Roz encouraged.

"I saw Alicia volunteering at Sunrise Tomorrow."

Roz thought about it. "That makes sense if she was abused."

"Do you know if she's still with her husband?"

"I believe they separated right after the reunion. She and her son are living in an apartment on their own. She sees her husband, though. I spotted them together at the Koffee Klatch. Maybe he's trying to reform his ways."

Old habits were hard to break. Personalities were difficult, if not impossible, to change. Old issues, even from childhood, could cause anger issues in adulthood that might never heal. That was a lot to fix in a union that was supposed to be intimate and forever.

Vince joined them again. "I like this place a lot, but Roz and I have to do some talking before I consider making an offer."

"Is this what you'd envisioned you'd buy?" Caprice asked.

"Not a chalet with an elevator," Roz joked. "I was thinking something a little more ordinary. I was also thinking the bedroom on the second floor could be turned into a nursery as well as a home office."

When Roz said the word *nursery*, Caprice was sure she saw fear come into her brother's eyes. But she had to be mistaken. Vince was fearless in anything he did, and he'd taught her how to be fearless too. Yet when it came to marriage and having a child, life took on a serious quality that Vince had never experienced.

More guests began arriving from the closed foyer into the game room. Caprice was the hostess just as much as the real estate agent was. Kayla Langtree was handling this house listing. Kayla had sold Caprice's sister Bella and her husband, Joe, their new home. Caprice usually worked with Denise Langford, a luxury broker, but this time she'd welcomed the chance to work with Kayla, who was sociable and easy to get along with.

Caprice leaned close to her brother. "I'll let you know if offers come in. If they do, you'll have to make a move if you want the place."

He gazed at the pool table, the counter where a dad or his teenagers could cook up a snack or warm up a pizza for friends. He stared out the beautiful French doors to the lawn and trees in the back and then upstairs where conversation was becoming louder, like a party he and Roz could throw.

Yes, she could see Vince was imagining himself living here.

Now what was he going to do about it?

Chapter Three

That evening, as Caprice sat at her computer at home, she thought about how the chalet she'd staged might fit into Vince's lifestyle. At present, her brother lived pretty much in the center of town and within walking distance of basic needs—like a corner grocery, the deli, the movie theater, the hardware store, as well as his law office. He didn't have a commute or the chore of mowing grass. Everything was maintenance free. He didn't even have to shovel snow. How would he cope with living farther out of town, having yard work to do, as well as everything else unexpected that a house dished up? On the other hand, if he was really ready to settle down . . .

She considered again her short conversation with Roz about Alicia. No, she and Alicia weren't close, but they had been around each other every few weeks for the meetings for the reunion. Could she have really missed all the signs?

Caprice had never really checked out Sunrise Tomorrow's Web site. She'd had no reason to. Tonight, however, she did.

The Sunrise Tomorrow main Web site page was set

up with everything a woman would need at a glance. There was a yellow warning triangle next to an "Escape This Site Quickly" box. Caprice suddenly realized that a woman in an abusive situation might be watched by her husband constantly. If she had a minute to use his computer, he could walk in on her. She also noticed the "Clear Web Browser" icon. Both were necessary for someone wanting to access the site in secret. There was a telephone icon on the other side with a toll-free hotline number. Volunteers staffed it twenty-four hours a day.

Under that, she spotted the logo for Sunrise Tomorrow, the words emblazoned in the middle of a yellow sun. There were three headings beside it—All About Sunrise Tomorrow, Learn About Abuse and Get Help, and How to Help.

An attractive banner underneath that of several women, all races and ages, with and without children, rotated constantly. Below that were several topics with a "Read More" suggestion—Sunrise Tomorrow's Programs and Services, Donate Now, Are You a Victim of Domestic Violence? and Become a Volunteer. There was much to read and discover about the site, about Sunrise Tomorrow, about a world she knew nothing about. She didn't particularly *want* to know about it. Yet the reality of domestic violence was out there. She couldn't help thinking about the children in those pictures . . . the children in those marriages.

Lady, who was sitting at her feet, stood and looked up at her. Sophia, her long-haired calico who was sprawled across the printer, meowed. Mirabelle, a white Persian and most recent adoptee who sat on her computer desk to the right of her keyboard, butted her head against Caprice's hand. Her pets always seemed to be able to sense her mood. They were such a comforting presence in her life.

Caprice was ready to turn back to the Web site and explore the "Read More" subject titles when her cell phone on her desk played the Beatles' "If I Fell." She couldn't help but smile. She'd fallen for Grant Weatherford big-time, and she thought he felt the same about her. She absolutely couldn't imagine what it would be like to be around a man she was afraid of, or a man who tore her down instead of built her up. She supposed she had her parents to thank for instilling in her the idea of what a life partner should be.

When she picked up the phone and checked the screen, she didn't recognize the number. It was a Maryland exchange. She might have thought it was just another telemarketer, but the name caught her attention. Vaughn Contracting. So she answered.

"Caprice De Luca," she said.

"Miss De Luca, this is Roland Vaughn. I build houses, mostly in Maryland."

Okay, so he'd caught her attention. "What can I do for you, Mr. Vaughn?"

"I'm hoping what you can do for me and what I can do for you will benefit us both. I've heard about you through the so-called grapevine. When you stage a home to sell, you have a unique theme. You throw quite a bash from what I hear. My architect attended an open house at your Hacienda Haven event. He was quite impressed. He even brought back photos on his cell phone that I studied quite thoroughly."

"I suppose that's a compliment," she said. "Why were you studying them?"

"I've heard you're straightforward, reliable, and inventive too."

She laughed. "Some people might use other terms for those qualities, but I'd like to think they apply."

"Plus you have a sort of urban-legend reputation. Several articles have been written about you in the *Kismet Crier* and other papers have picked them up. You solve murders and you take in animals."

"I have done both," she admitted, still not knowing where this was going.

"So you're perfect."

"That would be a first. Perfect for what?"

"I'm planning a promotion to advertise the houses I build. I'd like you to participate."

"How would I do that?"

"I have three model homes for sale, and right now they're standing empty. I would like you to decorate or stage, if you will, one home to sell. I've chosen two other interior designers to decorate the others. All of you would have three days to stage a two-bedroom, ranch-style home. A local TV cable station will cover the competition with a half-hour segment each evening, an hour on the fourth night. When the houses are finished, the public will vote on which they like best. The designer who wins will receive a contract to decorate another three model homes for me. If you agree, I can have the details set up in a week or so. What do you think?"

She thought the whole thing was very intense and public. But her contract with a builder in Kismet had run out and she was always looking for new ways to expand her business. Even if she didn't win, the publicity could be beneficial.

"You say I'd have to participate for four days?"

"That's right. The segments would air on a Tuesday, Wednesday, and Thursday, and the results show would be on a Friday. Your motel room, close to the homes, would be covered, of course. You'd have to cover meals yourself. I can send you an e-mail with photos of the houses and information about my company. But I need your answer by ten a.m. tomorrow morning. That will give you a chance to Google me, too, in addition to the brief bio I've provided. I understand you're going to want to make sure I'm legitimate and the offer is too. But there will be references on the e-mail if you'd like to call those. Derrick Gastenaux is a friend of mine, so I'm hoping you'll let him vouch for me."

She'd staged Derrick's houses to sell, and that was the contract that had run out. Derrick was in the process of negotiating another land deal where he could invest in a development.

"I'll call Derrick after I receive your information, and I'll let you know one way or the other by ten a.m."

"I should use the e-mail address on your Web site?" he asked.

"Yes, that would be fine."

"I look forward to hearing from you and working with you."

When Roland Vaughn ended the call, Caprice didn't waste any time exiting the Sunrise Tomorrow Web site and clicking on her e-mail program. She was more than a little curious about Vaughn and eager to study his material. When she opened her e-mail program, she saw the e-mail there and the attachment. After she clicked on it, she picked up her phone and dialed Derrick Gastenaux.

Everybody's Kitchen served residents from Kismet who needed a good meal. The food pantry that was attached dispensed food once a week to anyone whose cupboards were bare. Caprice, her nana, and her mom often signed up to volunteer to serve as well as cook. With school in session now, her mom, who was a high school English teacher, had less time to give.

On Monday at noon, as Caprice stood beside her nana dishing out beef stew and cornbread, she studied the faces of the women who passed through the line. After she'd spoken to Derrick last night about Roland Vaughn's offer and decided to participate in it, she'd gone back to the Sunrise Tomorrow Web site and read all the information there. Some of it shocked her. All of it informed her. Many women who escaped abuse were homeless because they had no place else to go. In Kismet and the surrounding area she hoped they could turn to Sunrise Tomorrow.

During the summer months, moms brought their kids in for lunches at Everybody's Kitchen. Now most of the kids were in school. She caught sight of two women with pre-kindergarten-aged children.

Caprice dished out a bowl of stew to a woman she'd seen at Everybody's Kitchen other times she'd volunteered. Her name was Marilyn. In the summer a child of about ten had been with her. Caprice wondered about Marilyn and her story. Was she getting the help she needed?

The line had thinned now and Caprice glanced around the room.

Nana nudged her shoulder. As always, her nana looked younger than her seventy-six years today. She wore her gray hair in a bun at the nape of her neck, a tortoiseshell comb holding it neatly in place. She wore no makeup, just a dash of light coral lipstick that matched her blouse. Khakis and sneakers completed her outfit.

"You're deep in thought today," Nana noticed. "What's on your mind?"

Nana noticed everything, and there was simply no point evading her.

"I recently learned one of my classmates might be an abused wife," Caprice explained in a low voice. "I never knew, even though I was around her planning the reunion. How could I have missed it?"

"You have to know what to look for," Nana told her. "Usually women are abused over a period of time. Many times it starts suddenly, with lots of criticism. That wears down a woman's self-esteem until she loses her independence. She's cut off from friends, either because her spouse controls that or because she's ashamed of what's happening."

"I'm not sure I'll know how to act around her now that I know."

"Be yourself. If she knows you know her situation, don't hide it. Just give her respect and listen to her. If you listen more than you talk, you can't go wrong."

"She's left her situation and is getting help."

"Well, good. Then all you have to do is listen. It's not unusual for a woman to leave her husband multiple times before she actually can find a new life without abuse. Fear and love for husbands often go hand in hand."

"Tell me something, Nana, did you ever fear Grandpa Tony?"

"Your grandpa could have a temper, but it was never, ever directed at me. He made me feel safe, *tesorina mia*. That's what a man should do. That's what a husband should do."

Caprice was quiet as she stirred the beef stew still left in the serving tray. Her nana used her "my little treasure" endearment when they talked heart-to-heart.

Leaning close, Nana asked, "Are you thinking about Grant?"

"I'm thinking about the type of man he is and how well I think I know him. I do feel safe when I'm with him. He'd never hurt me intentionally. But I imagine there are lots of women who go into a relationship thinking the same thing as I am. Don't you suppose?"

"I'm not sure about that," Nana admitted. "Human nature is a funny thing. But I do know you've known Grant a long time. Not in the sense you do now, but you knew him when he came home with Vince on weekends when they were college roommates. When he came to Kismet, you watched from the sidelines, I know, but you did watch him put a new life together. When the two of you became friends, at least in solving murders, you even saw shades of his grief and how he was swimming through it. You've seen him interact with our friends and our family and how he loves Patches. I think Grant is what he seems, inside and out."

"I think so too."

"There's another side to this, too, honey," Nana said. "Background counts. You have loving parents, no violence in the home, no substance abuse. Your family gave you a clear vision of what you want in a family and what you expect in a relationship. If a man took a poke at you, I truly don't believe you'd give him a chance to do it again. I hope you wouldn't. But some women—they don't think they deserve more. They might not feel that they can stand alone and face the world."

"From what I read on the Sunrise Tomorrow Web site, the counselors and groups try to give women back their self-esteem." That could be a long road, Caprice realized, seeing exactly why transitional care could be so important for victims of domestic violence.

The Wyatt estate could be integral in saving lives and building futures.

More than ever, she was determined to decorate the mansion in a way that would support the programs there and the women. She had a meeting there tomorrow morning with Wendy. Already Caprice had chosen furniture groupings and fabrics that she wanted to show her. Wendy had told her the renovations inside the house could take about a month. Caprice knew if she ordered the furniture, it would take that long to arrive.

After the last person in need of lunch went through the line, Caprice and Nana helped two other volunteers clean up. Caprice was wiping down the tables in the dining area when her cell phone in her pocket played her Beatles tune. It reminded her of Grant, so she smiled. But when she checked the screen, she saw Wendy was calling. Maybe she wanted to change the time of their meeting tomorrow morning.

"Hi, Wendy."

"Caprice, I need your help."

Caprice could hardly hear Wendy, so she turned up the volume on her phone and pressed it closer to her ear. "How can I help?"

"When we had dinner the other night, you mentioned you called Detective Carstead on the Kismet PD on occasion. I wondered if you could give his phone number to me. I really don't want to go through the menu and the public line."

Brett Carstead had given her his cell number because whether he liked it or not, she'd become involved in his murder investigations. She suspected that he expected her to keep it confidential.

"Wendy, I don't know if he'd want me to give it out."

Wendy's voice came back hushed and scared. "It's a matter of blackmail, Caprice. Please."

"Is there anything I can do to help?"

"Absolutely not," Wendy said tersely.

Caprice wasn't sure what to do, so she followed her gut instinct. Wendy wouldn't be asking her for the number on a whim. She knew that in her bones. She didn't have to look at her contacts to know his number. She had it memorized. She rattled it off.

Wendy repeated it back. Then she said, "Thank you, Caprice. I'll see you in the morning at ten at the Wyatt estate." The line went dead.

A matter of blackmail? She supposed Brett would investigate that.

Caprice wondered about Wendy's call into the following morning. Even if she saw Brett Carstead in passing, she knew he wouldn't tell her anything about his conversation with Wendy. He might wonder, though, why she'd passed on his phone number, especially if the matter Wendy wanted to discuss wasn't important.

Mirabelle meowed loudly at Caprice for her breakfast.

"Patience," Caprice warned her.

Mirabelle had been a bit neglected in her former home, and Caprice had to admit she'd spoiled her since the Persian had come to live with her. But now that spoiling was making itself evident. Still, when that little face looked up at her, and those golden eyes seemed to see into hers, Caprice just wanted her to feel loved. The same was true for Sophia and Lady, of course. The difference was, Sophia knew Caprice would feed her. She just stood at her plate waiting, sometimes stretching, sometimes waving her tail.

While the felines ate, Caprice let Lady outside for a bit of a morning romp. She allowed it to go longer than usual because she wouldn't be walking her this morning, not with her ten o'clock meeting. Maybe when she returned home. An Indian summer day would be perfect for a sojourn around the neighborhood.

Inside once more, she found both felines sitting on the dining room table and she knew what they wanted. Taking out the two brushes, one labeled for Mirabelle and the other for Sophia, she spent time brushing them both. Their full coats were coming in for winter and they needed brushing now as much as ever. The furnace heat would dry out their skin, and she wanted to keep them both healthy for many years to come.

After brushing them, she gave them treats designed for healthy skin and fur. She didn't give Lady any, though, because she'd be leaving a play ball stuffed with kibble for her when she left. Lady seemed to understand that as she followed Caprice up the stairs and approved her outfit for a business meeting.

Today she pulled on wide-legged cocoa-colored pants, like Katharine Hepburn might wear, adding a cream Oxford shirt and a boxy forest green jacket. Her suede saddle shoes were reminiscent of the fifties but were back in style now. She picked up her fringed leather purse with the jangling peace sign charm and hefted the strap over her shoulder. After a look in the mirror, and a quick flick of her brush through her straight, long brown hair, she was ready to go.

Her cats had already settled on the turquoise-carpeted cat tree in the living room. She quickly filled Lady's toy with kibble and tossed it into the kitchen.

Lady chased after it and rolled it around. After Caprice set the house alarm, she said good-bye, blew everyone a kiss, and went out her back door.

Last evening, she'd placed everything in her van that she'd need to show Wendy—from fabric samples to furniture catalogs. She had an itemized sheet printed out, as well as a copy on her electronic tablet. All she needed was Wendy's approval to get started.

This time when she headed to the Wyatt estate, she realized she was driving toward Country Squire Golf and Recreation Club. There were plenty of twisting back roads in this area, and she imagined that the estate, if the driver took a back road, wasn't that far from the housing development where Wendy and Sebastian lived. It was all in your perspective, and from which direction you drove.

It was five of ten when Caprice rounded a bend, passed a small church, and then veered right to head up the hill to the property. But as she turned to go up the hill, as she saw the Tudor mansion and the black wrought-iron gate surrounding it, she also spotted that something was definitely wrong. Police cars were parked haphazardly all along the curb! She noted two patrol cars, a rescue van, the coroner's van, and a forensic unit van. Yellow crime scene tape surrounded the whole property. Did they even have enough of it to go around? She'd heard sirens earlier but hadn't paid much attention to them. What was going on?

Her heart began thumping now as she parked across the street from it all. When she spotted Detective Carstead, she wasn't sure whether she should exit her car and approach him or not. After all, he'd warned her to stay away from crime scene banners before. Usually he didn't want her anywhere nearby. But this time, he saw her and soberly waved to her.

She parked, exited her van, and met him at the crime scene tape that led up the steps to the front door.

"What happened?" Caprice asked, her voice coming out shaky. With all these law enforcement officials here, and their vans, she was afraid she knew.

He managed to hold the crime scene tape over his head as he ducked under it. He looked her straight in the eye and asked, "Will you talk to me?"

"Why me?"

"Because you're on the list of people to call next. Wendy Newcomb is dead, and I believe you know why."

Chapter Four

Caprice had come to know Detective Brett Carstead because of her involvement in murder investigations. On a more personal level, however, he'd recently taken her sister Nikki out on a few dates. He was in his official capacity today and she read that in his expression. But she also knew he wouldn't bite her head off or suspect her of murder as Detective Jones was wont to do.

"Come sit in my car and talk to me," he suggested. "Soon the press will be here. I'm sure someone with a cell phone took a picture of all this commotion and the word will get out."

She felt as if she'd been sucker punched and could hardly catch her breath. She was having trouble believing that Wendy Newcomb was dead. It wasn't so long ago she'd been up for the same award Wendy had. Wendy had won and Caprice had sincerely congratulated her because she deserved it for her work at the shelter. Caprice just hated the idea that that work could have brought her life to an end. What else could it have been?

"All right. Let's go to your car," she agreed.

The detective led the way to his black sedan. As she slipped into the passenger side, she took a few deep breaths. She felt quivery inside. No, this wasn't her first crime scene, but a life being snuffed out could never be a common occurrence for her. Then again, maybe it hadn't been murder. Maybe it had been a horrible accident. That was a possibility, wasn't it?

The detective studied her, and asked, "Are you okay?"

"Just shaken up. Why did you want to talk to me?"

"Because Wendy Newcomb left me a message yesterday. I was out of town at a conference. I was going to get in touch with her this morning."

"What was the message?"

"She said you had given her my number. Why did you do that?"

Brett Carstead didn't dole out information unless it could help his investigation.

"I didn't do it easily," she admitted. "But Wendy did serious work. When she called me yesterday for your number, she said she was going to talk to you about a matter that had to do with blackmail. I thought it sounded serious enough to give her your cell number."

"Blackmail?" he asked. "She didn't mention that in her message or I might have called her back last night. She just said it was a matter of vital importance. I was beat. I'd been driving all day." He ran his hand through his hair.

"Don't beat yourself up," Caprice said. "You didn't know."

Without responding to that conclusion, he asked, "Why did you come to the Wyatt property this morning?"

"You know the house is being renovated to use as

a transitional shelter for domestic violence victims, don't you?"

"The workmen told me that."

"I had put together a proposal this week and given it to Wendy. She approved it and gave me a contract for the decorating work. I was going to meet with her this morning to go over purchases I was ready to make."

"Purchases like furniture?" he clarified.

"Exactly. I was going to have her choose materials too."

He took a small notebook out of his inside jacket pocket and a pen from the same pocket. Clicking it on, he rested the notebook on his steering wheel and jotted down a few things.

"So the workmen found her?" she asked.

"I'm interviewing *you*, remember, Caprice."

Oh, she remembered. "Right," she muttered. "You're interviewing me. You're in the middle of an investigation. You can't give out any information. I've got it, Detective. This isn't my first rodeo."

He arched his brows at that. Then he asked, "Do you know anything about the bequest and the money that went with it?"

"You mean the legacy that Sunrise Tomorrow received?"

"Yes, that one."

"No, I mean Wendy mentioned that Leona Wyatt's children inherited trust funds and that the rest of the money and the estate went to Sunrise Tomorrow. She also said Leona's children were squabbling about it, but there were no grounds to contest the will."

"So you *do* know something about it."

"My guess is anyone who belongs to the Country

Squire Golf and Recreation Club heard the same gossip. News like that gets around."

He nodded as if he agreed.

"I don't know any more than that." She added, "But I might know who a couple of the suspects are . . . if this is a suspicious death."

He gave her his full attention. "Who?"

She told him about Warren Shaeffer's meeting with Wendy and what she'd overheard. She ended with, "I never realized Wendy might be putting herself in danger by doing this work. When I stopped in at Sunrise Tomorrow the other day, another man was shouting at her over the phone and she hung up without even talking to him. I have no idea who that might have been."

Carstead was writing again.

"Have you ever been to the development Wendy's significant other lives in?" she asked him.

"Development? You mean like a housing development?"

"Yes."

He checked his notes. "Her significant other is Sebastian Thompson."

"Right. He owns the house in Poplar Grove. It's a co-housing development."

"And that means?"

"It means everyone cooperates with everyone else. They interact. They share meals and have meetings."

"Like a neighborhood with a home association?"

"More than that. These neighbors are interconnected. Grant and I had dinner with Wendy and Sebastian and his kids. I got the feeling that maybe the neighborhood could be involved in the work Wendy did. Grant thinks that I'm stretching, but I just got this feeling that it could be a network to help abused women find new lives."

"As soon as I'm finished talking to you, I'll be driving to Sebastian Thompson's to tell him about Wendy's death. I understand he's an architect and works from home."

After a moment, Caprice asked, "How did Wendy die?"

Brett Carstead never gave her any information. The last time she'd solved a murder, she'd given him some.

However, he studied her now, seeming to make a decision. "The whole work crew found her. The word's going to get out soon enough. That balustrade that looked down over the foyer gave way. She fell and broke her neck."

Caprice remembered how Wendy had mentioned the balustrade would soon be replaced and how she'd warned her against going near it.

"Wendy warned me about that balustrade, and she was smart enough not to go anywhere near it herself. What aren't you telling me? Is there something else that makes you think this is more than an accident?"

Again he stopped, hesitated, and cut her a probing glance. "It wasn't an accident. On preliminary examination, the coroner thinks someone hit Wendy Newcomb on the side of her head, possibly with one or more rolled-up window shades, and that's probably why she fell. We couldn't find the shade or shades in question, but the stack of them looked disturbed. Do you remember how many might have been stacked in that area?"

Caprice swallowed hard and felt her head spin a little.

"Caprice?"

"I'm fine," she insisted, yet she knew she wasn't.

Tears were close to the surface. "There were probably sixteen or eighteen shades stacked there from the upstairs rooms. If you count the windows on that floor, you'll have a fairly accurate number."

He made a note of that, then studied her again. "I need your help with something else."

His words gave her focus, and she swallowed back her emotions. "What?"

"We have a cat trapped in one of the rooms—a yellow one. I can't have him roaming over the crime scene. Can you help me with him, or should I just call animal control?"

"No, don't do that," she protested at once. "I saw him here when I met with Wendy. He's friendly."

"Yes, he is. He was rubbing against one of the officer's legs. But I don't want you going inside. Maybe you could go to Perky Paws and get one of those pet carriers for us."

"I can do that. Or . . . I have Lady's crate in the back of my van. It's bigger than we need, but if you need to remove him sooner rather than later, one of your men can use that. I'll call Marcus Reed at Furry Friends clinic and see if he can fit in an examination."

"Then what?" Brett asked.

"Then I'll have to find him a home."

"Do you think you can?"

"I can try."

Caprice waited with Sunnybud in one of the exam rooms at Furry Friends Veterinary Clinic. He was sitting on the exam table in what she called the "breadloaf" position, his front paws tucked under him.

He lifted his head and meowed at her.

"If I can't find you a home, I'll take you home with me. I have an idea of someone to call. It depends on how good my powers of persuasion are. But we have to get your health status first."

Sunnybud meowed again, obviously not pleased at being examined, as well as poked for a blood test. Marcus had guessed he was two or three years old.

The door to the room opened and Marcus came in. He was a burly African-American with a buzz cut and a wide smile. "His tests were clear. No FIV or feline leukemia. We can give him a flea treatment and other vaccines."

"Great," Caprice responded, blowing out a relieved breath. "Do you need the room right away? I want to call Bella and see if she'll take him."

"Bella? Are you kidding?" he asked with a grin, knowing from what Caprice had told him how meticulous her sister was about everything in her life.

"She has a new house now and more room. Her attitude is mellower since she had Benny. I'm going to give it a try."

"And plan B?"

Marcus understood her well enough to recognize the fact that she usually had an alternate plan. "Mom," she simply said.

He laughed.

The phone call was rocky to start. Explaining a possible murder was never easy. Then when Caprice suggested Bella take in a stray cat—

"A cat?" Bella squeaked. "You're kidding."

"I'm not. Think about it, Bee. All you need is a litter box and cat food. Sunnybud can teach Megan and Timmy responsibility. You know they've been begging you for a pet every time they visit me."

When Bella just remained silent and didn't squawk again, Caprice pushed on. "He's two or three, which means he'll sleep a lot, yet he'll still be playful. All you have to do is keep him in the basement for two days to make sure the flea treatment has worked."

Now Bella protested again. "Fleas?"

"Marcus says he looks clean, but we want to make sure. After two days, just wash up the basement and let him upstairs."

"I don't know, Caprice."

"Timmy and Megan can keep him company down there. It's heated. Old towels make a great bed and you can wash them. He's been sleeping in an empty house. He won't expect much."

Again Bella was silent.

"I'll wash the basement for you after two days."

After a few moments, Bella said, "And if this doesn't work out, Mom will take him?"

Caprice crossed her fingers. "Sure."

"What do I need?"

"I can get you a litter pan, litter, and food from Marcus. I'll be there in ten minutes."

"Wait! I should call Joe first. This should be his decision too."

Bella was right. "Go ahead and call him now. Then call me back."

Joe must have taken to the idea of taking in Sunnybud because Bella called back within five minutes with a "We'll try it."

That was all Caprice needed. She spent the next hour transporting Sunnybud to Bella's, introducing them, and helping Bella arrange towels in a cardboard box for Sunnybud's bed.

Her sister had looked Sunnybud in the eyes and said, "I'll take care of you. If you're a good fit, you can join our family."

Sunnybud blinked, then proceeded to sniff every foot of the basement, including the new litter box, water bowl, and dish with cat food that Bella had set on a plastic placemat.

When he began to eat, she said, "I can bring my sketchbook down here for a while and keep him company."

Caprice hoped her sister and Sunnybud would bond. That was possible, wasn't it?

After Caprice left Bella's house, she switched on her ignition and just sat there. She didn't know what to do next. That wasn't like her at all. But the shock of what happened to Wendy rattled her all over again. She respected Grant's work time and didn't want to barge in on him. But more than anything, she'd like to talk to him.

Taking out her phone, she texted him. Are you at home? Can you talk if I come over?

He must have had his phone nearby because he texted right back. At home working on a brief. Come on over.

Climbing into her car, she glanced over her shoulder into the back of her van where she'd stacked her sample books and catalogs all ready for Wendy's appraisal. What would happen to Sunrise Tomorrow now?

She felt as if she drove to Grant's in a trance state, cruising along his street before she knew it. His townhouse was one in a row of them, not too far from Nikki's condo.

Before she could even ring the bell, he opened the door. He took one look at her and opened his arms. After a long, strong hug, he shut the door against the September breeze and led her inside.

"What's going on?" he asked.

"How do you know something's going on? Maybe I just wanted to kiss you."

He gave her a crooked smile. "That's a possibility. But there was urgency in that text and I heard it without even speaking to you."

Patches ran over to her, sat at her feet, and looked up at her, tail wagging. Although he was Lady's brother, Patches looked nothing like her. His fur was curlier. He was cream-colored with brown patches on his face and flanks. His ears were shorter too.

She stooped over and gave the dog a good rub-down before she went to the sofa and plopped on it.

Grant made himself comfortable beside her. "Do you want coffee?"

"Maybe in a little. I had an appointment with Wendy Newcomb this morning at the Wyatt estate. When I got there, there were police all over the place and crime scene tape. Wendy's dead."

Grant's gray eyes went dark and his mouth tightened into a taut line. Without expression in his voice, he asked, "What happened?"

"Do you know the Wyatt estate at all?"

He shook his head. "Only from the outside."

"When you go up the stairway from the foyer, there's a balustrade across the hallway on the second floor. If you stand at it, you look down into the grand foyer."

Grant nodded as if he understood.

"When I toured the house with Wendy at the beginning of the week, she told me to stay away from it. Repairs hadn't been done on that house for years, and she said they were going to replace the balustrade because it was wobbly. Before I arrived, workmen had cleaned and were painting. Blinds, those old roller shades with the scallop and the fringe on the hem and a wooden bar across the shade, had been stacked near the balustrade. I don't think this is for public consumption, but Brett told me someone used one or more of those shades to hit Wendy and she fell through the balustrade. She broke her neck on her fall."

Grant was silent for a few moments. "Carstead thinks this is a homicide?"

"Yes, he does. After an autopsy, they'll know for sure. But I don't think he would have told me what he did if all the signs weren't there. The workmen found her and they think it's pretty obvious what happened. He'd already spoken to the coroner too. He asked me to take the stray cat that had been living on the property." She told Grant about taking Sunnybud to Marcus and then her trip to Bella's.

"Do you think Bella will keep him?"

"Only time will tell that. But I don't think she'll have much choice if Joe and the kids fall in love with him. I think they will."

Caprice and Grant were silent a few moments until he took her hand and squeezed it. Leaning close, he kissed her temple. "Wendy was doing important work."

"I know. I told Brett what I knew because he wanted to talk to me. He was going to call me. I forgot to tell you that Wendy phoned me yesterday. She wanted Brett's cell number. When I hesitated, she said it was a matter of blackmail. So I gave it to her. But he was away at a conference and just got back late last night. He was going to hook up with her today. I think he feels guilty he didn't call her back last night."

"Even if he'd called her back, he might not have prevented what happened today."

Patches rubbed against Caprice's leg and she stooped to pet him again. He circled and circled so she could pet all of him. His furry little body was a comfort, just as having Grant beside her was a comfort.

"I didn't mean to barge into your day like this, but I didn't know what else to do."

When she sat up again, Grant was gazing at her intently. He took her chin in his hand. "You can barge into my day anytime you want. The fact that we had dinner with Wendy and Sebastian on Saturday night makes this all the more real . . . and horrible."

"Brett was going to drive out to Sebastian's after he talked to me."

Grant dropped his arm around Caprice's shoulders. "So you and Brett Carstead are sharing information now?"

"I've always shared mine with him. He knows a lot about me. Now that he's dating Nikki, he knows even more probably."

"So he *is* dating Nikki? That's for certain?"

In the summer, Grant had voiced his opinion that Brett was interested in Caprice. But she knew better. Once the detective had questioned Nikki as a murder suspect, he'd been smitten with her, and her sister had been smitten with him.

Caprice told Grant the truth. "They've gone on a few dates, but they both have busy lives, and his work is his priority. So I don't think they're super involved yet. Given enough time, they might be. He's not interested in me, Grant, and I'm not interested in him. I told you that before, didn't I?"

He smiled. "You did."

Caprice had laid her purse on the coffee table, and now her cell phone sounded from inside of it.

"Go ahead and get it," Grant said. "I'll make coffee."

As he stood and then crossed to the kitchen, Patches

trailed after him, his toenails clacking on the linoleum floor.

Caprice checked the screen on her phone. The call was coming from a Sunrise Tomorrow line.

"Caprice De Luca here."

"Caprice? This is Lizbeth Diviney."

Caprice had been introduced to Lizbeth when she met with Wendy at Sunrise Tomorrow. The perky redhead, with a pixie haircut and huge wide smile, was Wendy's second-in-command.

Lizbeth charged on. "Do you know what happened to Wendy? I know you had a meeting with her this morning."

"The police were there when I arrived. Yes, I know what happened."

"I need to see you right away."

"About the Wyatt estate?"

"Yes, and about the facility here. I just need to talk to somebody. Everybody here is in tears." Lizbeth's voice broke.

"I understand. I'm going to make a suggestion that may seem a little odd. I need to stop at home and take care of my animals. Do you mind if I bring Lady, my cocker spaniel, along? She's well-trained and sometimes having a dog along, or a pet to focus on, gives people comfort."

"That's a terrific idea," Lizbeth said. "Yes, bring her. See you in about an hour?"

"An hour it is," Caprice said.

After Caprice ended the call, she saw Grant was standing in the doorway from the kitchen into the living room.

"That was Lizbeth Diviney, Wendy's right-hand person at Sunrise Tomorrow. She wants to talk to me.

Everyone there's upset and I told her I'd bring Lady. I think it might help."

Rising to her feet, she crossed to Grant and studied the expression on his face. "What's wrong?"

"I just had the very strong premonition that you might get pulled into another murder investigation."

He worried about her. She knew that. Wrapping her arms around his neck, she suggested, "I bet if I kiss you, you'll forget about your premonition."

He took her up on her offer.

Lizbeth met Caprice and Lady at the door of Sunrise Tomorrow and ushered them into what was once Wendy's office. Lizbeth couldn't seem to sit still. She paced around the office, stopped to pet Lady, then waved her hand across the desk that was stacked with documents. "I'm so upset I don't know what to do."

There were many things Lizbeth had to be upset about. So Caprice took a chair and waited for Lizbeth.

Flitting to the file cabinet, Lizbeth pulled open a drawer and selected a file folder. Then she plopped it on the desk. It was about an inch thick. "This is all the information on the Wyatt estate. Look at that folder. And this is only one aspect of the work we do here. Granted it's a big one right now. Wendy was grooming me to take it over. As she told you, I was going to be the director of the new transitional facility. But now I'm the director of this one, and that one, too, I guess. I just don't know how to absorb it all . . . and do it quickly. Maybe I should take up speed-reading."

Lady stretched out on the floor beside Caprice's foot.

"If Wendy was putting you in charge of the Wyatt

estate, then she knew you were capable of handling it," Caprice reminded Lizbeth.

"I'm familiar with most of the material. We want to be in the new facility by January. But Wendy played lots of things close to the vest, and there are so many details that I'm afraid I'll miss something. Not because I can't handle the Wyatt estate, but because I'm going to have to handle both facilities."

"Are you the acting director now?"

"I got the word from the board before I called you. I'm the interim director until they have a meeting and make a final decision. That should be in about a week or so."

"If you're the director over both facilities, then that means you can delegate, right?"

"The problem is, Caprice, there's no one with the level of responsibility or familiarity that I can delegate to. I assisted Wendy. No one assisted me. Not in the administration. Yes, in dealing with our clients and with the counselors and the advocates, Wendy and I oversaw the programs and chose the people who ran them. But each of those programs is an entity unto itself. Do you understand what I mean?"

"Yes, I do. You didn't have a right-hand person. The buck stopped with you and Wendy, and the two of you answered all the questions and solved the problems. Right?"

"Right," Lizbeth answered, finally sitting on the corner of her desk, or rather Wendy's desk, and looking at Caprice with big, wide hazel eyes that suddenly filled with tears. "I know I'm driving myself crazy over the details because I'm so upset about what happened. I can't believe she's never going to walk through those doors again."

Lady suddenly rose to her feet and went over to

Lizbeth. She looked up at her as if she wished she could comfort her too.

Lizbeth noticed. She hopped off the desk and crouched down on the floor with Lady, petting her while tears ran down her cheeks. Caprice didn't know what to say or do for her, and she knew probably the best thing was to just let her pet Lady and let her cocker comfort her.

Finally Lizbeth rose to her feet, went around the back of the desk, and sat in the chair—the chair that she realized now belonged to her, at least for the time being.

"How can I help you?" Caprice asked. "Do you want me to go over my proposal with you, give you my notes about the content of the meeting I was supposed to have with Wendy this morning?"

"That will help. You and I will have to sit down and do that, soon. But that isn't why I asked you to come over today."

"Why did you?"

"We have to be in that facility by January. I have to convince the board that I'm the person who can make it happen. But I'm afraid because of Wendy's death, contracts might have to be renegotiated with the renovating crew, with the groundskeeper, with the professionals we use here at the facility."

"That would be crazy," Caprice said. "As acting director, all of it should still stand."

"You'd think so, wouldn't you? But Wendy's name was on a lot of those agreements. Contracts weren't necessarily made with the foundation or even Sunrise Tomorrow. So I don't know exactly what's going to happen. I do know one thing—if this murder isn't solved, our plans to move forward could be held up, and I don't want that to happen. I know that you've helped solve other murder cases. I want you to look into Wendy's murder so that I can forge ahead."

Caprice knew exactly what she should say. "I'm by no means a professional in that field," she told Lizbeth. "The police will do everything they can to find out who killed Wendy."

"But will they do it sooner rather than later? Will they find the right person instead of hanging it on the wrong person? I know your friend, Roz Winslow, was almost railroaded for her husband's murder. I know your sister Nikki was a main suspect not so long ago. It's like they target someone and try to make their case against them, and I understand that. But they don't look around."

"I can't interfere in their investigation," Caprice told her.

"I know you can't, and I don't want you to interfere." Tears came to Lizbeth's eyes again. "Wendy saved my life and so many others. She would do anything to protect a woman in a domestic abuse situation. You have no idea how far our network extends."

As soon as Lizbeth said that, she clamped her hand over her mouth as if she shouldn't have.

Caprice thought about the co-housing neighborhood again and wondered if neighbors were involved in more than potluck dinners. She saw the stricken look on Lizbeth's face and felt it was sincere. She understood the importance of the work Sunrise Tomorrow did. She also knew, although Brett Carstead might have warmed up toward her, Detective Jones hadn't. He would view any misstep as a reason to throw the book at her.

The expression, however, on Lizbeth's face made Caprice's decision for her. "I'm not going to promise you I can solve this murder mystery. I'm not going to agree to take on the murder investigation."

When Lizbeth was about to protest, Caprice stopped her. "But what I will do is nose around a bit and see if I can find information that will help the detectives."

Lizbeth hopped out of her chair, rounded the desk, and gave Caprice a tight hug. "Thank you."

Caprice knew Grant wasn't going to like this new turn of events. Her family wouldn't either.

All she could do was assure them she'd be careful. And she would be . . . this time.

Chapter Five

On Wednesday, Caprice was having trouble concentrating on work. So in the afternoon when her uncle texted her that he was free to visit the kittens at Dulcina's house, Caprice texted her neighbor and was relieved to learn she was free too.

When Dulcina opened her front door to them, Uncle Dom said, "It's good to see you again." Caprice heard that note in his voice that said he really meant it. *Hmmm.*

"Come on in," Dulcina invited. "I can make coffee or hot chocolate."

After they stepped inside, Uncle Dom told her, "Hot chocolate sounds good. There's a chill in the air like fall is really moving in. Caffeine and sugar will do the trick."

Dulcina's smile said she agreed.

Uncle Dom glanced around the living room furnished with a gray and blue comfortable-looking couch and armchair, the attractive coordinating draperies, the gray-blue carpet.

"It's nice."

"I like it. We like it," she amended as Halo sauntered into the living room to see what was going on.

When the feline hesitated, Uncle Dom dropped into a crouch and held out his hand.

Halo came toward it, eager to sniff. Once she did, she butted her head against his palm.

"Maybe she remembers I fed her," he said.

"That's quite possible," Caprice agreed. "They remember who's kind to them."

Dulcina motioned to the sunroom. "The kittens are napping. Go ahead and visit them."

Caprice noticed that Uncle Dom looked as eager as a kid when he entered the sunroom and spotted the three kittens who were cuddled in a circle in a pink and blue plaid bed. The bed was positioned in front of the stationary French door in a stream of sunlight.

"Can I wake them?" he called into Dulcina.

"Sure you can," she called back. "They like to play even more than they like to sleep."

Caprice's Uncle Dom was younger than her dad. When he'd first arrived in Kismet back in March, his life had been on a downturn. He'd gained about twenty extra pounds and his outlook hadn't been sunny. Now, however, with the start of his pet-sitting business taking off quickly, the bookwork he did on the side for a couple of small businesses, and his new apartment, he'd lost ten pounds and wore a smile most of the time.

He pushed his oval glasses higher on the bridge of his nose and didn't hesitate to sit on the floor beside the kittens' bed.

Halo trotted over to check out what he was doing. She was still protective of her brood.

He lifted Tia onto his leg. "This is the princess," he said with certainty. "I can see her little crown."

Dulcina came into the room then. "It looks like a tiara. So her real name's Tiara, but Tia for short."

Tia looked up at him, opened her mouth and yawned, and then rubbed against his knee. He patted her gently. She wriggled a bit and then jumped up, eager to play.

Uncle Dom took a shoelace from his pocket. "I came prepared." He wiggled it on the floor and Tia chased after it.

Mason and Paddington were waking up now. They saw the string and jumped up out of the bed to pounce on it.

Uncle Dom laughed as they chased it around the floor.

"It's easy to see you're a cat person," Dulcina mused. "Tell me about your place."

"It's an older home, near Restoration Row where Roz Winslow has her shop. She's the one who heard about it and told Caprice."

Mason jumped high in the air to catch the string and did a little spin.

Uncle Dom kept his eyes on the kittens as he explained, "I have the second and third floors. There's a living room, small kitchen, two bedrooms. But there's also a stairway up to the finished attic for another bedroom. There's a lot of light up there, and I was thinking about just taking off that door. That way, the kittens would have the run of the whole place."

"Does someone live on the first floor?"

"Yes, a woman in her sixties. She owns the place." He nodded to Caprice. "She likes to bake as much as you do. When I moved in, she brought me home-made sticky buns. Since then, she also baked me an apple cake. If I'm not careful, I'll put back on those ten pounds I lost."

Dulcina said, "That third cup of hot chocolate should be ready now. I'll go get our mugs."

"I'll go with you." Caprice followed her, eager to hear her friend's thoughts.

In her color-blocked blue and white kitchen, Dulcina gave a little sigh. "I can tell your uncle's a cat lover."

"He is." Caprice didn't say more, waiting for Dulcina's verdict.

"I'm going to miss them."

"It's hard letting go. I know. It always tears me up when I find a home for an animal I've fostered. But if you know they're going to good homes, that's what matters."

"It sounds as if he'd provide a good home."

"I think Mason and Tia will have their own cat haven in the attic."

Dulcina smiled. "It does sound like that, doesn't it?"

"And you could visit them whenever you'd like. I'm sure he wouldn't mind."

"He's not dating anyone?" Dulcina asked.

"Not that I know of."

"How long ago was his divorce?"

"It was finalized about two years ago. As I told you, he was estranged from his family until spring."

"And he came to Kismet on his own to patch things up?"

"My dad had kept in touch with him. Uncle Dom would be the first to admit his life had gone south when he lost his job with a financial firm that went under and then got a divorce. He waited a good long time before he asked for help."

"Pride does that," Dulcina said as if she knew. "After I lost Johnny I was in a really bad place. I didn't want to ask for help. The house was too much for me to handle on my own. I'd let my work pile up and deadlines go by."

"What turned you around?"

"I found a letter Johnny had written me before we were married. He talked about our future and how bright it would be, and how we should look forward no matter what we faced together. When I read that letter, I realized he wouldn't want me wallowing in self-pity. He would want me moving forward. So I took one step at a time and put the house in York on the market to sell. Little by little I caught up with work. I found this place. I wasn't happy, but I also wasn't in the depth of despair anymore. Little by little, life became more fulfilling again. That old adage—'Fake it until you make it'—is good advice."

Caprice nodded, thinking about Grant and how he'd overcome loss and rebuilt his life.

Dulcina arranged the three mugs on a small tray. Then she plucked a can of whipped cream from the refrigerator door. After she popped the top, she spritzed it on each of the mugs topping the hot chocolate.

She lifted the tray. "Here we go."

Caprice suspected it wouldn't be long until her uncle had two kittens playing in his apartment, roughhousing, napping, and cuddling. She also had the feeling Dulcina might be visiting them often.

Time would tell.

Caprice was following Dulcina back to the sunroom when the cell phone in her pocket played. She took it out to check who was calling. It was Nikki. Caprice took a few steps back into the kitchen and answered it.

"Hi, Nik. I'm over at Dulcina's with Uncle Dom. Can I call you back later?"

"Were you going to tell me you were involved in another murder?"

"I'm not involved, exactly. I was going to call you later and talk to you about it. How did you find out?"

"Brett canceled our date for tonight. I guess he wanted me to know his excuse about work was legitimate because he mentioned you. He told me you were on the scene yesterday."

"Not until afterward. I was supposed to meet Wendy there for a meeting."

"How awful!"

"It is. And the thing is, I told Lizbeth, Wendy's right-hand person, that I'd nose around a little. She's afraid the investigation will drag on and on and she doesn't want it to affect the work at Sunrise Tomorrow."

"I can understand that. Brett sounded a bit harried as if there are lots of people to interview and maybe several suspects."

"There could be a score of suspects with abusive husbands and lots of anger floating around. The police have their job cut out for them."

"So what do you think you can do?"

"I'm not sure. The first thing I'm going to do is go back to the shelter and talk to Lizbeth again, maybe a few of the other employees. Then I'll go from there."

"Do you want me to keep mum about this and not tell Mom or Dad or Bella?"

"Bella knows. I convinced her to adopt a stray cat from the Wyatt property."

"You *are* kidding."

"Nope. I didn't get a call from her this morning, so I guess all is well. Don't say anything about the murder to Mom, Dad, and Nana. They'll just worry."

"But Grant knows you're involved?"

"He does. I went to him after it happened."

"Good. I'm glad. If you two are leaning on each other, then you really are getting closer."

"Is that a good thing? If I depend on him, I mean." She trusted Nikki to be honest with her answer.

"If you depend on him, maybe he'll come to depend on you. That is good, Caprice. You're strong enough that you won't lose yourself. I know you."

"Yes, you do. Probably better than anyone."

"Do you want to go to the Harvest Festival together on Saturday? You can catch me up on what's happening."

The Harvest Festival was a huge downtown event every September that brought tourists into their community. It helped rev up business for town vendors.

"That sounds good. Come over to my place around ten and we'll leave from there."

"See you Saturday. Don't get into any trouble until then."

"I won't," Caprice promised, then realized just how hard it might be to keep that promise.

Uncle Dom had been happy at how his visit went with Dulcina and the kittens. He was sure he'd be taking Tia and Mason home soon. He'd left, looking as if he had a new lease on life. After he'd driven away, Caprice had taken Lady for a walk and decided to start collecting information by stopping in at Sunrise Tomorrow. It was late afternoon when she arrived and Lizbeth was in a meeting with the staff counselor. Caprice realized she should have called first, but she wanted to look around the shelter on an impromptu visit rather than a planned one.

The receptionist, who'd recognized her from the

other day, let her in. Rena Hurley, in her early forties, with coal black hair and bright red lipstick, as well as rings on every finger, reseated herself at her desk. After she did, she waved to an alcove on the other side of the room. "There's coffee and spring water over there, if you'd like some while you wait."

Rena had an accent that sounded Midwestern, yet her style definitely wasn't small-town America. Everyone else Caprice had seen at Sunrise Tomorrow wore comfortable clothes, but Rena was dressed in a pretty burgundy suit with high heels to match.

"I'm fine," Caprice said. "I stopped in today because I talked to Wendy about sprucing up the facility here. I'd like to take another look around."

"Look around all you want, except of course in the private rooms. Did Wendy want to spruce those up too?"

"She did, but that can wait until another time. That's one of the things I need to talk to Lizbeth about. Wendy wanted a color scheme that included greens and blues and yellows—colors that are bright and soothing."

Rena motioned to the sitting area. "What we have now is mostly thrift shop special. Wendy never splurged. Even with the Wyatt legacy, she intended to keep changes frugal—though we'd have a little more leeway."

Caprice could see that Rena was talkative and that could be good. "How long have you worked here?"

"I've been here since the inception of Sunrise Tomorrow. I do everything from paperwork to receiving new clients to coordinating hotline volunteers."

"Are you from this area?"

Rena winked at her. "Did my accent give me away?"

Caprice just smiled.

"I'm from Nebraska. But my parents moved to Pennsylvania when I was in high school. I went to college here and got married here. But then . . ." She shrugged. "That didn't work out. So here I am."

Wendy had informed Caprice that Rena's position as well as Lizbeth's had been the first paid salaries at the shelter.

Rena lowered her voice. "I want to see us continue the work we've always done, but Lizbeth isn't Wendy."

Before Caprice could pursue *that* direction, women in conversation emerged from the hall that led to another area of the facility. There were about a dozen of them, and Caprice guessed they might have come from a workshop or a class. She noted many of them held rolled-up mats under their arms. Caprice had taken yoga classes years before, and the mats looked like those she had used.

One of the women separated from the others and came over to Rena's desk. She was wearing camel-colored, loose-legged yoga pants along with an oversized off-white T-shirt with Sunrise Tomorrow's logo printed on the front. She wore the type of shoes that Caprice associated with rock climbers that were close-fitting and flexible. Her light brown hair was short, curly on the top of her head and above her ears, and straight, close to the neck in the back. Practical.

Rena motioned to her. "Caprice, this is Evelyn Miller, our yoga instructor. Evelyn, Caprice De Luca. Wendy hired her to decorate the Wyatt estate and spruce up our space here."

Evelyn stretched out her hand and Caprice took it, looking into very blue serene eyes. Evelyn's hand was warm and dry, and she had a friendly grip.

"I've heard about you," Evelyn said with a smile.

"You have the reputation for helping to sell houses quickly. Do you use feng shui when you stage?"

Feng shui decorating was all about harmony. "I don't call it that," Caprice said. "But I always try to create a good flow of energy and let in plenty of natural light. I declutter as much as the client will let me and create good vibes with color too. I think we all want our house to be a place that lifts us up."

"You'll use those concepts at the Wyatt estate?"

"Most assuredly, and here too. The public areas are sometimes hard to clear of clutter."

Evelyn nodded. "Exactly. Fresh flowers in vases help too. I try to bring in a bunch at least once a week."

Caprice noticed a tall vase, filled with yellow and white chrysanthemums on one of the side tables by a sofa.

"Do you arrange them yourself?" Caprice asked.

Evelyn nodded. "I do. In fact I teach a class on flower arranging at Green Tea Spa. I teach yoga there too."

"I took yoga a few years ago and enjoyed it. It's better exercise than most people believe when they think about yoga. I try to swim laps twice a week, but yoga would be a nice change."

"I have one open class at Green Tea for anyone who wants to drop in when they feel like it and then another that's progressive with committed students."

There was something very calm about Evelyn, and very steady. She imagined the woman was a good presence to have in a place like this where emotions as well as activity could become chaotic.

The door to what used to be Wendy's office opened and Lizbeth emerged. She introduced Caprice to Heather Davis, one of the counselors. Heather was in her fifties, gray haired with plenty of lines around her eyes and her mouth. She looked like a woman who had seen it all. She excused herself and crossed to the door that led outside.

After Caprice said good-bye to Rena and Evelyn, Lizbeth motioned her into her office. "Heather's in a hurry because she's meeting a client for a cup of coffee. Sometimes women don't want to come here, or become associated with Sunrise in any way. Heather tries to accommodate that."

"This really is a wheel with a lot of spokes," Caprice noted. "And you're going to be the center of it, making it all keep spinning."

"That's what I hope to do. How can I help you today?"

Lizbeth seemed calmer than the day when Wendy was murdered. But Caprice could tell energy was bubbling just below the surface. This was a woman who liked to keep moving.

Just as Caprice thought that, Lizbeth went to the bulletin board on the wall, plucked a sticky note from it, crumbled it, and tossed it into the waste can.

"I know something about Wendy's present-day life, but nothing about her past and her family," Caprice explained. "Can you fill me in?"

With a spin around on her brown flats, Lizbeth moved to the front of her desk. "I'll try. Wendy and I became close over the years. You can't work beside each other like we did without sharing things."

Caprice supposed that was true. You became almost like family when you worked long hours together.

"Wendy lost her mother when she was around five," Lizbeth began. "But even back then, her father was successful, working in finance, something with hedge funds. His father before him had been successful, too, so she came from money and she was used to moving in the best circles. She'd gone to private schools and socialized with other wealthy families. She was attending college at the University of Delaware—Delaware is where she was from—when she met and married a man whose family had money too. He moved them to York to open a branch of his family's business. But money can't buy happiness, and the longer they were married, the more he abused her."

"But if she had the means to get away—" Caprice began.

"You'd think that would help, wouldn't you? Even if her husband controlled all her money, you'd think the fact that her dad was wealthy would have saved her sooner. It didn't. She stayed in the marriage because she loved her husband. He'd go for months acting as if he loved her, but then he'd hit her. Afterward he'd be remorseful and he'd say he'd change. But of course he didn't. It's an old story."

One Lizbeth was familiar with? "I've been doing reading on domestic violence, and that's the pattern, isn't it?"

Lizbeth nodded. "So many things kick in with that kind of situation. Background, former treatment by males, the way your dad raised you. Wendy had a good dad, but she was too proud to go to him. Nevertheless, she was smart. She devised a plan and managed to see a lawyer. Together they came up with an exit strategy."

"Explain *exit strategy*."

Lizbeth perched on the corner of her desk. "Her exit strategy was to leave her marriage without putting herself or her loved ones in any danger. That's often difficult to do."

"So what *was* the exit strategy?"

Lizbeth's eyelids fluttered down for a moment as she pulled together her thoughts. "Wendy saved everything her dad sent her for gifts. She took a post office box and asked her father to send all of her mail there. He didn't question it because he just thought it was part of her lifestyle. If her dad or any other relative sent her presents, and she could keep them secret from her husband, she returned them for the cash. Since she was home alone a lot, she managed to sell some things on an auction site. She set up bank accounts in her own name. In some ways, she was luckier than most because her husband didn't suspect a thing."

"Why do you think that was?"

"He thought he was in total control, that Wendy wouldn't dare do anything he'd disapprove of."

"Because of threatened retribution?"

"Exactly."

"Was that enough to get her out?"

Lizbeth shook her head. "She found out the combination of her husband's safe. Once a month he stashed more cash in there to use for gambling in Atlantic City. She began siphoning off a little at a time. One night he gave her another battering because he didn't like what she'd cooked for dinner. She'd had enough. She felt she had enough money saved. She went to the ER, had photos taken, filed charges, rented an apartment, and left him."

The courage that must have taken, Caprice thought. It was hard to imagine the fear and survivor's instinct that must have run through Wendy.

"What happened with her husband? I also read that so many women are in danger *after* they leave because their exes go after them."

"Rick begged her to come back, but she remained steadfast. She'd kept a journal from the first time he'd hit her, and she'd taken her own photos so that she had a record of everything. She warned him if he did anything to hurt her or her dad, she'd go public with her journal and the photos and his family would be humiliated."

"That could have revved up his anger."

"She was taking a chance and she knew it. But I think she also knew him. Apparently he had some sense of reason. He didn't want to hurt his business or his reputation, or his family's pedigree. Wendy finally told her father what happened. He was a heavy investor and sponsor when she started Sunrise Tomorrow. It's grown to this—a safe haven, counselor advocate programs, and group meetings so that women and their children can break free of the cycle of abuse."

"You said the network extends far beyond here. What did you mean?"

Lizbeth hesitated as if she didn't want to give away too much, and Caprice could understand that. But she must have decided she could trust Caprice, at least a little.

"I'll just give you an example. Wendy's father lives in Delaware. He's helped provide safe passage and shelter for women who need to escape this area. Wendy created a network so no woman or her children have to fear the man they're escaping from. But she could be pushy and determined and relentless. She made enemies. There's no doubt about that."

"And her ex-husband still lives in York?"

"Wendy took back her maiden name when she divorced. And yes, he still lives and has his business in York. His name is Rick Grossman. He met with Wendy last week. I told the detective that when they questioned me. So I'm sure he's going to be on their suspect list."

"What is his business?" Caprice asked.

"His family's company builds on Add-a-Rooms. You know, sunrooms, that type of thing."

"Can you give me the address?"

"Sure," Lizbeth said. She pulled a sticky note from a stack on the desk and jotted down the information.

Right then and there Caprice decided she might have to look into the prospect of considering adding a room to her house.

Chapter Six

Although the leaves on the elms, poplars, maples, and sweet gums showed no hint of the change of seasons yet, yellow, white, purple, and cranberry-colored chrysanthemums bloomed in pots on porches and along garden walks as Nikki drove Caprice and Lady toward downtown and the Harvest Festival.

Parking for the mid-September celebration was always a problem with the downtown area cordoned off. The public parking lots filled and the streets on the outskirts of downtown became lined with cars. Many residents near the downtown area opened their yards for cars to park and charged for the privilege.

Caprice and Nikki were lucky to have their brother living downtown. They drove to Vince's condo building that had been an old school renovated into apartments. Fortunately, he had a guest parking space and Nikki slid her car into that. His condo building was located in the heart of downtown so they wouldn't have to walk far for access to the crafts and vendors, the food stands, and the shops that had enthusiastically decorated for the day.

After Nikki parked, Caprice let Lady jump out of

the back seat and they walked along the path that led out to the street.

"I can't believe Roz and Vince are skipping this," Nikki said as they walked. "They actually left town."

Lady trotted beside Caprice, her nose high as she caught the aroma of food cooking at the fest.

"Vince said he found another winery in Spring Grove to take Roz to. But I think the bottom line is that he just wants to be alone with her, not in the middle of a crowd of people," Caprice guessed.

"Do you really think he's going to buy the house you staged?"

"He's still thinking about it. I'm supposed to call him if any other offers come in."

"But he doesn't want Roz to put money into it too. So what kind of commitment is that?"

"A practical one," Caprice maintained. "At least for him. That's the lawyer in him. I mean, think about it, Nik. If they put their money together and bought the house, and then their relationship didn't work out, they'd have to sell the house and split the proceeds. Or one person would have to buy the other out. It would be like settling a divorce."

"I suppose," Nikki responded. "But it seems to me as if they're doing everything backward. Does he think living together is going to be a trial run for marriage? Because it's not. Living together just means neither of them is sure they want to stay."

Nikki and Caprice were on the same page with this line of thinking. To Caprice, living together was like playing house. It wasn't real life. She didn't want to pretend to be married when the time came. She actually wanted to *be* married. Vows were not something she'd ever take lightly.

"Did Brett set up another date with you since he canceled?"

Nikki frowned and shook her head. "No, I haven't heard from him. But then I guess solving this murder is on his mind twenty-four/seven."

"It wouldn't hurt for him to text you or something," Caprice muttered.

"We're not that far yet."

"You mean you're not thinking about each other every hour of the day?"

"Nope. In my case, I think about him every few hours of the day, but I don't even think he's at that point with me. I certainly don't want to get my hopes up. He could decide dating is just too difficult with his profession. His job interfered in his last relationship."

"He told you that?"

"It was like pulling teeth, but I wanted to know a little bit about his romantic history. I think that's important."

"And?" Caprice prompted.

"And, he admitted his girlfriend broke off their relationship after about a year because she was tired of canceled dates and his late hours."

Caprice thought about Seth Randolph whom she'd dated for a while before she'd made her mind up about Grant. "He's sort of like a doctor on call, only with law enforcement instead of patients."

"Exactly. The thing is, you didn't break off with Seth because of his profession. You broke it off because you knew you'd never come first."

"Among other things. I don't think Seth was really ready to settle down. He's still pursuing his dream."

"Have you heard from him since you broke up?"

"He e-mailed me last month to tell me he was extending his stay in Baltimore past the fellowship to fill in for a doctor who was on leave. He just said he'd let me know when he decided where he was going next. I appreciated that."

"Do you still have feelings for him?"

"No, not in the way you mean. But I'll always be fond of him. I'll always wish him well."

"Just as Grant wishes Naomi well?"

"Probably. But I see that as a good thing. Don't you think it's better to have an amicable relationship with an ex than a bitter one?"

"I suppose."

"That's why Grant and Naomi saw each other this summer. They worked out a lot of the old stuff, the baggage that was still weighing them both down."

"You weren't okay with it at the time."

"No, I wasn't. But I am now."

They'd reached the street and there were residents of Kismet and surrounding communities everywhere. They turned left, passed in front of Vince's condo building, and stopped to admire the white and cranberry-colored mums in the window display at Cherry on the Top, their favorite ice cream shop.

"I guess it's too early in the morning for a sundae," Caprice teased.

"It's never too early for a sundae, but I think I'd rather have chili fries or a burger first. Did you see the sign for fried ice cream in the store window? We could always try that."

As they passed by the movie theater, they noticed an Alfred Hitchcock festival was playing. The stands along the side of the street were filled with crafts. They stopped before a beeswax candle-maker booth.

"I don't light candles at all anymore," Caprice said. "Because of the animals. I miss them."

"What do you and Grant do for romance?"

"I have flameless candles now," Caprice responded reflexively and then was sorry she had.

Nikki elbowed her. "Have you and Grant taken the romance to the bedroom yet?"

Caprice shook her head and said seriously, "We both know what a commitment that would be. We're not in a hurry. We want to make sure our relationship is solid in every way."

Nikki studied her. "That's smart."

Caprice leaned close to her sister and whispered, "But that doesn't mean we don't make out by flameless candles."

They both laughed and moved on to the next stand, which sold beautifully embroidered scarves for dressers and tabletops.

Lady nosed around at the boxes underneath the stand. Caprice saw she was just sniffing, not doing any harm, so she examined a few of the scarves. "Do you think Nana would like one of these for that table in front of the window? Her birthday's coming up."

"She'd like that pink and green one with the lace edge," Nikki decided.

In no time at all, they'd bought the larger scarf and two smaller ones in case Nana would like to spread them under a vase or a picture frame.

"Have you spoken to Bella lately?" Caprice asked.

"She's so busy, between All About You, her online business, and the kids. She hardly has time to breathe."

"She seems to like it that way, though. And Joe's helping her a lot more with the kids."

"I guess the old adage that you can't teach old dogs new tricks isn't true," Caprice mused. "Counseling with Father Gregory has really seemed to help them. Joe's attitude has made a hundred-and-eighty-degree shift since a year ago. I think Bella's loving the house, and Joe doesn't complain too much about having to traipse down the yard to the garage."

Joe and Bella had needed room for their family to grow. They'd given up a one-floor ranch house for a two-and-a-half story older home near their mom and dad's. It had beautiful old woodwork, a refurbished kitchen, and the four bedrooms they needed. For the time being, Bella used her sewing machine in the nursery. But Joe intended to finish off the basement so Bella could run her kids' costume-making business from down there. It had its own outside entrance and would even be accessible for clients who wanted to explain what they preferred in the design of costumes or christening outfits.

Lady stopped at the curb as they came to the intersection of Sixth Avenue and White Rose Way, the main thoroughfare.

"Should we stay on this side of the street?" Nikki asked her. "Or cross over?"

"Let's stay on this side for now. I can peek in the window of Secrets of the Past." It was one of Caprice's favorite dress shops where she found many of her vintage-style clothes. Today with her fringed sweater poncho reminiscent of the '60s, she'd worn deep purple flannel slacks that flared at the ankles. Her purple pinstriped blouse with its Peter Pan collar picked up the color of purple in the poncho. Her fringed purse jangled with its peace sign charms. She made her own fashion statement.

Before they window-shopped at Secrets of the Past, both she and Nikki were distracted by the aromas emanating from the chili vendor that Lady had caught the scent of early on. Caprice was about to ask Nikki if she wanted to sample a small cup when she spotted Alicia Donnehy walking up the street. At first Caprice thought Alicia was just going to pass her right by and avoid making eye contact altogether. But then as if she knew that would be rude, and Caprice would probably confront her about it at some point, Alicia stopped, crouched down, and patted Lady. Lady licked her hand and rubbed against her leg.

"She remembers me," Alicia said.

"I think she remembers everybody she meets. But you actually sat with her for a while on the sofa during the reunion meeting. I'm sure she remembers you."

There were people milling all about and Alicia rose to her feet.

"I saw you at the shelter," Caprice said in a low voice while Nikki wandered on to the next stand that happened to be selling baked goods.

Alicia took Caprice's elbow and led her to a quiet spot near the side of the Secrets of the Past building. Nikki saw where they'd gone and she waved that she'd just be looking at the baked goods until Caprice was finished.

Lady sat at Caprice's feet and looked up at her, imploringly.

As usual, Caprice took a treat from her fanny pack and said to Lady, "Sit." Lady sat and Caprice gave her the treat. Then she gave her full attention to Alicia.

"Lizbeth told me you're going to investigate Wendy's murder," Alicia said in a low voice.

"That's not precisely true. I told her I'd see what information I could find out, and I'd give it to the police. She wants their investigation to move along and I don't blame her. But I'm not going to interfere in what they're doing."

After a few moments hesitation, Alicia nodded. "We should talk somewhere privately. I have to pick up my kids now. They're at my sister's. But how about tomorrow after church?"

"Sure. Why don't you come over to my place?"

"It probably won't be until about noon."

"That's fine. I'll go to early Mass, and then I'll make something for lunch. You'll join me, won't you?"

Alicia thought about it and then nodded again. "Okay. Thank you. I'll be there around noon."

As Caprice watched her high school classmate walk away, she wondered what Alicia had to tell her. There was no point dwelling on that for today. She and Lady wandered back over to Nikki.

"Let's cross over," Nikki said. "The Blue Moon Grille has a stand with some of their crab and cheese pretzel bits as samples. They advertised online this morning. It was posted on the same site where Helen told me to buy an ad."

A few months ago, another high school classmate had offered to check into the best social media positioning for Nikki's business. "Have you gotten any new clients since you posted there?" Caprice and Lady waited at the curb until the light turned, then she crossed the street with Nikki.

"Three new calls for catering gigs for October and November: an engagement party, a baby shower, and a luncheon. All new faces that could lead to more new faces."

As they strolled up the street in front of the arts and crafts mall, they spotted the Blue Moon Grille's stand. The Grille was located on top of the mall and had an outside deck that was already filled to capacity. As Nikki snatched a crab and cheese pretzel sample, Caprice noticed Sunrise Tomorrow had a booth of its own. That was a good idea to get the word out. Rena was manning it and was occupied in earnest conversation with a woman who held a pamphlet in her hand.

Nikki came closer to Caprice. After she finished her bit of crab pretzel, she said, "The murder came up when I was having my hair done at Curls R Us yesterday."

"Did you hear anything interesting?"

"No one was speaking from personal experience. Everything seems to be hush-hush about the facility. But I heard snippets about the main players, how Wendy and Lizbeth made such a great team. Lizbeth only came onboard about four years ago, but Rena has been working there since it opened. One thing interesting—my hair stylist said she'd heard there were hard feelings between Lizbeth and Rena, but nobody knows why."

"Lizbeth and Rena, not Wendy and Rena?"

"That's what she said."

Caprice was so engrossed in thought watching Rena and the woman having a serious discussion that she almost didn't notice the tug on Lady's leash. Lady barked and Caprice jumped as somebody's arm snaked around her waist.

She turned to find Grant staring down at her, Patches on a leash close at hand.

"I didn't even have to text you," Grant said with a smile.

Caprice leaned into his shoulder for a moment as their dogs sniffed recognition of each other.

"Didn't you have an appointment this morning?"

"Actually, I had two, but I brought Patches into the office and met with my clients there. Both were cut-and-dried wills, living wills, and powers of attorney."

"And Patches settled in okay?"

"I took him on a long walk before I brought him in with me. He was good."

Patches, Lady's sibling, was a cutie. His heritage must have come from his father. Caprice had rescued his pregnant mother, who Lady resembled, and then

found her owner. Ace's daughter Trista had adopted
another of the pups. One had gone along with her
mom, and the fifth had been adopted by a house
painter Caprice knew.

Nikki said to Caprice, "Now that you have company,
I'm going to check out the leather jackets on sale."
She pointed up the street to a small leather boutique.

"You don't want my opinion?" Caprice asked.

"I think I can find a bomber jacket on my own. I'm
not as colorful as you are. Will Grant give you a ride
home?"

Always going out of his way to include her family
when they were together, Grant said, "I'll see that she
and Lady get home safely. Are you sure you don't want
to have lunch with us? I passed a pulled pork sandwich stand. It smelled delicious."

"No, I'm good," Nikki said. "I might grab chili fries.
But I have a catering gig tomorrow, and I need to
whip up a carrot cake. You two have fun." She gave
Caprice a hug and Grant a smile and then walked up
the street.

"I didn't mean to run her off," Grant said.

"You didn't. She knows she can hang with us if she
wants. Do you really want pulled pork sandwiches for
lunch?"

"Why don't we get them to go and walk to the dog
park? We can eat in the picnic area there."

"Sounds good. What about something to drink?"
Caprice asked.

"While you buy the pulled pork, I'll stop at the
fresh lemonade stand."

And that's what they did. The dog park was about
a quarter of a mile away, but the sandwiches were

wrapped in foil and the lemonade cups held plenty of ice.

They walked through the crowd at a good pace, slowed down to view an artist's corner where paintings were on display, and then continued to the dog park.

As they left the Harvest Festival behind, Caprice told Grant, "Sunrise Tomorrow had a booth back there. Did you see it?"

"I did. It's a good way to spread contact information if anyone needs help. I asked a friend I have in the D.A.'s office about Wendy, and if the investigation was making any progress. She was murdered, by the way. The autopsy confirmed it. She was struck by something long and cylindrical, most likely one or two of those shades, and she fell into the banister and down to the first floor."

"That's just horrible." Caprice really didn't want to think about exactly how it had happened.

Grant bumped her arm with his. "Are you okay?"

"Just thinking about Wendy a lot. It wasn't as if I knew her that well, but something about this murder just really gets under my skin."

"Because you sympathize with the women who were abused and the work she did?"

"Possibly. It's not as if I ever experienced domestic violence, thank goodness. It's difficult to even imagine staying with someone who would hurt me."

"You have a strong sense of identity and good self-esteem."

"From what I learned of Wendy's background, she did too. Wendy mentioned that Warren Shaeffer has a Jekyll-Hyde personality. I wonder how many people that's true of?" Caprice asked rhetorically.

"It seems whatever Wendy's experience was didn't

keep her from trusting. She and Sebastian seemed to have a life together."

"That's true."

"My friend at the D.A.'s office said Wendy was instrumental in helping many women acquire protective orders," Grant said. "She also helped with relocations. She even rented storage units for women to store their belongings until they could find a safe place to stay."

"Alicia Donnehy's coming for lunch tomorrow. I ran into her earlier, and she said she thought we should talk."

Suddenly Grant stopped walking, and Patches looked up at him inquiringly, as did Caprice and Lady.

"Whether you say you're just gathering information for Detective Carstead or not, I know you're going to get involved in this investigation. This one worries me more than all the others did. Wendy Newcomb interfered in marriages, and that could be dangerous."

She could tell Grant again she'd be careful, but he'd heard that before. He also knew what had happened before. After all, he'd saved her life once.

When she remained silent, he gently clasped her arm. "I don't want you to make promises you can't keep. But I do want you to promise to depend on me to help you this time."

Gazing straight into his eyes, she nodded. "That's a promise I can make and keep. I *will* depend on you."

"Are you free for dinner tomorrow night? I'll cook," he offered.

"I'll bring dessert," she said.

"It's a date."

* * *

When Alicia arrived Sunday at noon, Caprice broke any awkward ice by saying, "Come on into the kitchen. The timer just went off on the casserole."

Mirabelle meowed from the lowest shelf of the cat tree, saying hello in her own way. Sophia looked down from the top shelf, blinked her eyes, and swished her magnificent tail.

Lady looked up at Alicia as if she expected attention.

With a smile, Alicia stooped to give Lady a couple of pats, then went over to Mirabelle and said, "Aren't you pretty?" Turning to Caprice, she remembered. "You were still keeping her separated upstairs the last time I was here."

That was true. The animals hadn't yet been acclimated to each other. Now they were for the most part, but Caprice knew their relationships, just like interactions between humans, would take time to develop.

In the kitchen, Caprice slipped one hand into an oven mitt and picked up a pot holder with the other. Then she opened the oven and took out the casserole she'd made in a lasagna pan.

"Oh, my gosh," Alicia said. "That's a lot for two people."

Caprice laughed. "I'll have leftovers for the week. I never know who will stop by. It's a beef and sausage base with tomato sauce and then a shredded potato concoction that I spread on the top."

"You come up with these recipes all on your own?"

"I just mix and match favorite ingredients. My mom and Nana were always cooking, and I picked it up easily. So did my sisters. Vince, not so much. He's our wine connoisseur."

"That's right. You get together with your family

for a dinner once a month and everybody brings something. Do you know how lucky you are?"

"I realize it more and more each day. Did you have a big family?" She really didn't know that much about Alicia. Even though they were classmates, she hadn't hung around with her during their teenage years.

Alicia slowly laid her purse on the counter. Next she pushed up the sleeves of her long-sleeved sweater as if she needed something to do. She'd pinned back one side of her hairdo with a wood barrette. She'd been pretty in high school and was pretty now. Her honey-blond hair had darkened a bit through the years, but it still shone with golden strands.

Her green eyes were somber now, though, as she said, "I have a brother who moved far away. My parents fought all the time when we were kids. He tried to protect me and my mother."

"Protect?" Caprice asked, though she felt she knew the answer.

"Can I do anything to help with lunch?"

This was a subject that probably needed to be entered slowly. "Sure," Caprice answered. "The salad's in the fridge. Just pull it out. I have salad dressing and a peach balsamic vinegar that's really good by itself."

"That sounds good."

Caprice already had the table set with her brightly colored dishes in turquoise, lime, and fuchsia. From her buttercup yellow appliances in vintage style to the sunny yellow and white linoleum on the floor, the room was a more than pleasant place to be.

Caprice had warmed slices of cheddar-pepperoni bread in the oven. She pulled out the tinfoil pack and placed it on the table.

After they were seated and Caprice was dishing out the casserole, Alicia poured balsamic vinegar on her salad. "My dad was abusive when he drank. My mother finally divorced him when I was ten and my brother was fourteen. But there were a lot of years that we were unhappy and fearful. I guess that's why I fell into the situation I did."

"I don't mean to pry," Caprice said sincerely. "But are you and your children safe now?"

"We are. Sid is in counseling and goes to anger management classes. We'll never get back together, and for now his visitation time with the kids is supervised. But I'm getting into a better spot than I was in a year ago. Everything about domestic abuse is so hidden. When I was in the middle of it, nobody knew. I sure wasn't going to tell anyone and risk humiliation and more of Sid's anger. And the kids—it's like they made a pact not to talk about anything bad and maybe that was my fault. Maybe if their teachers had known what was going on, we all would have gotten help sooner. Sid never touched the kids, never even yelled at them. He took all of that out on me. I would have left much sooner if I felt they were being harmed. At least that's the way I thought then. Most of our arguments took place after they were in bed at night. But they knew. I'm hoping counseling through Sunrise Tomorrow will help them recover so they can have good relationships when they grow up."

They turned to eating for few moments, then Alicia added, "I wanted to get together because Wendy was smart about protecting the women she took under her wing."

"What do you mean by *smart*?"

"Do you know about Wendy's marriage?"

"Some. I know she kept a record of her abuse and took photos."

"Exactly. Which is what she counseled me to do as soon as I contacted her. She recorded other data too."

"Data on the women she helped?"

"More than that. Because of the information she collected, she often had leverage when she had to deal with an abusive spouse. She did deep background checks and even used a P.I. on occasion. That way she had some control—or rather the wife in danger had some control."

"Did you have first-hand experience with Wendy collecting this information?"

"Absolutely. Somehow Wendy found out that my husband had secretly sent out an e-mail blast campaigning against his boss to have him ousted. The boss didn't know it was Sid doling out everything he'd done wrong to everybody in the company. Sid used some kind of anonymous e-mail server. Anyway, if the word had gotten out that Sid had done it, he would have lost his job. He didn't want to lose it. He just wanted a promotion. So after I left him, Wendy threatened him with public exposure if he didn't agree to my terms."

"Wow," Caprice responded. "That's not just leverage, that's almost blackmail." She remembered Wendy's phone call when she asked for Detective Carstead's number. She'd said it concerned blackmail. Was somebody blackmailing her? Or had she gotten herself into trouble by blackmailing someone else?

"I guess you could say it was blackmail," Alicia agreed, without being defensive at all about it. Maybe because Wendy's information had kept her out of harm's way and helped her set up a new life.

Suddenly Caprice thought of something. "Where did Wendy keep this information?"

Alicia shrugged. "She probably stored it on some Cloud, or if she really wanted to be secure about it, a backup drive. I heard the police took her personal computer from her home, but I'll bet the information isn't on there."

"Do you think Sebastian knows where it is?"

Alicia shook her head. "I doubt it. Wendy was too careful to keep it someplace obvious."

Caprice hadn't paid a condolence visit to Sebastian and his sons yet. She was going to make a coconut cake for dessert with Grant tonight. It was a recipe Bella had given her. Maybe she'd just bake two and take one to Sebastian.

Alicia took a big forkful of the casserole as if she was really enjoying it.

If the police found wherever Wendy kept that storehouse of information, they'd probably have a whole list of suspects.

Caprice knew a list of suspects would be a good place to start to find Wendy's murderer.

Chapter Seven

Grant's townhouse, comfortably appointed and decorated with a masculine feel, looked lived-in and comfortable. Caprice and Grant had spent many nights on his faux suede gray couch watching movies and eating popcorn with Lady and Patches at their feet. As both canines ushered Caprice into the kitchen, she caught the scent of frying bacon and meat broiling. Grant was setting a salad bowl on the table when she entered the room.

"I let myself in," she said.

He smiled at her. "Good. I should give you a key, then if the door's ever locked you can still get in."

His words surprised but pleased her. She'd already given him a key to her place as well as the alarm code. If he was trusting her with a key, that meant he was really opening his life to her.

"Something smells good," she said, setting the cake on the table, then taking off her poncho.

"The porterhouse steak needs about another minute under the broiler. I have toppings for loaded baked potatoes and the salad for something healthy. What's for dessert?"

"Coconut cake. You seemed to like it when Bella brought it to our family dinner."

"It was delicious," he said, coming toward her. "Bella's recipe?"

Caprice nodded as he took her poncho from her and hung it on a peg near the back door. Then he came to her again and pulled her into his arms, giving her a huge hug and a kiss.

Afterward, he leaned his forehead against hers. "I'm glad you're here. I have a bottle of Chardonnay that Vince suggested. Wine with dinner?"

"Sounds good. One glass should wear off before I leave."

The timer on the microwave went off.

"Steak's done. You like yours medium well, right?"

"I do, but you like yours done a little less."

"The thicker side for me. The thinner side for you. It will be just right," he assured her. "Steak is the one thing I do know how to cook. My dad would let my mom splurge once a year for Christmas and buy steak. When most people were having ham, we were having the best cut of sirloin she could find."

"Steak was rare in our house too. When Mom splurged, she'd buy round steak to make Swiss steak that stretched a little further with parsley potatoes."

"Parsley potatoes. You just boil them and then put butter and parsley on them, right? I could probably manage that sometime."

Grant was wearing a light blue Oxford shirt with the sleeves rolled up and what looked like new jeans. No holes in the knees for him. With his black hair waving across his forehead, his gray eyes always coming back to hers when he spoke to her, her insides twittered with the recognition that this was the man she wanted to be with.

"Parsley potatoes would go with steak too. Next time," she agreed.

Patches and Lady had already made themselves comfortable under the table as if they were sure they would be getting bites of steak. Caprice motioned to them. "Ready, willing, and able to eat our dinner if we don't want it."

Grant laughed. "We'll save them some scraps. Patches already had dinner. How about Lady?"

"She had hers before we came. I didn't want her to beg."

Grant turned off the broiler and removed the broiler pan, setting it on the stove burners. The steak sizzled, investing the kitchen with its deep aroma.

A few minutes later, Grant opened the wine and poured a glass for Caprice as well as himself. "Did you have lunch with your classmate? Alicia, wasn't it?"

"I did, but are you sure you want to talk about it tonight?"

"I figured if you had lunch with her, you're thinking about it. So we might as well get it out of the way first, then we'll have the rest of the night to concentrate on us."

He really did know her very well. Her mind was still buzzing about everything she and Alicia had discussed. If she told Grant what was on her mind now, maybe she *could* just relax and forget about it for the rest of the evening.

"Stories around murder are never simple, are they?"

Using his steak knife adroitly, Grant cut his portion into pieces. "Premeditated or not, the motives behind murder are rarely simple."

Caprice didn't know quite where to start and obviously Grant could see that. He reached across the table and covered her hand with his. "Start at the beginning."

"I don't know where the beginning is. Wendy could have been racking up enemies ever since she started Sunrise Tomorrow a decade ago. But her instincts for survival had taught her lessons she used in her work."

"Explain," Grant said, taking a bite of his potato topped with sour cream, cheddar cheese, and bacon bits.

"Lizbeth told me that Wendy kept a journal while she was being abused. She wrote down details and she took photographs. She threatened to expose the sordid details and ruin her ex-husband's reputation. She blackmailed him to let her go."

Grant stopped eating, fork in midair. "I think I know where this is going. No place good."

"No place good," Caprice agreed. "Alicia told me her own story. Essentially, Wendy blackmailed Alicia's husband into letting Alicia go, and to get him into counseling. It worked. Many of these men are bullies. Their ego is everything. They don't want to be humiliated, especially if they have high-profile reputations, and especially if they'll lose their jobs. Wendy dug into backgrounds. Alicia said she even used a private eye on occasion."

"As I said before, interfering in marriage is dangerous, especially if these men are obsessive about their wives."

"But if they're bullies, they back down. Some of them even get help. Maybe we can't approve of Wendy's methods, but they worked."

"Yeah, and they probably got her killed," Grant protested.

"She probably felt she was giving these women tools to defend themselves, tools that weren't lethal like buying a gun and learning how to shoot, which is what some people might recommend in this situation."

Grant stabbed at his salad and shook his head. "Harmful information on paper might seem like a good self-defense mechanism. Even blackmail too. But in the end, don't we have the same result? Someone died."

"I'm not disagreeing. If we found Wendy's journal, we might have a whole score of suspects."

"If you found all the dirt she kept, you might have another score."

"Alicia didn't think she'd keep it on her personal computer. The police took that. She didn't believe Wendy kept it on the one at work either. There's all kinds of confidential information on the Sunrise Tomorrow computers. The detectives would probably have to get a search warrant."

"If the info isn't on Wendy's personal or work computers, that leaves . . ." Grant left his sentence open-ended.

"That leaves either a secure Cloud site or a flash drive."

"And that's what you're looking for?"

"That's probably what the police are looking for too. I think I'd like to talk to Sebastian about it."

"Is he ready for that conversation?"

"I'm going to find out. I'll pay him a condolence call tomorrow and just feel him out on the subject. I would think he'd want Wendy's murderer brought to justice just as much as the police do."

"And if he doesn't want to talk about more than the food you bring to comfort him?"

"Then I'll find someone else to talk to."

Grant arched his brows. "Of course, you will." He

waved at her dish and the steak she hadn't touched. "But for tonight, let's concentrate on good food, a fabulous dessert, and each other's company." The look in Grant's eyes said there might be a few kisses in that mix too.

Caprice picked up her fork and took her first bite of the steak Grant had broiled to perfection.

Early Monday morning, Caprice had just fed her felines and taken Lady out to the backyard for a run when Bella called. Her phone to her ear, Caprice watched Lady roll in the grass as she took a deep breath of the crisp air.

"I need your help," Bella told Caprice.

When the sisters needed each other, they called, and they never turned each other down.

"With Sunnybud?"

"No, he's made himself at home since we let him come upstairs from the basement. I need help packing up orders. Do you have any time you can give me today? I have the morning to work because my neighbor is watching Benny. My Halloween costume orders are ready to send out, but I'm behind packing them up. I have a video consultation at ten."

"I can probably be there around eleven. How does that sound?"

"Eleven sounds good. We should be able to get a lot done before I go get Benny."

"I'll leave Lady at home this time so she doesn't spook Sunnybud."

"Sounds good. I'll see you at eleven."

It was only a few minutes after eleven when Caprice arrived on Bella's doorstep. Bella waved her inside and

Caprice could see the long table she'd set up in the family room with collapsible cardboard boxes, tissue paper, and larger boxes the others could be put in for mailing. Tape and supplies were on the table too. Bella had set up an assembly line that was ready to go. In the living room, there stood a dress rack that held costumes from a pirate to a gypsy to a bumblebee.

"Where do we start?" Caprice asked Bella.

"I just pressed them all. I'll line the boxes with tissue paper if you fold each one carefully. We'll do one at a time so nothing gets mixed up and I'm sure the right address is on the right package."

"Sounds good," Caprice said, taking the hanger with the pirate costume off the end of the rack and crossing through the French doors to the table in the family room. Bella followed her and readied a box with tissue paper.

"You have about twenty orders here."

"And another ten for next week. Halloween is approaching fast. I did the mail-out orders first. There are some parents at school who wanted costumes for their kids and I'll be finishing those next week."

Bella's comment reminded Caprice that she had a long acquaintance stretch because of her kids at school and her involvement with the parent-teacher organization. Maybe Bella could fill in some background she didn't have.

"Do you know anything about Poplar Grove Co-housing Development?"

Bella squinted at her. "Why?"

"Wendy Newcomb lived there."

"Tell me again why you're getting involved in a murder investigation."

"Lizbeth Diviney, Wendy's assistant director, asked

me to get involved. She doesn't want the work at Sunrise Tomorrow to get stalled."

"And that's why you're asking about the housing development?"

There was something in Bella's tone that alerted Caprice she was about to learn something new. "It's a cooperative neighborhood and I wonder exactly what they cooperate with. I think Wendy and her significant other, Sebastian Thompson, are two of the leaders."

"I've heard of the development," Bella admitted. "One of Timmy's classmates and his mom were involved in a custody dispute after a divorce. They went to live with someone in that neighborhood. But the odd thing was, they disappeared."

"What do you mean they disappeared?"

"They went to the neighborhood to live with someone at the end of the week, but after that weekend, no one could find them. The police questioned the couple they were staying with, but they said one morning the mom and child went grocery shopping and didn't return. The thing was—they disappeared the day before they were supposed to appear in court for the ruling on the custody dispute."

"How long ago was this?"

"About a year ago," Bella answered.

"What was the rumor on the court decision?"

"That the judge was going to give the father the advantage and custody."

"That would have been unusual."

"Unusual, but not impossible. The father was rich and well-connected."

"Was there any buzz about it afterward?"

"There was a lot of supposition about the kind of

father and husband he was. If the woman was fearing for her child at all, that could be why she ran."

"But they disappeared from Wendy's neighborhood," Caprice murmured. "I wonder if it was possible that she helped them disappear. I heard she has a network that extends far beyond what anybody expects."

"Just how would you disappear in this day and age?" Bella wanted to know. "It's like Big Brother is watching you everywhere. Any trace on the computer and they'd be found. Credit cards can be tracked and phones can be pinged."

"Maybe. But if someone's smart enough and knows exactly what they're doing, I imagine new identities can still be bought. Fake IDs can be made. A new identity, a new social security number, a fake driver's license. It would all be possible with the right kind of help."

"That stuff actually happens?" Bella asked.

"I'm not sure, but it's possible."

While Caprice mulled over the information Bella had provided, she heard a meow in the kitchen.

Bella immediately went to the dining area of the room. Caprice followed her.

"He's hungry. It's almost lunchtime."

Bella went to the refrigerator, took out a can of cat food, and plopped half of it on a ceramic dish she pulled from the cupboard. Then she set it on a placemat on the floor where a water dish stood.

"Hey, Sunnybud. We have company. Remember her?"

The cat gave Caprice a look, then began eating.

"You should see how the sun glows off of him when he sits in it. And he's become everybody's buddy."

Sunnybud stopped eating and looked up at Bella with trusting green eyes.

She stooped down to pet him. "I'll give you crunchies later."

"I think you like him," Caprice said with obvious surprise. She'd expected Joe and the kids to befriend Sunnybud, not Bella. But from her manner with the feline, Caprice could tell her sister was already attached, whether she'd admit it or not. "I'll help you pack up the orders; then I'm headed over to Sebastian Thompson's house."

Bella shook her head. "I can only imagine what he's going through. Do you want to stay for lunch? I made homemade tomato soup, and we can have tuna sandwiches to go with it. Joe stocked up on tuna."

There was a twinkle in Bella's eye, and Caprice liked seeing it there. She imagined someone was sneaking Sunnybud tuna . . . and that someone was Bella.

When Caprice arrived at Sebastian's home, she spotted his Land Rover in the carport and knew he was there. When he answered the kitchen door, she could see the grief in his eyes. He didn't hesitate to invite her inside.

"It's good to see you," he said.

Although they'd met only recently, she couldn't help but set the coconut cake on the counter and give him a hug. Tears came to her own eyes, and she said, "I'm so sorry."

"I know. Everybody's been saying that and I don't know what to tell them in return. *Sorry* is about what sums it all up. If Wendy had died of natural causes, maybe I could understand it. But this?"

"It's senseless. The work she did was so noble."

"Downright gritty and dangerous sometimes too," Sebastian supplied, as if he wanted to talk about it with someone. "Can I get you a cup of coffee? I've kept a pot brewing ever since all this happened. People have been stopping in. The neighbors thought I needed company that whole first day and the next. And they were probably right. But at some point I have to deal with it on my own with the boys." He nodded toward the living room.

Kevin and Cody were on the sofa, remote controls in their hands, playing a game on the flat-screen TV. Dover sat between their feet, gazing up at the screen.

"I've kept them home from school this week. I figure mindless video games will help them process. Maybe I'm wrong. But at least I know where they are and what they're doing. If they have questions, I'm here to answer them. Not that I have any answers."

"Nobody does in a situation like this. And yes, I'd be glad for a cup of coffee."

He poured her a mug and they sat at the round oak table under the wrought-iron chandelier. She could hear the *blip, blip, blip* and the *bong, bong, bong* of the video game the boys were playing, and she imagined they could hear her conversation with Sebastian too.

He took the milk carton from the refrigerator and set it on the table beside the sugar bowl. "Wendy would have poured this into a little creamer, but I just can't work up the energy to think it matters."

"It doesn't, Sebastian. Not now. This isn't about prettying things up. It's about dealing with what happened."

While Caprice added milk and sugar to her coffee, he poured his black and sat down across from her. "Did you know Wendy was Catholic?"

"No, I didn't."

"Sometimes she would go out to the six a.m. Mass at St. Francis."

"I never get to that one," Caprice admitted with a smile.

"If we were helping somebody relocate, we often did that on Sundays. In some ways, I think Wendy's work was her religion."

"I can understand that. From what I've learned since she died, this was a very personal cause to her."

"It certainly was."

The dog suddenly stood, stretched, and meandered into the kitchen. He went to Sebastian first and propped his muzzle on Sebastian's knee.

"Even he knows."

"They do, and pets are a great comfort. My guess is, your boys talk to him."

Sebastian gave her a weak smile. "You're right about that. Sometimes I go into Cody's room and he's talking to him like he never talks to me. Kevin began spending more time with Wendy. They often took bike rides together. Cody is the quieter one."

Confirming what Caprice had guessed, Cody looked their way as if he'd heard what his father had said.

Sebastian lowered his voice. "He's a computer geek and happily admits it."

Cody called in from the living room. "I'm going to major in computer science and artificial intelligence when I go to college. Why hide that fact?"

"It's good he knows what he wants to do," Caprice commented.

"I suppose so. Wendy had already downloaded college catalogs online. We were going to tour campuses in the spring."

Caprice realized that when a loved one died you

didn't only lose them, you lost your hopes and dreams for the future.

"I think my neighbors decided they needed to support me because the detective interviewed me that first day for hours. He wanted to know so many details of our life."

From past experience Caprice realized the spouse or significant other was always considered the prime suspect. "Did you call a lawyer?" she asked.

"No, I didn't have a lawyer. Wouldn't that make me look guilty?"

Caprice shrugged. "That's one way of looking at it. On the other hand, you need to protect your rights. If they decide you're on their persons of interest list, you need to have good advice."

"I can't believe they'd suspect me."

"I've been in several situations where the detectives do suspect an innocent person. And once they make you their target, it's hard to divert their attention again."

Sebastian looked worried now. "So you really think I should get a lawyer? Would Grant help me?"

"Grant isn't a criminal defense attorney and neither is my brother. But I'm sure they could recommend someone."

He shook his head again and glanced toward his boys. "I'm all they have."

"I think you should know that Lizbeth asked me to look into Wendy's murder. I've done a bit of mystery solving in the past. She thinks I might be able to gather information the police can't, and she doesn't want anything to stand in the way of renovating the Wyatt estate and having the facility up and running by January."

"Lizbeth asked you to do this?"

"She did. I think she's feeling quite overwhelmed."

"Yes, she is," Sebastian agreed. "It's a lot for one person to take on. So you're really going to look into this?"

"Already I have some information that I don't know if the police have. I learned that Wendy kept a journal."

"Yes, she did. But it's not here."

"The police took it?"

"No, she always had it with her."

"So it might have been with her the day she was killed, and the person who did it might have stolen it?"

"I suppose that's possible."

As the dog came over to Caprice now for an ear rub, Kevin nudged his brother, set the remote control aside, and wandered into the kitchen. "You're talking about Wendy's journal?" he asked.

Sebastian eyed his son quizzically. "We are."

"She hid it somewhere."

"I don't understand," Sebastian said. "Why would she do that?"

Kevin shrugged. "I think it was an old habit from when she was married. She didn't keep it on her because her husband would search her and her things."

"I'd never do that."

"I know you wouldn't, Dad. But Wendy was afraid of a lot of things, and having her privacy violated was one of them. She felt it was safer to hide the journal someplace else so we couldn't stumble across it accidentally, I guess."

"Do you know where she hid it?"

"Nope, that's not something she'd tell *anybody*."

Caprice supposed the teenager was right. But then there was another matter to consider. "One of the women I spoke with told me Wendy kept information about the abusive husbands she came in contact with. She used that information for leverage."

"If she kept it on her computer," Sebastian said, "the police took that."

"Get your geek on, Dad," Cody scolded his father from the living room. "It's information she needed and wanted and didn't think anybody else should look at. She's not going to keep it on her computer."

"He's right," Caprice agreed. "Lizbeth told me she didn't keep it at work."

"*Get my geek on?* What does that mean?"

Cody practically scowled. "You've been around me long enough to know how I operate. If I don't want anybody to see something, I put it on a flash drive. Then I can hide that someplace safe. She probably put it the same place she keeps her journal."

"Do any of you have any idea where that might be?" Caprice asked.

As Cody began to think about it, she could practically see the wheels turning in his head.

He began eliminating possibilities. "Not at work. Not here. Someplace where nature can't get to it, and no one else could either. But I'm blank right now."

"We'll think about it," Sebastian assured her. "If the boys and I put our heads together, maybe an idea will generate."

"One big puzzle," Kevin murmured.

Caprice discovered that's exactly what solving a mystery was like—putting together a 5,000-piece jigsaw puzzle. She just hoped with everybody working on the same board, they could do it.

Chapter Eight

Caprice's stop at Perky Paws on Tuesday morning was a strategic move. She needed time to think about what she was going to do next in collecting information, and the pet supply store was open earlier than the office of the man who could be the main suspect in Wendy's murder. The front case at Perky Paws was always lined up with snacks that looked good enough for humans to eat. But they were for dogs with their peanut butter base, bacon and cheese biscuits, the yogurt topping. Some were as fancy as any wedding cookie. Others were to be gulped down with a snap of a finger. She always bought a few and had them on hand when Patches and Dylan came over. Lady received one on special occasions.

After picking out a few that she knew they'd all enjoy, she had them boxed up and then told Gretta she needed to look for a few catnip-infused toys. Sunnybud, as well as her felines, would enjoy them.

Since Gretta knew her family, Caprice told her, "Bella took in a stray cat. I thought he'd appreciate a few toys."

"Bella? She doesn't like fur on her dresses, on her stockings, on her clothes, or on her sofa."

Caprice shrugged. "She seems to like this cat."

"What color is he?"

"Yellow tabby."

"They can be beauties and sweet ones too. So you need a carrier?"

"I had one that she's using. If I know Bella, she'll make a designer carrier for him."

"Maybe she could get into the business. There's big bucks in pet clothes and pet toys."

"I don't know if I even want to tell her that."

"Ace and his daughter were in here last weekend with Brindle." Brindle was the name that Trista had given to Lady's sister.

"I haven't seen Trista for a while. How's she doing?"

"She and that dog are like one. They're insepa-rable."

"I can see they would be. Brindle's probably Trista's best friend. With her dad on the road again, visits not as frequent as she'd like, her mom with her own concerns, she probably tells Brindle all her thoughts and dreams."

"She does, and she buys her the cutest leashes and collars. And Ace buys the best food. You surely did him a favor getting him away from Detective Jones's clutches when his fiancée was murdered."

"I knew Ace didn't do it. I had to do everything I could to help."

"You helped your sister last time around. That's five. I think I see a pattern. Are you changing your life's work?"

"Oh, no, nothing like that. Somehow I just get pulled in."

"Are you pulled into the latest? You knew Wendy Newcomb, didn't you?"

"I didn't know her well, but I did know her. I was going to redecorate the Wyatt estate."

"Is that still happening?"

"I surely hope so. I signed the contract. Tell me something. Do you know anything about her ex-husband?"

"You mean that Rick Grossman who owns the Add-a-Room place?"

"So you *do* know. I thought Wendy's first marriage was kept hushed up."

"Hushed up is one thing. But when they were getting a divorce, he had a loud shouting match with her at the Koffee Klatch. Lots of witnesses. After the fact, that's the kind of thing nobody wants to talk about."

"You say that was about the divorce?"

"Rather about the settlement. Like many men, he didn't want to give her her due. But I was there on my coffee break. I saw her take out this little blue book."

"Like a notebook?"

"Sort of, maybe smaller than a notebook. It looked like it had a leather jacket, not a cardboard one. She opened it up and turned it around and showed him. He turned so red that I thought he was going to have a stroke. But then she grabbed it back, closed it, and put it in her inside jacket pocket. There wasn't any more shouting after that."

"Wow. Have you ever been to his store?"

"Nope, no need to do that. We don't have any place to add a room onto."

Their conversation ended, Caprice wandered to the aisle with the cat toys. Then she pulled her phone from her pocket, playing a hunch. Usually a man like

Rick Grossman was a control freak. So better to let him have some control at the beginning.

She searched for his Web site to find his phone number, then called his store. A receptionist answered. Caprice asked if she could make an appointment for this morning. The receptionist didn't hesitate, probably because she thought Caprice wanted to buy a room. They set up the appointment for nine-thirty, as soon as she finished here.

After a few pointed questions for Mr. Grossman, maybe she could figure out if the man had the temperament to commit murder.

As Caprice drove south of York to Loganville where Grossman Rooms and Stoves was located—apparently they sold and installed wood stoves, too—Caprice phoned Grant and left him a message. She told him where she was going to be, just in case. He'd asked her to depend on him, and she would. He would be her safeguard as she tried to unravel some of the circumstances surrounding Wendy Newcomb. Maybe after her meeting with Wendy's ex-husband, she'd stop at Brown's Orchards and pick up vegetables and fruit. The store had so many varieties of apples this time of year. It teemed with fresh produce, baked goods, and even a wine room. Maybe she should surprise her brother and take *him* a bottle from Logan's View Winery for a change.

She kept her mind on the task before her as she pulled into Grossman's stand-alone building with its parking lot. When she opened the door to enter the business, a bell dinged and the receptionist sitting behind an L-shaped oak desk looked up and smiled. "Can I help you?"

"I'm Caprice De Luca. I have an appointment."

The receptionist pressed a button, announced into

the intercom, "Your appointment's here," and went back to her computer. A few seconds later, a tall, thin man with sandy blond hair, a beakish nose, and a friendly smile emerged from an office.

He held his hand out to Caprice. "I'm Rick Grossman. You're interested in an Add-a-Room?"

Caprice didn't know what she'd expected, a monster with two heads? No, that was just the point. From what she'd been reading, an abusive husband could be charming, solicitous, and more than friendly in many situations. It was when his buttons got pushed he turned into someone else. Did Caprice want to push this man's buttons?

Caprice had thought about her answer to his question, and she'd decided that in the future she might want to add a room to the back of her house. She had plenty of yard there. It wouldn't hurt to visualize it and talk to this man about it. She couldn't just plunge into pointed questions.

"I *have* been thinking about adding a room. My neighbor has a sunroom and in the winter, she enjoys sitting in there."

Rick said, "We like to call them all-seasons rooms. They do warm up a house in the winter. You could even put a wood stove in one, or a space heater to make it especially toasty as well as bright. Do you want to come into my office to talk about it?"

"Sure, let's do that," she said.

He was wearing a white Oxford shirt and gray dress slacks and he looked professional. As he motioned her to a wood chair at his desk, he went behind it. "How large a room were you thinking about?"

"That's why I'm here—to collect information. Do you have any pamphlets, how small the rooms start and how large they get?"

"Of course, I do." He swiveled his chair around to a file cabinet, opened a drawer, and took out a glossy packet. He handed it to her. "This will give you preliminary ideas, but I can do that, too, if you want to discuss what you need."

"I have a porch on the back of my house now. The question would be whether I want to enclose that or whether I would add the room onto the garage side. I'm really just in the thinking stages."

"I see. Can I ask where you heard about my company?"

There it was, the perfect opening. "I first heard about it from Wendy Newcomb."

His eyes widened and then narrowed. "You did? That surprises me. She wouldn't give me a recommendation if her life depended on it."

She could hear the bitterness in his voice, and she decided to probe into it. "I knew Wendy. I was going to decorate the Wyatt estate for her and update the original Sunrise Tomorrow shelter."

"Because you knew Wendy you decided to come here and ask me about an Add-a-Room?" He sounded suspicious.

Caprice didn't lie. It wasn't in her nature. But she could bend the truth just a little. "I'm gathering information to help the police investigation into Wendy's murder."

Grossman sat back as if he wanted to remove himself from her. "You're an investigator for the police?"

"No, not exactly. But I have worked with them solving a couple of other murders." That was true enough, she supposed.

"I don't know what you want from me. Wendy and I were through. No contact. Those were the terms of our divorce."

"I know the reasons you divorced," she admitted.

"You do?" he asked, as if daring her to tell him what they were.

She couldn't turn down a dare. "You abused Wendy. She kept a record of it and she used that to blackmail you into the terms of the divorce."

His mouth tightened into a line that made him go silent. He stood. "I think you should leave."

Caprice didn't move. "If I leave, that means you don't want to cooperate."

"I don't have to cooperate with you. I don't have to cooperate with anyone." Grossman might be tall and thin and lean, but by the way his hands gripped into fists, the way his muscles bunched under his shirt, she could see he'd have the strength to whack Wendy with a shade and knock her over that balustrade.

"Tell me something, Mr. Grossman. Is it true Wendy had a journal where she wrote everything down?"

He gave her a sidelong glance. Then he muttered, "Yes, she had a journal. I didn't know about it until it was too late. I would have found it and destroyed it."

Whoa. He was angry enough to be honest with her.

"What color was it?" Caprice asked.

"It was blue . . . leather . . . not very big. I saw it once or twice and thought it was just some kind of reminder notebook she kept in her purse. Little did I know that it was a detailed account of her life."

Seeing that Caprice hadn't budged, the bluster seemed to go out of him, as did some of the ruddiness in his face. He sat on the corner of his desk. "Look. I'm not that man anymore, not the man I was when I was married to Wendy. I got counseling. Yeah, I had anger issues, but now I know what to do with them. I'm involved with someone and we have a good relationship. My past with Wendy is just that, the past."

He was saying all the right things, but that didn't mean he was innocent. "So you have had no recent contact with Wendy, say within the last month?"

"No contact." He held up his hands in front of him like a barrier as if that was proof.

"I heard the two of you were spotted meeting."

"We just ran into each other at the deli. We said hello. I told you I've changed and Wendy knew that. We were civil."

Had they been civil?

"Have you ever been to the Wyatt estate?" Caprice asked.

"No, I haven't, but I've seen photos of it. I don't imagine they'd need an Add-a-Room."

If that was his attempt at humor, it fell flat.

He glanced at his watch. "I have another meeting in ten minutes. We need to wrap this up. Is there anything else?"

"There's nothing else . . . for now," Caprice told him. "Thank you for your time. And I will think about that Add-a-Room." She lifted the packet on her lap, stood, and left his office.

Adrenaline was running full and strong through her, and she felt a little shaky as she went outside. She didn't like being in the same room as Rick Grossman. She didn't like the vibrations that had emanated from him as he'd gotten angry. Wendy had lived with more than those vibrations. Had he really changed? Was that even possible?

As Caprice drove to Brown's, she gave it more thought, but she didn't come up with a conclusion.

Caprice had pushed her cart loaded with apples and other produce, two bottles of wine, and cheese bread into Brown's parking lot when her cell phone buzzed. She had an inkling who it was going to be even before she checked the screen. She pushed her cart along the side of her car and answered Grant's call.

"I got your message," he said judiciously.

"Good. I just wanted you to know where I was . . . in case."

"I'm glad you did, though I can't say that makes me feel a whole lot better that you interviewed Grossman to begin with."

"His receptionist was there and the store was open for business. It was safe, Grant, honestly."

"Where are you now?"

"I'm outside of Brown's. I bought great produce. How about an apple pie and cheese bread for supper? Are you busy?"

"Not too busy for apple pie and cheese bread," he returned with a smile in his voice.

"Come over around six?" she asked.

"That sounds good. I had another reason to call you other than checking up on you."

"Oh, you did. What was that?"

His voice turned serious. "Wendy Newcomb's body was released, and her funeral's being held in Delaware on Thursday. From what I understand, Sebastian and his boys will be traveling there for it. On Saturday, Sebastian's planning a memorial service and a get-together at his house afterward. Wendy touched so many lives here that he wants to affirm that and give the people she helped a chance to share memories."

"How did you find out about all this?"

"Sources."

"The D.A.'s office?"

"Giselle has her ear to the ground."

Giselle was Vince and Grant's secretary at the office downtown. "Does she know Sebastian?"

"She's friends with one of Sebastian's neighbors. I

just thought you'd like to know. I can get more details from her closer to the time."

"Lizbeth will probably have those details too. Of course, I want to go to the service and stop at Sebastian's afterward."

"I knew you would. Where are you headed now?"

"Back home." Her phone beeped that another call was coming in. She checked it. "Grant, Dulcina's trying to get hold of me."

"I'll let you go," he said. "I'll see you tonight. I'm looking forward to it."

Caprice was smiling when she pressed the icon for Dulcina's call to come through. "Hi, Dulcina. What's up? Is Lady wreaking havoc with the kittens?" Dulcina had offered to pup-sit while Caprice ran errands.

"No, and I'm glad she's here," her friend responded, sounding as if she might be near tears.

"What's wrong?"

"Your uncle picked up Mason and Tia."

"Aww, Dulcina. You miss them?"

"The house seems empty without them."

"It's a hard choice to make, to foster animals and then let them go to forever homes."

"He said I could visit them."

"That's something, isn't it? Will you want to?"

"Yeah, I think I will. I'm attached. Besides . . . your uncle stayed for a cup of coffee and we chatted a while."

Hmmmm, Caprice thought. *That's interesting.*

"His life's been very different from mine."

Dulcina had been in the perfect marriage. Her uncle had been in a nightmare marriage. Dulcina worked at home. Her uncle had been out in the financial world meeting with all types of clients, including venture capitalists.

"I imagine if your lives are very different, you have a lot to talk about."

"That's true, we do. Who would have thought?"

Exactly. Who would have thought?

"He's a very practical man," Dulcina went on. "He said I should give the kittens a few days before I visit so they can settle in. That makes sense, don't you think?"

"Yes, that makes sense. You want to give them time to bond to him, and to get used to being without Halo and Paddington. They'll form their own little family."

"Just as we will," Dulcina said.

"I'm just leaving Brown's in Loganville. I'm still in the parking lot. They have the most luscious baked goods. Are you interested in anything? I'll bring it along and we can have it with coffee."

Dulcina thought about it.

"Or," Caprice said, "I have my cooler in the car. I can pick up a container of their chicken pot pie or their bean soup and we can have it for lunch." Her friend sounded as if she needed a shoulder to lean on, and Caprice could do that for her.

"Are you sure you don't mind?"

"I don't mind."

"Get them both. I'll pay you. We'll have bean soup and chicken pot pie."

Caprice laughed. "No, you won't pay me. You pup-sit for me all the time." She hesitated a moment and then said, "I know you're going to miss Tia and Mason, but think about how much happiness they'll be giving my uncle. And if you do talk now and then, you can share all their antics."

"You're right. I suppose time will help. If it doesn't work out for them, I can always take them back."

"Uncle Dom will be a good cat dad. I'll check on him myself in a day or two and see how they're faring."

"You're a good friend."

"I'll see you soon."

Caprice ended the call, then loaded the groceries she'd already bought into her car. She was heading back into Brown's for the luncheon entrées when she considered her schedule for the week. She could afford to take time for a comfort chat with Dulcina, bake this afternoon for her date with Grant, and then spend the evening with him. Soon she'd be out of town for a good part of the week, working on the house competition. Somehow she'd fit it all in. The situation with Wendy's murder had made her truly realize how important it was to tend to family and friends.

Maybe she could fit in a phone call to her nana this afternoon too.

Sebastian Thompson held Wendy Newcomb's memorial service at the Dunbach Funeral Home in Kismet. Funeral homes still had that cold atmosphere, but Wilbur Dunbach had modernized this facility, not only with better interior design but with technology. Sebastian had decided to have a morning service with a reception at his house afterward. The word had spread through Sunrise Tomorrow, from Lizbeth and Rena, to the counselors and victims' advocates, through the workshops, and into the community. Caprice suspected not all would go back to Sebastian's house afterward. If they did, he'd need crowd control. She'd never really seen a line like this flowing into the funeral home before for a wake. This morning, there was a line, mostly women but a few men, too—relatives of women who had needed Sunrise Tomorrow's facilities, workshops, and groups most probably.

Like most funeral homes, Dunbach's had more than one room for its services. Caprice had never realized that a portable wall divided the reception room into two. After she finally reached the threshold and signed the guest book, she was led to one huge room with at least fifteen rows of chairs in four aisles that could seat at least a hundred and fifty. There was no casket, of course, or an urn. But there was a flat-screen TV on which flowed video of Wendy in a continuous loop. She was playing baseball with Kevin and Cody and romping with the dog. She and Sebastian stood at the door of the house waving at someone. There was video of her walking into Sunrise Tomorrow, briefcase in hand, as well as footage of her sitting on the sand at a beach with Sebastian and the boys in the background playing Frisbee.

So huge and lifelike, the images of Wendy brought tears to Caprice's eyes. That was Wendy, playing and working . . . and living.

Besides that showcase in the front, there were easels placed at intervals with collages of photos. Here Caprice saw a glimpse into Wendy's childhood, the beautiful property where she was raised, the luxurious house. College photos decorated one easel, and Caprice got a glimpse of Wendy's friends. The only time period that was missing would have depicted Wendy's marriage to Rick Grossman.

Would he come to the service to pay his respects?

Instead of taking a seat, Caprice kept wandering around the room until she finally spotted Sebastian and the boys seated in the front row. She went to them without hesitation.

After hugging them all, she asked, "Who edited the video?"

Cody raised his hand a bit shyly.

"He did a wonderful job, didn't he?" Sebastian asked. "Wendy recognized his skills and it's only fitting he could contribute this way."

Kevin said in a husky voice, "I picked out all the photos and put them on the boards. Granddad helped me." The teenager nodded to a man in a black pin-striped suit who was talking to another gentleman in the side aisle.

"You did a fine job," Caprice told Kevin. "Wendy would be proud."

"I asked Father Gregory to speak about Wendy, and he said he would," Sebastian explained. "He should be here any minute. We spent a couple of hours together yesterday, so he'd really know her before he talked about her. I thought about asking people to share stories, but I didn't know if I wanted to get into that here. It could get pretty serious. So I figured at the house afterward if people want to share, they can."

"It's probably a good idea."

"You are coming, aren't you?"

"I'll be there," Caprice assured him.

Taking a quick glance at the chairs filling up, she suddenly saw someone she knew, someone she should talk to.

Kevin asked, "Do you want to sit next to me?"

She could tell he was missing Wendy, and maybe a little scared of everything going on around him.

"Sure, I'll sit next to you. Do you want to save me a seat? There's somebody I need to talk to before I settle in."

Kevin nodded and put his hand on her chair.

Brett Carstead had appeared in the back and Caprice decided she'd better talk to him while she could. When he saw her approaching him, he nodded.

They moved out of the crowd into a quiet corner, and he said, "I'm supposed to be unobtrusive."

"I'm not sure that's possible at a time like this."

"What do you have to tell me?"

"How do you know I didn't come back here just to say hi?"

"I know you better than that."

She took a step back. "Don't be so sure you know me." Just how many dates had he and Nikki gone on? And what had Nikki told him? That was a conversation she had to have soon with her sister. But she wasn't going to play coy with him.

"I might have found out a few things you don't know."

His brows arched. "Do I look surprised?"

At least his tone was resigned rather than outraged. "I spoke with a woman who got to know Wendy pretty well. She also sought help from her. Did you know Wendy kept a journal documenting her own abuse as well as information on abusive husbands?"

"Is that the blackmail she was talking about the night she called me?"

"I don't know, but I do know there's a journal that's leather-bound, small, and blue. Sebastian and the boys confirmed that and so did her ex-husband."

"You talked to her ex?"

"At his place of business. I stopped in to look into Add-a-Rooms."

"I just bet you did. What else do you know that I don't?"

"Sebastian's boys seemed to think Wendy might have kept the information on a flash drive or a thumb drive, and that she wouldn't keep it in a normal place. So I thought you should know."

"I'll have to talk to Sebastian and his boys again.

I'm glad you told me." Brett ran his hand over his face as if he was tired from not sleeping well the past week . . . or longer. "We almost have too many leads to follow with this case. More than a few people didn't like Wendy Newcomb. She protected women for their own safety but interfered in their lives. Her actions tore people apart."

"It all boils down to motive," Caprice mused. "And if all their motives are the same, you're going to have a tough time deciphering which is the right one."

"Yes, we are. But it's our job, not yours. So stop nosing around now. If you get an inclination to do more, remember what happened the last time, and the time before that."

She could back down, really she could, but what was the point? "I do remember what happened," she said. "We caught murderers."

"Don't start thinking in terms of *we*," he warned her. "You and I are not a team."

"Maybe not," she acquiesced. "But we could be on the same team rather than adversarial. Don't you think that might help?"

"What I think is that the De Luca women are stubborn."

That comment meant Nikki had done some pushing back too. Caprice wondered what about. She also wondered when Brett Carstead would ask her sister out again. But biting her tongue, she didn't bring it up and felt very proud of herself for her restraint.

She said, "I'm going to sit with Sebastian and his boys."

Brett gave her a probing look. "Be careful."

"I will."

And she would be. More careful than she'd been in the past.

Chapter Nine

Since so many people had come to pay their respects to Wendy, Sebastian hadn't given an open invitation to everyone to come back to his house afterward. But word had gotten around to those closest to him and the boys. He'd hired Nikki to cater the reception and she'd kept it simple. She'd made crab ball and ham puff hors d'oeuvres, was serving chicken rice soup and hot cider to ward off the chill, then added a selection of deli meats, broccoli salad, and macaroni salad. She'd kept dessert simple, too—a sheet cake of chocolate with peanut butter icing and a yellow cake topped with a fluffy white icing.

Rena seemed to be helping everyone connect. Sebastian looked lost as he migrated from one person to another. Caprice caught bits of conversations, then realized Kevin and Cody were spending most of their time with their neighbors. Cody was assuring one gentleman he'd help ready his garden for winter. Kevin was speaking to a boy his own age about home-schooling. Apparently his friend Jeremy didn't attend public school but followed a syllabus for an online school. The trend of the future? Caprice imagined that would work only for parents and kids who were self-starters and motivated.

Crossing to the kitchen for a mug of hot cider, Caprice spotted Nikki filling the meat tray. "Everything looks great."

"Sebastian told me he didn't want anything out of the ordinary because people really didn't care about food at something like this. And if you notice, everyone's eating kind of absently. They're too busy sharing memories."

A woman who had been standing nearby scooping broccoli salad onto a plate smiled at Caprice. She asked, "Did you know Wendy well?"

"We were acquaintances, not friends," Caprice said honestly. "But I was going to be working with her more closely, helping her with the Wyatt estate."

The woman nodded, set down her plate, and extended her hand. "I'm Penny Claussen, a neighbor of Wendy and Sebastian's."

Caprice had been wanting to talk to some of Sebastian's neighbors, and here was her chance to learn more about the neighborhood and Wendy's relationship to it.

Nikki moved away to give them privacy and Caprice was grateful for that.

"I really hadn't heard much about co-housing developments until I talked with Wendy and Sebastian," Caprice admitted.

"It's a way of life reminiscent of bygone years," Penny explained. "Families weren't as mobile then and they lived nearby and helped each other. Of course, in the sixties there were communes, but this is a practical way of looking at life."

"How long have you lived here?"

"Four years now. I owe being happy here to Wendy."

Aha. The chance she'd been waiting for to find out more about women Wendy helped. "How so?"

"She connected me with another single mom. I couldn't afford a security deposit and rent to get out of my situation, and Wendy hooked me up with Carly, who I live with. We both have little girls. We both have jobs that we like but don't cover enough expenses. So living together and splitting household fees as well as food costs and sometimes even gas give us both a leg up."

"You say you're renting your house? Who owns it?"

"Why, Sebastian does." She lowered her voice. "Apparently he was a bigwig architect in Chicago. He made really good investments. When his wife died, he wanted to move somewhere safe and wholesome and have a different kind of life for himself and the boys. So he invested in this community. That's what it is— a community within the larger community. I think he pulled in another investor who believes in this kind of concept, but he's a silent partner."

That was news.

"I wonder how Sebastian chose this area," Caprice mused.

"Something about him spending time in Pennsylvania with an aunt on a farm in Lancaster County. Maybe the Amish way of life gave him the whole concept. He put a real estate agent on it and this is what they came up with."

"Do you know how he and Wendy met? I've never heard that story."

"They met at a local charity event. They were seated next to each other at dinner. Just one of those fate kind of things. It's a shame they didn't marry."

"I suppose marriage isn't for everyone."

"Sebastian kept hoping," Penny said in that low

voice again. "But Wendy had sworn she'd never marry again. Lately, though, I wondered if Wendy was seeing someone else."

"Really? She and Sebastian seemed so connected."

"You never know what really goes on in somebody's relationship. She was staying at the shelter overnight many nights. I noticed because her car wasn't in the carport by the time I went to bed . . . or in the morning when I left for work."

"That doesn't mean she was seeing someone else."

"Maybe, maybe not. But Sebastian has just seemed different lately, like he has something on his mind."

"What do you mean by *lately*?"

"The past few weeks. We neighbors see each other often, so we can tell mood shifts or when changes are coming. After all, one person's troubles can affect the whole community. Sebastian has just been . . . off-kilter."

Wasn't that interesting? If Wendy was having an affair, had Sebastian known about it? Had there been signs? He seemed to be an easygoing guy, but if neighbors had noticed a difference in him—

Still waters did run deep. Could Sebastian have had a reason for killing his significant other? That was hard to believe. Nevertheless, Caprice had been surprised by killers before.

Kevin came into the kitchen then and Caprice's conversation with Penny stopped. He went straight for the chocolate cake.

Taking the biggest slice set out on one of the plates, he took a fork and cut off a bite, popping it into his mouth. "This is really good," he managed to say around the icing.

Caprice motioned to Nikki, who was standing at the sink. "My sister baked it."

"I liked the coconut cake you brought too. I don't get cake much," he admitted. "Wendy was only into healthy food. She wouldn't bring sweets into the house."

Caprice picked up a slice of cake of her own but much smaller than his. "Do you want to sit somewhere and eat?"

"Can we go outside?" he asked. "It's getting too crowded in here."

The end-of-September day had warmed up with Indian summer sunshine. "Sure, let's go out on the porch."

Caprice knew crowds could give a claustrophobic feeling, especially at something like this. Kevin seemed like he needed a break from condolences and sympathetic glances.

They exited out the front door and crossed to two caned rockers that had a small, round table positioned between them on the porch. There was a breeze, but Caprice ignored it for the sake of conversation with this boy who seemed to need it.

"If you don't eat many sweets, that cake could give you a sugar high." She popped a bite of her own cake into her mouth. Nikki's chocolate cakes certainly were luscious.

"A sugar high is the only kind of high I'm ever going to get, so I might as well take advantage of it," Kevin told her.

"That's good to hear."

The teenager rolled his eyes. "My clean-cut way of life doesn't make me a hit at school."

"But if you really believe in a clean-cut way of life, it seems to me you'd only want friends around you who believed in it too."

He groaned. "You sound like my dad."

Caprice laughed. "Maybe we're both just speaking from experience. I followed the beat of my own drummer in school and wasn't that popular. But the friends I did make were good friends. I could rely on them."

He forked up another bite of cake. "I have a couple of good friends I can rely on, and there's always Cody," he said with a shrug.

"My sisters are my best friends."

"I can't say that. Cody thinks he knows everything about everything."

"I have one of those kinds of sisters."

Kevin finished his cake and gave Caprice a sideways look. "I don't really mind not having sweets all that much. I mean, Wendy made other stuff to make up for it, or she'd bring home something unusual to try and tell us to taste the spices because they were better than sugar."

"You're going to miss her."

Looking away, Kevin swallowed hard, and Caprice suspected he was fighting tears. But it was important that he let himself feel.

After a minute or so, his voice was husky when he said, "I'll miss our bike rides."

Giving him time to recover, Caprice explained, "I haven't ridden a bicycle in years. I don't even know if I remember how."

"Oh, you'd remember. It's true you never forget how to ride a bike. Wendy said so too."

"Did you ride around the neighborhood?"

"Oh, no. When we rode we'd go at least five miles at a time. We rode a lot around that old Wyatt place."

"The one Sunrise Tomorrow inherited?"

Caprice had realized that as the crow flew, the Wyatt estate wasn't all that far from here. Still, she remembered the wrought-iron fence that surrounded the property. "There's a fence around that yard and quite a hill leading up to it."

"There is," he admitted. "But we rode into the back. The gate's kind of falling apart back there so we could ride around inside too. There's all kinds of cool statues back there. There's a shrine to Saint Antonio de Padua. Wendy told me if I ever lose anything, I should go to the shrine to pray to him and he'll help me find it."

Caprice's nana believed strongly in Saint Anthony's help, and Saint Francis's help. Other saints too. But they were the two most popular.

"So have you ever done that?" Caprice asked. "Prayed to Saint Anthony?"

Looking sheepish, Kevin nodded. "When I lost my phone, I did. It turns out it had slipped out of my pocket down the car seat. My dad found it two days later, so I guess the prayer helped."

"My nana taught me that saying prayers to Saint Anthony for finding things works."

Kevin cocked his head. "Do you really believe that stuff?"

"Actually, I do. Not just because I was raised with it, but because prayers and wishes and affirmations are all positive energy. It certainly can't hurt to send that out into the universe even if you don't believe in a direct prayer to a saint who might intervene for you with God. There's a lot of different ways to look at it."

"Wendy used to tell me that too."

"It sounds like you learned a lot of good things from Wendy, things you can hold on to for a long time."

After Kevin set his plate on the table between them, he stared out into the yard at the leaves on the trees in the distance. "I wish she was still here. I wish . . . I wish we had a chance to go on another bike ride."

There really weren't any words to help Kevin with his grief, so Caprice just sat with him, letting the breeze toss around his memories, letting him come to terms with the reality he had to live with now.

Caprice sat with Kevin until he said, "I'd better go back in. I don't want Dad to worry that I ran off somewhere. Since Wendy died, he worries about every little thing. He hardly lets me and Cody out of his sight."

"He doesn't want anything to happen to you."

"Maybe when Wendy's killer's caught, he'll feel better. I sure hope so. Are you coming back in?"

"In a few minutes. Go ahead."

Caprice was thinking about everything Kevin had said when a voice from the other side of the porch startled her.

"It's a nice thing you did, talking to him like that."

She didn't know where the man had come from, maybe from the other side of the porch, or maybe from in the yard. She recognized him from the funeral home. Kevin had pointed him out as Wendy's father. He wasn't a tall man, perhaps five-ten, who looked to be in his late fifties or early sixties and was wearing an expensive suit. The black pin-striped jacket fit him impeccably well.

He came close to her and extended his hand. "I'm Daniel Newcomb, Wendy's father."

"Mr. Newcomb, I'm so sorry for your loss."

"Everyone is," he said with a frown. "I wish that helped. I came out here for fresh air before you and Kevin did. Those boys need someone to talk to, and when Kevin started in with you, I didn't want to interrupt."

"Do you spend much time with Kevin and Cody?"

"I was in the habit of visiting Wendy every couple of months, and I'd stay overnight. She drove to Delaware when she could, and sometimes Sebastian and the boys came with her."

"Are you going to stay in touch with them?"

"I'd like to. But that depends on Sebastian. At a time like this, I wish I'd had ten kids. Not that losing one would be any easier, but the other nine might fill in the void a little. I was waiting for Wendy and Sebastian to get married, maybe give me a grandchild." His voice cracked and he stopped.

"One of Wendy's friends told me she said she'd never get married again," Caprice offered.

"I suppose that was true. That girl never did back down—not from a fight and not from her own determination. It was a strength, but it was a fault too. That made it impossible to undo something she put into motion." After a pause, he said, "I heard you tell Kevin you have sisters."

"And a brother. I'd do anything for them."

"That's the way it should be. But that's the same attitude Wendy had toward the women she helped. She would do anything for them."

"Anything, Mr. Newcomb? I'm thinking maybe that's what got her killed."

His jaw hardened before he nodded. "That's quite possible. She couldn't always follow the letter of the law. She had to skirt around the edges now and then."

"Have you talked with the detectives on the case?"

"I have, though that Detective Jones rubs me the wrong way. The Carstead fellow seemed to understand better. He knew about the protective orders and the way Wendy found living accommodations for women who needed them."

Caprice took a chance on discovering a little more.

She lowered her voice, even though no one was in earshot. "I heard that she helped spirit women away who had no other alternative."

Newcomb's brow creased as he studied her. "I didn't go into that with the detectives."

"Do you think you should have?"

Newcomb had an authoritarian look about him, and was obviously used to running his own show, which included his financial services firm. Caprice could tell he was about to get all blustery, so she added, "There's nothing on the books with names, no suspects for the police to look at. How are they going to catch Wendy's killer?"

Newcomb shook his head. "I don't know names. I don't know any specific information. Do you honestly think Wendy would give me that? Sure, I did favors for her. I know people who can create new identities, if that's what you're asking about. But Wendy would just pass on vital statistics to me, and I would relay the information. In return, with the right amount of money, I'd receive a packet ready to go. That packet would contain a social security number, a driver's license, a passport. Could be all three. Wendy only did that for the most severe cases, for women in danger for their lives."

"Women who had children?"

"Now and then."

"Are you sure you shouldn't tell the detectives about that?"

"Are you going to?" he returned, seriously.

"I already hinted at it with Detective Carstead. If they go down that road, they might come looking for you."

"Let them look for me. I'll help them however I can, except, of course, I won't give up the name of my source for the work he does for me."

"I suspect whoever killed Wendy was somebody she wasn't afraid of."

"My girl had learned not to be afraid of much, so I don't know how far that theory will get you. If an angry man on a dark street confronted her, she knew self-defense and knew it well. She even had a carry permit for a Lady Remington."

"Did she always carry it?"

"She kept it locked up in the house, I know that. Sebastian has a safe. But when she went to that shelter, yes, she carried it. So I suspect she also carried it on errands, especially at night."

A gun. If Wendy had a gun and her life was in danger, she would have had to get to it. On the other hand, if she met with someone she didn't suspect would hurt her, she hadn't seen the attack coming. Premeditated? Or had anger gotten out of control and blown up in a few minutes?

A car pulling into the driveway had both Caprice and Wendy's dad looking that way. Lizbeth climbed out of the Acura and hurriedly started up the front walk.

Wendy's father said, "I'd better get back in. I'll be leaving later today and I want to spend as much time as I can with Sebastian and the boys."

Caprice nodded and said, "It was good to meet you." He said the same and went inside.

Seconds later, Lizbeth was on the porch. She was wearing a tailored black suit and heels and looked flustered. That seemed to be her ongoing state these days. Caprice had seen her leave the memorial service early and had wondered why. Now she was about an hour late getting to the reception.

Lizbeth said, "I almost wish it was after five and I could have something strong to drink."

"What's wrong? I saw you leave the service."

"It couldn't be helped. I had a meeting with the lawyer who'd settled the Wyatt estate."

"Who is it?"

"Mr. Silver. He's in York and I had to drive there and back."

"Is there anything that's going to be a roadblock in getting the transition facility ready?"

"I sincerely hope not. I had to sign so many papers I feel dizzy. As acting director, Wendy signed your proposal for redecorating. I just had to approve it. Another month on the renovations should do it, and then you can really get started."

"That sounds good. I'm going to have a project out of town the first week in October, but my assistant can answer any questions you might have while I'm gone. I'll put through the orders for the furniture. I was holding off on that before I knew for sure you were going ahead with everything."

Lizbeth bit her lower lip and something still seemed to be bothering her.

"Is Mr. Silver easy to work with?" Caprice asked, wondering if that could be the problem.

"Yes, he is. He did a lot of work for Wendy pro bono. He's semiretired and just likes keeping his hand in. He did tell me one thing, though, that worries me."

"What's that?"

"He told me not to talk to Leona Wyatt's two children, Scott and Doris. Apparently they're still furious that their mother didn't leave the whole estate to them. But he reiterated again, they didn't have grounds to contest the will. And if they had and lost, they'd inherit nothing. So they are bitter. They can't understand why their mother believed in Wendy's cause, why she believed in Sunrise Tomorrow, why she believed in Wendy."

"Did she believe in Wendy because of the way she ran Sunrise?" Caprice asked.

"Oh, it was much more than that. Leona took Wendy under her wing after Wendy's divorce. They met at a luncheon at the Country Squire Golf and Recreation Club and just hit it off. I think Leona was lonely because her own children ignored her. She and Wendy developed a friendship that became really strong. Wendy was the one who took her to her doctors' appointments. She was the one who held Leona's hand through chemo and was by her side when she passed on. *Not* her children."

"And now they regret they didn't do more?"

"Goodness no," Lizbeth said with certainty in her voice. "They're just mad they didn't inherit the entire fortune. They claim blood's thicker than anything else. With some families that might be true, but Leona apparently valued loyalty and friendship as much as she did ungrateful kids. And from what I've heard and seen, they can be mean, so it wouldn't surprise me at all if one of them killed Wendy."

Lizbeth was vehement about that, and Caprice wondered if that wasn't where she should dig a little more. As Lizbeth drew a deep breath and tried to find her composure again, she said, "I need to give Sebastian and the boys condolences. I'll see you inside."

Caprice nodded. Yes, she was going to spend a little bit more time inside too. Conversation could reveal a lot about people there. But first she was going to call Roz.

"Hey, there," Roz said, answering on the first ring. "Where are you?"

"I'm at the funeral reception for Wendy."

"Oh, that's tough."

"Where are you?"

"I'm at the dog groomer waiting for Dylan to get finished."

Dylan, part Pomeranian and part shih-tzu, needed periodic grooming.

"I have a question for you," Caprice said. "Do you know Doris and Scott Wyatt?"

"I don't think anyone 'knows' Doris and Scott Wyatt," Roz returned in a dry voice.

"Meaning?"

"They're cold, both of them. I've been to lots of functions around them at the Country Squire and they're just not sociable. When I was married to Ted, he and Scott would play golf. After Ted was killed, I thought maybe Scott and Doris just didn't want to associate with me. You know, the stigma and all? But I've seen them snub other people too."

"What can you tell me about them?"

"Scott Wyatt is married, and his wife is quiet, younger, and seems to constantly look to him for approval. At least that's my impression."

"And Doris?"

"Doris has been married and divorced twice. She took back her maiden name after the second divorce."

"I wonder what the best way would be to meet them?"

"I'm surprised you want to."

"I don't necessarily want to, but I'm curious as to whether either of them would have the wherewithal to have killed Wendy."

"Are you going six for six?"

It took only a moment for Caprice to figure out what Roz meant. She'd been involved in five other murder investigations. This was number six. "I'm just collecting information."

"In that case, I might know a convenient way for you to meet them. The Country Squire's Masquerade Ball is next weekend. It's not too late to buy tickets because they're not getting the response they hoped for. Maybe people just don't want to dress up anymore, or want to go to the expense of renting costumes. But you and Grant could dress up like a famous couple. Vince hasn't given me his answer on going yet, but if you and Grant go, I could probably convince him. We might have a good time."

Yes, they might. She hadn't spent much time with Roz lately and this would be a good opportunity. "I'll talk to Grant about it."

"Sounds like a plan. Oops, I think the groomer is finished with Dylan. I've been thinking that he needs a buddy, so when I do have to leave him at home, he wouldn't be so lonely."

"If you and Vince move into a house together, the timing could be perfect."

"Yes, it could. I'll call or text you about next Saturday night. Caprice, don't dig around too hard. I worry about you."

"I know you do. But you don't have to worry this time. I'm staying on the periphery. Honest."

However, after she ended her call, she thought about Sebastian and his boys. They needed answers. She knew if gathering information led her deeper into motives for murder, she was going to explore them.

Chapter Ten

Caprice glanced at her Uncle Dom, who was guiding her and Dulcina up the back stairs to his apartment on Monday evening. Apparently he was eager to show off the place to Dulcina. Either that or he wanted to reassure her the kittens were settling in. And the timing had worked out perfectly. She and Dulcina had signed up for a yoga class at Green Tea Spa that began at seven-thirty.

Caprice wasn't exactly sure why she was here. She sensed there was a liking between Uncle Dom and Dulcina. Maybe he didn't know if he was ready to date, or maybe he was concerned Dulcina wasn't ready to date and that's why he'd asked Caprice along too. When she'd gotten his call, she'd been surprised but pleased he wanted to show off his new digs.

The deck at his door was large enough for two lawn chairs with a small wrought-iron table set between them. They were Adirondack-style and bright blue. Caprice approved.

Her uncle winked at her. "What do you think?"

"I think you can watch the sunrise in style."

He laughed. "Believe it or not, lots of mornings I'm awake for it. Somebody likes to bite my toes."

This time Dulcina laughed. "That must be Tia."

"Yes, it is. I thought about closing the kittens in a room of their own at night, but it just didn't seem quite fair. The first night I let them out because I thought they needed the comfort. The second night, I realized I missed them if they weren't with me."

He opened the door and motioned them inside.

Dulcina hadn't said much on the ride over and Caprice thought she might be a little nervous, or maybe anxious about how the kittens were faring.

But as soon as they crossed her uncle's threshold, Tia and Mason came running.

Uncle Dom motioned to the door hanger—leather with sleigh bells. He rustled it and the bells jingled. The kittens backed away from the door.

"I don't want to take any chances that they're going to get out, so the bells are training them to stay away from the door. It seems to be working."

They walked through the galley-sized kitchen with its small table for two and entered the living room. The kittens had chased each other to the top of a cat condo positioned in front of a window.

Dulcina went right over to pet them. They must have remembered her because they butted their heads against her hand and let her stroke them. Mason stretched out and Tia sat prettily.

"Are you two being good?" she asked them.

"As long as they're entertained," Uncle Dom said with a wry smile. "They're good company for each other. I play with them three or four times a day. That seems to satisfy them." He motioned to a length of brown packing paper on the floor. "They love chasing their toy mice on that and hiding underneath it. I think it's the sound."

"I'll have to try that with Paddington and Halo," Dulcina decided.

"Can I get you something to drink? I have iced tea, convenience-store-made."

"That sounds good," Caprice said, and Dulcina nodded too.

Her uncle went into the kitchen to fetch it.

Caprice noticed Dulcina looking around at the green and burgundy plaid nubby-material couch, at the oversized recliner positioned for the best view of the flat-screen TV. There was a clover-leaf table at one end of the sofa that Caprice thought looked like an antique. The coffee table was a small cedar chest.

When her uncle returned to the living room, he set napkins on the chest to put under their glasses. Caprice motioned to the table. "That looks like an antique I saw in Isaac's shop."

"I found it at Older and Better," her uncle responded. "Isaac gave me a good deal because you two are friends. He has some nice furniture in there and his prices are reasonable."

"He likes to move his merchandise, so he doesn't overprice it. And he's honest."

"He seems to be. I was going to go to the thrift store, but I stopped there first. I bought a headboard for my bed and a dresser. I figure I'll furnish the place slowly and pick the pieces one by one."

"That's a great idea," Caprice agreed.

Her uncle shrugged and looked at Dulcina. "The divorce pretty much wiped me out. When the financial services company I worked for downsized and I lost my job, that led to the downfall of the marriage."

"How long were you married?" Dulcina asked.

"Twelve years, but most of them weren't happy ones. I was just too stupid to admit it . . . or too proud."

"Did you know your wife a long time before you got married?" Dulcina asked.

"No, I didn't. Mistake number one."

"Maybe, maybe not," Dulcina said. "I didn't know Johnny long before I married him, but we just knew it was right. Relationships are complicated."

"I suppose," Uncle Dom agreed, sitting on the sofa and motioning to the recliner. Dulcina picked up Tia and took her along with her to the recliner.

Tia let her pet her for about a minute; then she hopped onto the arm and climbed up the back.

"I guess the older you get, the more you realize what the warning signs are," Dom went on. "I didn't realize Ronnie respected my job more than she respected me, that she liked the idea of a nice car more than the idea of children. She didn't want anything to do with my family, when all they wanted was to get to know her. I thought she'd change and grow into a warmer person. But that never happened."

"I'm not sure anyone can change their innate nature," Dulcina said. "As much as I want to be an extrovert, I never will be. I like working at home. I like having meaningful conversations instead of surface ones. And sometimes I like cats more than I like humans."

Uncle Dom laughed. "I suppose I'm social by nature. I miss not going to an office and having other people to talk to during the day. On the other hand, I have the best of both worlds right now. The pet-sitting and bookkeeping are both home-based businesses. I have to work around the pet-sitting, but I can set my own hours with the bookkeeping. The spare bedroom is my office."

Uncle Dom looked a bit anxious for a few moments;

then he looked Dulcina straight in the eye. He said, "Caprice told me you broke up with the man you attended the concert with."

"He wasn't willing to let me be around his daughters more. I'm not exactly sure why. The older one was resisting him dating me, and he could have been waiting for her to come around. But he wouldn't include me in their activities. It just wasn't working."

"Are you still hurting from the breakup?" her uncle asked.

"Not as much as I should be." Dulcina's hands fluttered. "That didn't come out right. I guess our breakup didn't hurt as much as it could have because I wasn't as invested as I thought I was."

Caprice was remaining unusually quiet because she could see dynamics at work here. Whether her uncle and Dulcina knew it or not, they were sharing on a level that didn't happen after just a first or second or third meeting. Something was brewing. She found that she liked that idea. Her uncle needed someone in his life and so did Dulcina.

Mason ran off down the hall, and Uncle Dom said, "He's probably going up to the third floor to watch the birds. Do you want to see what I've done with the place?"

When Tia jumped off the back of the chair and ran after her brother, Dulcina agreed, "Sure."

"I took the door off so they could go up and down as much as they wanted. There's another cat condo up there, a few rugs, more brown paper, and lots of toys. They carry them up and down. Come on, I'll show you the view from the third floor."

Caprice followed her uncle and Dulcina, smiling all the way. You never knew when something might work out for the best. She was just glad it sometimes did.

* * *

Dulcina had been quiet as Caprice drove to the Green Tea Spa for their yoga class. They'd both signed up by phone and intended to go to the class that wasn't progressive. It was rather a refresher exercise each time they would attend. From what the receptionist had told Caprice, the poses were basic and the class would concentrate on breathing, stretching, and relaxation. Who didn't need all those in her life?

They grabbed their duffel bags. Dulcina had wanted to wear street clothes to visit Uncle Dom, then change at the spa. Caprice had agreed to make Dulcina feel more comfortable.

As they walked in the door of the Green Tea Spa, the first thing their gazes went to was a black fountain dripping water down at least five shelves, each a different size. Soft instrumental music played in the background without a distinctive melody. The reception area was painted a dreamy green, somewhere between aqua and seafoam. Ergonomic furniture, upholstered in shades of blue, surrounded large hassocks where anyone waiting could put up their feet and relax.

The receptionist sat at a Plexiglas desk that looked as if it were floating in air. It wasn't, of course, and it housed a computer. The effect it gave to the space was light, airy, in keeping with the décor. A metal sculpture of a yin-yang symbol hung on one wall. Another wall held a grouping of photographs from the purple and blues of a beautiful Grand Canyon shot to the red rocks of Sedona, Big Sur, and the rocky shore of Maine. All places of power in Caprice's estimation.

After they told the receptionist why they were there, she directed them to a dressing room, explaining their class would take place in the room next door.

As they went inside, Dulcina said, "Tia and Mason seem very happy with your uncle."

"Yes, they do. They have each other, and now they're bonding with him." That was easy to see.

Dulcina suddenly stopped and took Caprice's arm. "Do you really think your uncle wouldn't mind if I visit?"

"He said you could come whenever you'd like."

Dulcina shook her head. "I know, but sometimes people say things just to be nice."

"I think Uncle Dominic had too many years of just being nice and not saying his mind. That didn't make him happy. From the moment he decided to come to Kismet and reunite with his family, I think he had a new outlook. He's always been completely honest with me, and I have a feeling he would be with you too. Are you interested in visiting him or the kittens?" Caprice teased.

Dulcina blushed. "I like him."

Her uncle was about the same age as her neighbor—maybe a year or two older. "Would you like me to hint to him that you'd like to be invited over for a date?"

"Absolutely not," Dulcina protested in practically a whisper. "I'll give it a couple of weeks and then I'll call him. No harm in that, right?"

"No harm in that," Caprice agreed.

They quickly changed into yoga wear in the dressing room. Caprice's slouch pants were flowered in lime green and turquoise, her loose cardigan the same color turquoise. When she didn't wear vintage, she wore color. Dulcina's outfit was navy.

As they entered the room where women were already positioned on yoga mats, Caprice spotted Rena Hurley, who waved and grinned.

Immediately, Evelyn Miller crossed to them. "I saw your names on the list. Hi, Caprice. And you're Dulcina?"

Evelyn extended her hand and Dulcina took it.

"Yes, I am. I've mostly done yoga videos at home after a class years ago."

"No problem," Evelyn said, and Caprice had a feeling she said that a lot. She waved to the back of the room where mats, a few duffel bags, and purses sat. "Just pick up a mat and find a space on the floor. We're ready to start. Think of this room as your safe haven where you leave all your thoughts and any problems outside the door. Here you're just going to concentrate on being in the moment."

Like a cat, Caprice thought, but didn't say it out loud because Evelyn would probably think she was crazy.

Caprice picked up a mat and placed it beside Rena's, introducing the receptionist from Sunrise to Dulcina.

Rena explained, "I come to Evelyn's class here to get away from work. She's good. You'll enjoy it."

The other women in the room were welcoming, too, as Caprice and Dulcina found their places on their mats.

Class began with an alternate nostril breathing exercise. That progressed into the participants doing warm-up exercises—forward and back bends, seated forward bends and arm swings. Caprice had heard yoga called meditation in motion. She tried to empty her mind of everything but her breath and moment-to-moment body movement. Posture and breathing went hand in hand. Evelyn reminded them to breathe through their nose, not their mouths.

They ended the session that lasted about an hour and a half with a guided imagery meditation. On their mats, they closed their eyes, arms relaxed by their sides. Evelyn played a recording of her voice that took them through the exercise, from relaxing eye muscles and cheek muscles and neck muscles to low back, knees, calves, and feet. Caprice had forgotten how good relaxation could feel. Right now, she felt like a limp jellyfish.

At the end of the exercise, they were supposed to lie there with their eyes closed. Caprice obeyed the sound of Evelyn's voice. She was on the mat closest to the door and Evelyn's voice, in a different tone, interrupted her relaxation. Apparently the yoga instructor had stepped outside the room when she'd begun the recording for them. She was speaking to someone else and at first two women's voices were just a whisper.

But then Evelyn's voice rose in tone. "I thought we could make this work together. Our own studio would benefit us both."

"Yes, I know it would," the other woman agreed. "But I just don't have the capital to make it happen. Perhaps in a year or two."

There was silence again and Caprice kept her eyes closed. After all, she did sometimes follow directions. Still, although her eyes were closed, her senses were alert now. She noticed that Evelyn stayed in the hall and soon it sounded as if she was talking to someone else. But the conversation was one-sided, which probably meant Evelyn was calling someone on her cell phone.

Her voice rose again. "I need it now and not six months from now."

That did it. Caprice opened her eyes and sat up. She caught a glimpse of Evelyn just beyond the doorway. She didn't look so Zen now. Her expression was anxious and lines cut deep around her eyes and her mouth. It was possible that she was older than Caprice thought she was. So who was the real Evelyn? The yoga teacher who could remain calm, or the woman in her forties standing outside the door who looked as if her world had just collapsed around her?

Dulcina sat up now too. "What's wrong?"

"Nothing's wrong. I think it's amazing how it takes so long to relax our bodies and how it can be revved up in about a minute."

"So you're revved up again?"

"I am. I'm thinking about all the people who surrounded Wendy and who among them would have wanted to hurt her. One particular person comes to mind. Wendy was arguing with him the first time I met with her about the Wyatt estate. I know him in another context, and I think I'm going to have a talk with him."

She and Warren Shaeffer could always begin talking about business and then let the conversation wander into the territory where she wanted to go.

"Will you have someone with you when you talk to this person?"

"That won't be necessary. I'll go to his place of business. There will be people around."

"You can't take Lady?"

"I could try, but then I might not get in. Grant wants me to depend on him, so if he's free, I'll keep my phone line open."

Dulcina gave an approving nod. "That sounds like the best idea of all."

Caprice hoped Grant thought so too.

Warren Shaeffer had saved his printing company from becoming obsolete. Once, the company had produced hobby magazines as well as a few medical journals. When journals went digital, he'd discovered a way to keep his business thriving. The self-publishing business had taken off and he'd tapped into older residents of the area who wanted to save their life stories for posterity. Sure, they could have self-published online with an impersonal company, or had the ingenuity to do it themselves by finding formatters and cover artists and the myriad other services necessary to jump into the venture. On the other hand, Shaeffer's company had made it easy. He charged exorbitant fees but set up signing parties, had the events catered, and was keeping his business viable in the area.

Caprice had to give him props for that. Oh sure, he still printed pamphlets and programs for any locals who wanted to use him, but savvy business owners knew the best deal to get online like she did. Still, Millennium Printing had its place and Warren did too. As president of the Chamber of Commerce, he had some power in the town. His recommendations went a long way and so did his veto.

She hadn't made an appointment because she knew the best way to get into his office. After she phoned Grant and left the line open, her phone hooked on her wide leather belt, she simply appeared in front of his receptionist on Tuesday morning and said, "I have Chamber business to discuss with Warren." She could have been stalled if he'd been in a meeting, but he wasn't. His receptionist, Danita Ottman, who'd been with him at least five years with his newer ventures, was pretty, young, and friendly.

"Chamber business? I know he'll want to talk about that. Let me buzz him." And she did. Caprice could hear Warren's voice over the intercom when he said, "Tell her to come on back."

Now the problem was, Caprice had to think of Chamber business to start their discussion. Chamber business. Just what could she talk about? Then she thought of it. She and Bella had sort of been discussing an idea.

Warren's office door was about ten feet from the

receptionist's desk. She took a last glance at Danita and then knocked.

He came to open the door himself instead of just yelling, "Come in."

"It's good to see you, Caprice. Danita said you had Chamber business. How can I help?"

So helpful. So charming. Did he really have a Jekyll and Hyde personality?

She took a seat in front of his desk while he went around to the high-backed leather swivel chair, very similar to the one Rick Grossman had used. A commonality among CEOs? Or a commonality about men who had egos and wanted other people to know they were important?

"I was speaking to my sister Bella about raising more revenues for the town and the businesses in it."

"I'm always open to discussing that," he said with a smile.

"You know there are many houses downtown that have historical status. Some of them even have plaques."

"Yes, I do know that."

"With the holidays coming up, maybe we could take advantage of that."

"I don't understand."

"My family once drove to Williamsburg after Christmas. It was a beautiful sight—old-fashioned decorations on the doors and lots of candles. But the big thing was that tourists flocked from everywhere to come see the sights."

"We certainly don't have the quaintness of Williamsburg," Warren said wryly.

"No, we don't. But we do have the wherewithal to put a weekend together with tours of historic homes. Most people decorate for Christmas anyway, and I imagine the residents of historic homes decorate

according to their character. It wouldn't be that much
more bother for them. But they would have their
homes open to groups of tourists. I was thinking that
if they did that, we could have a bartering of sorts with
services in the area. The homes could promote local
businesses one way or another, and in return, they'd
receive coupons for gas or a discount at the food
store, a free ham, snow removal at their date of choice
in the winter, house cleaning, discounts at restaurants.
The list could go on and on. Say we picked a Saturday
the second week of December and said that was Historical Home Tour day. We could have a banner or
two across White Rose Way and still have time to get
the advertisement out."

"And just who would coordinate all this?" Warren
asked, sitting back in his chair.

"I'm not sure, but we could bring it up at the next
Chamber of Commerce meeting. We might even want
to coordinate with the Garden Club. Maybe they
would want to make arrangements to put in the
homes. It could be a whole community effort."

Warren nodded. "I can see that it would be. Can
you write this up into something I could hand out?
How much we might charge per person?"

She really didn't need more work right now with
everything else that was going on. But besides it being
an element for discussion with Warren today, the
whole tour idea could catch on and be a valuable asset
during the Christmas season. How long would it take
for her to jot down the ideas? Then she could hand
the project to Bella and she could add her input. Bella
always had input.

"We have a Chamber of Commerce meeting in a
week. I could have it ready for you by then, if that
would be all right."

"I'd like to look at it the day before."

"I'm sure I can manage that."

"This is a good idea, Caprice. I'm glad you came to me with it."

"I also came for another reason."

"More ideas to increase revenue?"

"No, I'm helping to move the Wyatt project forward for Sunrise Tomorrow."

While Warren's expression had been open, now it became closed. His brows knitted together and he frowned. "What does that have to do with me or the Chamber?"

"It could affect the Chamber because it affects the town." She decided to plunge right in and see what happened. "And it could affect you."

"In what way?" he asked belligerently.

"I overheard your argument with Wendy. I imagine it's possible that you could become a suspect."

Warren stood, pulled himself up to his full five foot nine, and glared at her as if he wanted to sock her. "I don't know what you're insinuating. You didn't hear anything. And if you say you did, it's my word against yours."

Aha. The Mr. Hyde side was coming out—the bully side. She felt the phone on her belt. "It might be my word against yours, but what would your wife say?" That was a shot in the dark, but an intuitive one that seemed to hit home.

"You leave my wife out of this," he said with gritted teeth.

"Warren, I have a feeling Wendy's murder is all about wives and husbands, control and power, and freedom."

"You know nothing. Just because you've been written up in the paper a few times, you think you're an expert. You're not, and certainly not about this. I think you should leave."

After all, it was his office and he could call security or the police to have her escorted off the premises. She didn't want that. But she wanted him to know she knew he was a bully and she wasn't going to let him cow her. "I've already told the police about your argument with Wendy."

"So you're the one who put my name on that detective's list. Well, when he interviews me, I'll show him he has no cause to have me on that list."

"When do you see the police?"

He looked as if he wasn't going to answer, but then he admitted, "This evening at seven o'clock."

"Detective Carstead or Jones?"

"Jones is the one who called me. He seems to be efficient and quick. I'll be in and out of there in no time."

Jones might be efficient and quick, but he was also thorough. If Warren Shaeffer was seriously on their suspect list, he could be at the police station for hours. But she wasn't going to aggravate him more by telling him that. She knew Grant was probably scolding her through her phone for what she'd done already. Her line was open, as she'd promised it would be.

"Have you known Wendy long?" she asked.

Again Warren hesitated, but then he gave a shrug. "Only the past year when my wife decided to get a spine."

At least he'd noticed that.

He added bitterly, "Thanks to Wendy Newcomb, I don't know where she is. My guess is she's with a cousin in North Carolina. I haven't followed up on that yet."

If he hadn't followed up, just how important was his marriage to him? On the other hand, if he hadn't followed up, maybe his wife wasn't in any danger. Maybe if she wanted a new life she could find it. Caprice couldn't say she was sorry he couldn't find his wife because it might be a good thing.

"I'm sorry you're having problems, Warren."

"Don't be sorry for me. Just mind your own business."

"I will do that," she said, and from the expression on his face, she knew he realized she wasn't giving in. She was challenging him. If her business included him, especially in the aspect of Wendy's murder, so be it.

When she turned to leave, he said to her, "You women think you own the world. Maybe it's about time you find out you don't."

If Grant heard that parting shot, he was going to be pacing his office. She was so tempted to toss back a comeback, but she didn't. She smashed one lip tightly against the other one, and she left Warren Shaeffer's office and the building.

Outside, she unlocked the mute button and put her phone to her ear. "Are you there?"

"I'm here. What did you think you were doing baiting him like that?"

"I wanted to see if Mr. Hyde would come out and he did. Warren isn't all Mr. Nice Guy."

"No, he's not, and from now on I want you to stay away from him."

Sometimes Grant's protective attitude frustrated her. "Is that an order?"

There were a few seconds of silence while they both considered what they'd said.

She heard him sigh. "No, it's not an order because it does no good to give you orders. Don't you think I know that by now?"

"Just asking," she said, a little playfully. She didn't

want to argue with him. But because this was Grant and because she loved him, she told him, "I don't have any plans to see Warren again, not unless it's at a Chamber of Commerce meeting. I can e-mail him the Historical Home Tour proposal. Really, Grant, you don't have to worry."

"Really, Caprice, I do."

She smiled. "Are you looking forward to the masquerade ball? I am. I love the idea for our costumes." They'd come up with a theme on the phone last night.

"Yeah, well, I have a feeling the masquerade ball and the costumes have more to do with you investigating and connecting with someone than they do with having a good time."

"It's true, I want Roz to introduce me to Leona Wyatt's children. They bought tickets and are supposed to be there. But, on the other hand, I'm looking forward much more to dancing with you."

"Okay. I give up. You win."

"Win what?"

"You win the prize for knowing exactly what to say at just the right time because now all I'll think about until the ball is the idea of dancing with you."

"I can blow you a kiss."

"Better yet, I can get a real one tonight."

"Come over for supper. I'll make some of Nana's minestrone soup and we can light a fire."

"I can be there by seven."

Caprice ended the call, forgetting all about Warren Shaeffer and thinking about an evening with Grant.

Chapter Eleven

The Country Squire Golf and Recreation Club had been elegantly decorated for fall for a few weeks. Yellow tinted twinkle lights draped around the entrance and the trees. A harvest theme spread across the entrance portico with a huge pumpkin, a stand of hay decorated and wrapped with orange and black ribbon, and a scarecrow that looked welcoming. The same yellow twinkle lights wreathed the inside of the lobby. Orange and yellow mum flower arrangements sported gold lamé wired ribbons while multicolored dried corn ears along with orange and green gourds filled a giant cornucopia on the credenza along one wall in the reception area. Other cornucopias, similarly filled, decorated marble-topped tables as well as wall shelves in the huge dining room.

Each of the tables in the expansive room was covered with yellow linens. In the center of each stood crystal vases with cranberry, yellow, orange, and white spider mum arrangements.

A crowd already milled about when Caprice and Grant entered Country Squire. Roz and Vince must have been watching for them because they hurried to them and smiled at their "costumes." Grant had rented a shadow-striped suit from a costume shop. It was fashion from the forties—double-breasted with a wide collar and lapels in silk. The pleated suit pants were designed with wide legs and a rolled cuff. With the shoulders padded and the jacket fitted at the waist, his muscular, lean figure was emphasized. With his gray felt fedora tilted at a rakish angle, he could have stepped straight out of an old-time movie.

Caprice's gown, also from the costume shop, was golden like the color of fine champagne. It had long sleeves, a deep V neckline, and a tight bodice that flared into a calf-length skirt. She'd worn strappy gold high heels with it and carried a beaded purse from her vintage collection. Grant's eyes had seemed to pop when he'd seen her and that's what had mattered.

Now Vince studied the two of them as Roz grinned and said, "Humphrey Bogart and Lauren Bacall."

Caprice nudged Grant's elbow. "See, people will know who we are."

"Roz isn't *most* people," he returned wryly. "But if *she* guessed, a few others will too." He studied Vince, who was dressed in jeans, a snap-button shirt with a bolo tie, boots, and a Stetson. Roz's fringed suede skirt, boots that sported high heels, and a puffed sleeve blouse complemented his outfit.

"There's no mistaking the two of you," Grant said. "Roy Rogers and Dale Evans."

Vince laughed. "Got my country groove on."

"He convinced me," Roz assured them. "Not too outlandish, but not over the top either. Lots of folks here aren't into masquerading. They're just here for the food and the dancing and the party atmosphere, I guess. We snagged four chairs at a table far away from the music so we can talk if we want. Ready to head that way?"

"How's the food?" Caprice asked. "Nikki went all out trying to come up with harvest fare. She said she added cayenne to the deviled eggs and made pumpkin cupcakes with a cream cheese glaze dribbled on top and a chocolate stem so they resemble pumpkins. She actually baked crackers that resemble leaves."

Roz explained, "She has a sausage, potato, and red pepper combination that looks fabulous, sweet potato chips for that spinach dip, and white pizza with cheese and mango slices. I can't wait to try that one."

"Don't forget the apple cake with the cinnamon crumble topping," Vince added. "And the stuffed peppers with the little faces. She's got a great imagination."

If Nikki kept securing gigs like this, she might have to rent a place to cook out of instead of using her own kitchen.

"Considering the amount of people you two probably know here, it will take a while to walk to our table. Let's get started," Vince suggested, "or we'll never have dinner."

"He thinks about his stomach a lot," Roz joked.

"In all the years I lived with him, Mom couldn't keep up with his appetite and stock enough food in the fridge," Caprice teased.

"Don't give me that," Vince said. "You and Nikki used to raid the refrigerator at midnight too. You both had healthy appetites."

Caprice knew she could eat all the low-fat yogurt and celery in the world and it wouldn't erase the curves from her hips or thighs. That was hereditary. But swimming did help keep her fit and a little more trim than she used to be. Walks with Lady helped too.

She had to admit she liked food as much as Vince did, and exercise was a way to prevent pounds from settling in the wrong places.

Vince had been right about the residents she and Grant knew in Kismet who stopped them to talk as they walked through the dining room on the way to their table. They passed a baby grand where a pianist was playing dinner music, but in a corner on the other side of the room, a DJ was setting up for later.

"A DJ instead of a band," Caprice said. "That's unusual for the Country Squire."

"Everybody's cutting back expenses," Vince decided. "A DJ's probably cheaper. Besides, he can pull anything from a playlist. It's more practical too."

Her practical brother. She wondered if he'd made a decision about the house yet. If he had, he hadn't told her.

After they'd gone through the buffet line and waved to Nikki, who was headed toward the kitchen, they settled at the table with two other couples. Caprice was pleased to see one of her tablemates was Judy Clapsaddle, who owned the Nail Yard, a manicure business located near Vince's office downtown. She and her husband were dressed as gypsies. She introduced her husband, Tom, to everyone. He fiddled with the black bandana tied around his head and said to Caprice, "You're the one who takes in stray animals."

"I do now and then," she responded, eager to dig into Nikki's food. After a few moments of conversation, it was easy to see Tom was an animal lover, too, and the discussion turned to the care of cats and dogs. When Judy and Tom, Roz and Grant excused themselves to fill their plates with desserts, Caprice took the opportunity to nudge her brother, who was sitting next to her. "So what are you going to do about the house?" she asked him.

After a couple of beats, he said, "I'm still thinking about it."

"Thinking or procrastinating?"

"It's a big step, Caprice, and I don't just mean buying the house."

"You mean living together."

"Yes."

"But you asked her."

"Yes, I did. But when I started looking at houses, I realized the full implication of it all. I could be setting foot into something long term I can't easily pull my foot back out of."

"Are you serious about Roz?"

"I am."

And Caprice knew that was the problem. Her brother had never been serious about anyone. He'd dated lots of women, but he hadn't been this captivated or fully emotionally involved. Now he knew he couldn't play around with Roz's heart. She'd been hurt in her marriage, and he wasn't about to take the chance on hurting her again.

"If you're worried about Roz, she's stronger than she looks. As long as you're honest with her about everything, you'll both be okay."

"That's what a relationship's all about, honesty?" He looked as if he really wanted to know.

"It's a huge part of it. Honesty and trust go together. Don't look at this as Mount Everest to climb, just think of it as one little hill at a time."

A smile broke across Vince's face. "Leave it up to you to put it in picturesque terms. I did go to the bank. I don't think it will be any problem getting a loan."

"So you have started the process for loan approval?"

"Yes, I have. So don't worry, little sister. Your big brother is just fine. I'm just a little shell-shocked by the idea of all of it."

She could understand this was a big step for Vince, and for Roz too.

Grant and Roz returned to the table then, dessert plates loaded with goodies that the couples could share. Suddenly, however, Roz reached around Vince and put her hand on Caprice's arm.

"You said you wanted to meet Doris Wyatt, right?"

"Yes, I do."

"She just disappeared into the ladies' room. Do you want to go in?"

That was a rhetorical question if Caprice had ever heard one. She stood and whispered to Grant, "I'll be right back."

He gave her one of those warning looks. "Don't get into trouble."

"Not me."

Then she joined Roz and they wove around three tables to the other wall and the ladies' room. After they went inside, they were glad to see it was empty except for one woman standing at the mirror refreshing her lipstick. Her blond hair had obviously seen several years of touchups. It was cut in one of those haphazard, along-the-cheek with a short back styles. She was wearing a black sequin cocktail dress with a neckline a little too low and a hemline a little too high for her weight and height.

Roz unobtrusively checked the other stalls in the bathroom, then nodded to Caprice that they were empty. Doris was self-absorbed at the mirror and didn't seem to notice them at all, not until Roz stepped up beside her at the sink next to hers.

"Hello, Doris, it's good to see you again."

Doris looked over at Roz and Caprice standing beside her. She gave a nod and then studied Caprice. "You're that woman who's been interviewed several times in the *Kismet Crier*, aren't you? The one who rescues animals and solves murders."

Caprice wondered if that was going to be her epitaph someday. What a morbid thought. "I do rescue strays, and I've been involved in a few murder investigations. Marianne Brisbane wrote the articles."

Doris waved her hand as if that wasn't important at all. She had something else more pressing on her mind. "Are you looking into Wendy Newcomb's murder?"

Caprice supposed that was a logical leap. Or had Doris heard she was asking questions?

"I knew Wendy, and I'd like to see her killer brought to justice. She did such important work."

Caprice's words must have hit the wrong chord in Doris because the woman scowled, making her broad face absolutely unattractive, as unattractive as her next words.

"Wendy Newcomb was nothing but a meddler who should have minded her own business. I told the police as much. That woman stole my inheritance."

Caprice intended to stay neutral and tried to keep a perspective on the whole matter. After all, how well did she know Wendy? She'd never even met Leona Wyatt. So it wouldn't hurt for her to play along with the way Doris saw things, at least for the moment.

"I can understand how you might think that. You and your brother were your mother's only blood relatives. But I've heard how important Wendy was in your mother's life. Couldn't you and your brother see how Wendy was insinuating herself into your mom's day-to-day living?"

Doris brushed the hair that swayed along one cheek behind her ear. "We didn't see it until it was too late. If we had known what was happening, we would have put a stop to it."

Just what did that mean? Did that mean Doris and her brother would have taken their mom to her chemo appointments? Would they have sat by her and taken care of her when she was sick from those treatments? Or would they have just pushed Wendy out of their mother's life and left her to handle her cancer alone?

Caprice's family was close and that's what she had known all her life. She believed that if Doris and her brother had been in touch with their mother often enough, they would have seen Leona's friendship with Wendy developing. But she couldn't say all that, not without gaining herself an enemy. And she tried not to make those.

"I'm so sorry for your loss. Losing a mother has to be a life-changing event. I just can't imagine it." And she couldn't.

"Thank you," Doris said, looking a bit surprised, as if maybe many people hadn't offered her their condolences. "My mother and I didn't talk often, but she was a driving force in my life . . . and my brother's. I just wish everyone could understand what a conniving witch Wendy Newcomb was. She wasn't this person with a halo who saved the world. She could be harsh and manipulative, and I'm sure that's why someone killed her."

Could that someone have been Doris? Caprice wondered, exchanging a look with Roz. With that much vehemence behind her words and that much passion, it was entirely possible.

"Does your brother feel the same way?" Caprice asked.

"Absolutely he does. As far as we're concerned, Sunrise Tomorrow doesn't deserve a penny of our inheritance. But we've been told there's nothing we can do about it. No grounds, they say. Too much risk to contest, our lawyer told us."

At that moment, the door to the ladies' room opened and two more women strode in.

Doris muttered, "I'd better get back out there. Scott and his wife will wonder what happened to me." After she stomped from the ladies' room, Caprice checked her own lipstick and said in a low voice to Roz, "I wouldn't want to meet her in a dark alley."

"I told you she was cold."

"I don't think cold quite covers it."

After they'd both freshened up, they exited the ladies' room. On the way back to the table, Roz said, "I forgot to tell you, Vince said he worked a corporate merger between Doris's brother and his client. He said he'll snag him if he can for you. And, by gosh, he's done it. Look over there."

Grant was nowhere to be seen for the moment, but Vince was talking to a tall, thin man in a dark suit and a red power tie. Beside him was a petite blonde who might have been in her mid-twenties. She was wearing a bright orange sheath with a black color-blocked hem.

As Caprice approached them, she saw that Scott Wyatt looked to be near fifty. The woman beside him was probably a quarter century younger. That was quite an age difference.

Vince saw Caprice coming and smiled. While Roz went to stand beside him, Vince said to Scott Wyatt,

"You know Roz. And this is my sister Caprice. Caprice, Scott Wyatt and his wife, Darby. Scott and I did some business together about a year ago."

Scott said wryly, "Yes, your brother wasn't my lawyer, but maybe he should have been. He knows how to negotiate."

Scott's wife, Darby, smiled politely at Caprice, but then said, "I see an old friend over there. I'm going to go talk to her."

But Scott didn't seem to like that idea and he grabbed his wife's arm. "You can talk to her later. We're having a conversation here."

Darby seemed cowed by his words, went still, and stayed put. Scott's gaze swept over Caprice with one of those male looks that made her skin crawl.

"I understand you're a celebrity in this town. You've made the paper a few times."

Apparently everyone in Kismet read the *Kismet Crier*, page to page, top to bottom. She forced herself to be pleasant to this man whom she already didn't like. She would love to get his wife alone and have a conversation with her.

Darby seemed to suddenly realize who Caprice was too. She said, "You're a decorator, aren't you?" She snapped her fingers. "Not a decorator, but a home stager."

"Yes, I am."

"She staged my house to sell," Roz said, jumping into the conversation. "She's good at what she does."

"Do you still decorate houses? I'd love to redecorate our living room," Darby said.

As if women having a conversation bored him, Scott muttered, "I see an old golfing buddy over there. Stay put," he ordered his wife. "I'm going to ask him if he could hook up for a game this week."

Apparently intuitive enough to figure out that Caprice would like to talk to Darby alone, Vince added, "And I see Grant's talking to one of our clients. Roz, I'll introduce you."

After the others moved away, Caprice asked Darby, "What kind of décor do you have in mind?"

"I'm not sure. I just know I don't like what Scott has there now, something his first wife picked out. It's all dark and gloomy. I'd like to brighten up the room."

Caprice opened her purse, realizing this wasn't the place to talk to Darby. But a consultation in the woman's own home might be. She always carried business cards and she took one out now and handed it to Scott Wyatt's wife.

"Give me a call if you want to generate ideas, or if you want me to give the room a makeover. I mostly stage houses now, but I still enjoy redecorating."

After a furtive look at where her husband was standing with his golfing buddy, Darby lowered her voice. "I will call you. Scott shouldn't disapprove of bringing our living room up to date."

Caprice realized Darby didn't sound sure of that, didn't sound sure of that at all. She was certain the young woman would check with her husband before she consulted with Caprice.

Just what sort of marriage did the couple have? Caprice thought about the kind of marriage *she* wanted. Yes, she'd consult with her husband. But she didn't want to have to rely on his approval to make decisions. She wanted to make decisions on her own.

Caprice was on her way back to the table when Grant stepped up beside her and wrapped his arm around her waist. "Miss Bacall, may I have the pleasure of this dance?" he asked with a smile.

"Yes, you may," she said in her best Lauren Bacall raspy-voiced imitation.

He laughed and led her to the dance floor that was set up in front of the DJ's dais where other couples were already dancing. Then he took her into his arms easily, holding her in a ballroom position in sync with their character portrayal.

They'd been dancing a few minutes when Caprice asked him, "Do you believe married couples need to make all of their decisions together?"

"The important ones. Why are you asking?"

She nodded toward Scott and Darby, who were still mingling and talking with people. "Darby seems almost afraid of Scott, like she won't make a move without his approval."

"What kind of decision are we talking about?"

"A consultation about redecorating their living room."

Grant shrugged. "It could be a matter of budget. She wants to consult with him first to see how much money she has to spend. Then again, she could get into your favorite bailiwick, asking him his favorite colors and the kind of chair he wants to sit in to watch TV."

"I suppose that could be it. But it just seemed that she didn't even want to talk to me without checking with him first. Doesn't that seem odd to you?"

Grant studied her. "Each marriage is unique. My mom probably wouldn't think about redecorating or a new color scheme unless she consulted with my father first, though she might have a side conference with a decorator to find out what her options were before taking it to my dad. What about your parents? What would your mom do?"

"My mom would probably bring home a selection

of fabrics and wallpaper samples and paint colors, check off the ones she liked best, and then ask my dad what he liked. Then they'd compromise."

"Exactly. Every couple's unique. That doesn't mean one does it the right way and one does it the wrong way."

"No, I suppose not. But I just get this feeling about Scott Wyatt—"

Grant pulled her a little closer. "Do you really want to talk about Scott Wyatt tonight?"

When she gazed into Grant's gray eyes, she forgot about the murder investigation and thought only of him. He seemed to be thinking about only her because he said, "I'm going to miss you this week when you're in Baltimore."

"You can watch me each night on TV."

He squeezed her hand. "I like reality better than reality TV."

"You can join me in Baltimore the last night."

"The night when the results come in for the vote? You bet I'll be there, because win or lose we can celebrate."

"Celebrate what?"

Bending his head, he whispered, "Celebrate being together."

For the time being, Baltimore, house decorating, and anything but the two of them seemed light-years away.

On Monday evening, Caprice stopped in at her parents' house on her way to Baltimore. As she climbed the steps to the side porch, rounded the rope-type pillar supporting the porch roof, she thought about her van packed with everything she'd need for the week. Nikki was going to be staying at her house to pet-sit until the results were in from the model home competition and Caprice was back home.

When Caprice walked in the side door of her childhood home into the foyer, a cuckoo clock just ahead on the wall of the dining room cuckooed six times. She smiled, remembering that clock from her childhood.

Her mother called from the living room to the left of the foyer. "In here, honey."

A burst of laughter came all the way through the dining room from the kitchen. A round of applause went up and then there was more male laughter.

Poker night.

Crossing to the sofa, Caprice unbuttoned her poncho. "Did you get the info I e-mailed you about the motel where I'll be staying?"

"Sure did. You should be comfortable there."

"I'm just hoping I can sleep. We have to stop work on the rooms every night by nine. So theoretically I should get some rest, especially since I won't have to feed cats or walk a dog. They won't wake me in the middle of the night either."

"But you'll miss them."

"Yes, I will. And not only them. I'll miss everybody here too."

"You'll only be gone four days. Think of it as a vacation from the De Lucas and everything in your ordinary life."

"I can try and do that."

"Most of all you're going to miss Grant, aren't you?"

"I am." There wasn't any more to say than that. "I can't stay. I'm just going to go say good-bye to Dad and then stop in at Nana's."

After a hug and a kiss from her mom, she made her

way through the dining room, turned right into the kitchen, then through to the eat-in area. There she found not only her dad, but Chief Powalski and three other friends of her dad's . . . along with a beautiful white Malamute.

"Hi, honey. You're leaving for Baltimore?" her dad asked.

"After I tell you if you have a winning hand or not."

Her father chuckled and motioned to the man beside him. "You know Chris Merriweather . . . and Blitz."

The chief said, "He's hard to recognize without his white beard and wire-rimmed glasses."

Caprice grinned as she remembered Chris Merriweather's twinkling blue eyes. "You play Santa Claus in that little cabin they bring into the community park. And Blitz is your loyal sidekick."

Chris nodded solemnly. "That's us."

"You've been playing Santa for a long while."

"I have for the past decade."

"I brought Megan and Timmy in to see you for the past three."

"Yes, you have. Your sister Bella doesn't want them to think she overhears when they tell me what they want. The truth is, I think this is Timmy's last year believing. He just pretended to believe last year for his mom's sake."

"That's probably true."

Her father went on to introduce the other two men at the table. He said to them, "She's pretty good at poker. She can bluff with the best of them. She does have a few tells, though."

Mac joked, "But we won't let on what they are." He said to Caprice, "So tell me the scoop on Brett Carstead and your sister Nikki."

"Scoop? I should be getting that from you. What does Brett tell you?"

"You are joking, right? That man is as tight-lipped about his personal life as he is about the investigation he runs. He's a good man. He just doesn't open up much."

"I know nothing. Honestly, I don't. I do know Brett had to break a date because of the Newcomb investigation."

"And I know you're asking questions about Wendy Newcomb."

Because she didn't need another warning, she adroitly reminded him, "I won't be asking any questions for the next four days. I'm going to be too busy to think. You can watch me every night on TV and see my progress."

"You want me to watch some decorating show?" The chief sounded horrified at that idea.

"You don't have to watch a decorating show. All you have to do is look at all three houses and decide which one you like best . . . which one *you'd* like to live in. Of course, you're going to like mine best and vote for that one on Thursday night."

Her father punched Mac in the arm. "You can come over here. We'll watch together and then I can make sure you vote for Caprice."

"I'll see what else I have on my schedule that night," the chief responded sagely. Then he said to Caprice, "I just took a few hours tonight to get away from the investigation so I can go back to it with a clear head. I can understand why Brett broke his date with Nikki—I heard him call her. I hope she's not too upset about that. We've all been up to our eyeballs with interviews. I think Brett even slept in his office the last couple of nights. He's taking the lead on this one, and he's meticulous."

"Any headway? I know you can't tell me specifics, but do you have a suspect list?"

"We have more suspects than we can count. This one's a puzzle that's going to take quite a bit of sorting out, let alone leg work and running down the leads."

"I'll share with Brett anything I learn and he knows it."

"You do have a knack for pulling information out of people. It must be the way you seem to care about them."

Her dad interjected, "She doesn't *seem* to care, she does care."

The chief pointed his finger at her. "Don't care too much."

She knew what he meant. She wouldn't be impulsive. She wouldn't be reckless. And for the next week, she was going to keep her mind on decorating a house and winning the competition.

Chapter Twelve

Tuesday, the first day of the house competition, had flown on by. From the moment Caprice had seen the ranch-style model homes this morning through the initial taping, she'd been thoroughly excited with adrenaline shooting through her. She had set a budget, deadlines, and a plan for winning.

All of the competitors had access to three local furniture stores that would be supplying furniture and getting plenty of advertisement for their efforts. Each designer also had access to a handyman to help with painting and anything else that was necessary. This wasn't a renovating project, but rather a decorating one.

Still, accents could be added that would enhance the whole look, and that's what Caprice was intent on doing. She didn't know what the other competitors would come up with as themes for their model homes, but she had settled on hers. "Flair for Wood" was her theme and, in addition, she'd develop a color scheme. But the richness and warmth of wood would make her house stand out—from the furniture to crown molding to a chair rail. The question was—could she accomplish all of it by the deadline of Thursday at five? The Thursday and Friday night segments would be live.

She wasn't thrilled by live TV, especially after a day of frazzled working to decorate the house. But hair and makeup wasn't usually a concern of hers. She wouldn't make it a concern now. Her vintage bell-bottoms and tie-dyed T-shirt would just have to make a statement of their own.

She stopped at one of her favorite burger places on the way back to her motel. She'd have a salad tomorrow for lunch to make up for the Five Guys burger and fries that were hand-cut on the premises. Taking the delicious-smelling bag of food to her motel room, she was sitting on the bed cross-legged, dipping a warm fry into ketchup, when her cell phone played. She'd laid it on the nightstand next to her.

Wiping her hand on a napkin, she picked up the phone and blinked. Caller ID said it was Seth Randolph's number! She'd dated the handsome doctor until last spring when she decided Grant was the man who owned her heart. Seth's career choices were driving his life decisions and Caprice had known she'd never come first. Seth's love of medicine would. When he'd e-mailed her this summer to tell her he was extending his stay in Baltimore past his fellowship, she'd e-mailed back that he should keep her informed. After all, she'd liked Seth and wanted to keep him as a friend. Was that possible when they'd been romantically involved?

She answered the call just before it would have gone to voice mail. "This is a surprise."

"A welcome one, I hope," he said smoothly. "When I saw you on TV tonight, I couldn't believe it."

"Believe it. I could win a contract to decorate model homes. I couldn't pass up the opportunity."

"It looks as if you have your work cut out for you in three days."

So he had actually watched the whole segment when the competition had been explained as well as the designers introduced. "You know me—go with the flow. I just have to make sure I don't sink."

"You'll do great. I wondered if while you're in the area you'd like to meet for coffee or a drink? We can catch up."

"Do you have time for that?" As a doctor with a specialty in trauma medicine, he was constantly busy without much time to even grab a bite to eat let alone sleep.

"I'm on a rotating schedule right now—three days on, two off. Thursday I'm off."

"I'm tied up until at least eight on Thursday with the live show and taping afterward."

"Where are you staying?"

She told him and then added, "There's a coffee shop here."

"I can meet you at the coffee shop Thursday night if you won't be too tired. I'll buy you supper."

She and Seth really hadn't had closure. She'd made her decision about Grant and she'd told Seth what she'd decided. He'd left the family gathering afterward and they hadn't really talked since. Just as Grant had needed closure with his ex-wife Naomi, she needed it with Seth.

"I won't be too tired. And I have to eat."

He chuckled. "All right. I'll meet you at the coffee

shop at your motel about nine on Thursday for a late supper."

"That sounds good. If I'm going to be held up, I'll text you."

"I'll see you Thursday night, Caprice. I'm looking forward to it."

After she ended the call, she stared at the phone. Should she tell Grant about the meeting?

She would tell him. But maybe not until after she saw Seth. She wanted to find out what he wanted. Then she'd tell Grant all about it.

When Caprice entered the coffee shop on Thursday evening, she caught sight of Seth right away. There were only a few people in the small restaurant and Seth would have stood out anywhere, with his blond hair, blue eyes, and handsome face. He was wearing khakis and a cream Oxford shirt with the sleeves rolled up. His wardrobe choices hadn't changed. Had he?

Caprice was grateful to see and feel that her heart hadn't sped up when she'd spotted him. No pitty-pat anymore for Seth Randolph. All of that romantic anticipation and excitement was aimed toward Grant now. She did wish, however, that she'd told Grant about this meeting. She hadn't wanted to cause him worry or any anxiety, but they'd promised to be completely honest with each other. Would he think she'd hidden this meeting because she still had feelings for Seth?

Too late to worry now. It all depended on how much Grant trusted her.

Seth stood when he saw her. As a De Luca, it was natural for her to give him a hug. It was a quick hug, just one of those kinds a family member gives another family member.

He motioned her to the booth seat across from him and she slid in. He sat too.

"You look terrific," he said.

She didn't know how true that was. It had been a long day and she might even have a couple of splatters of paint in her hair. She'd worn her red bell-bottom jeans and a Bohemian-style top with a lacy red and blue swirled bodice that was crocheted across the shoulder line.

"You're too kind. I probably have sanding dust in my hair. The crown molding arrived today and I was helping to saw it as well as paint it."

"You use power tools?"

"All part of the expertise," she said with a shrug. "I'm glad my dad taught me how."

"How *is* your family?"

Just then the waitress came over to take their order. Caprice ordered coffee, a turkey club, and a tossed salad. She had to get those salads in. Seth ordered the mushroom-bacon cheeseburger and coffee.

After the waitress returned to the kitchen window with their order, Caprice answered his question. "My family is good. Bella and Joe bought a house they seem to be enjoying. Nikki has gone on a few dates with Brett Carstead."

"The detective?"

Caprice nodded.

"How did that happen?"

That launched Caprice into an account of the last murder she'd been involved in and an explanation of how Nikki had been a suspect. That's when her sister and Brett had "noticed" each other.

"And how are you?" Seth asked, gazing straight into her eyes.

"Busy."

"Are you happy?"

Is that what this get-together was all about? Finding out if she'd made the right choice? "I am happy. Grant and I are dating."

"Getting serious?"

"I hope so. At least I am."

Seth nodded. "You made the right decision. Not that I didn't care about you. But you were right—I'm not ready to settle down. I guess I wanted to see you to tell you I'd always care about you because above everything else, we had a really good friendship. I'm taking a position in Chicago at a trauma center. I'm starting out on the night shift, which will really turn life upside-down. But it will be a good experience."

"You sound as if you might not stay there."

"I'm not sure Chicago is where I ultimately want to end up. I've always wanted to live on a houseboat in Seattle."

"You never mentioned that before."

"Maybe I thought that would chase you away."

"Because I'm such a small-town girl?" she asked wryly.

"No, because you want to stay close to your family. You need a guy who wants to do that, too, and I think you found him."

Studying Seth, knowing how he cared about his patients, she asked, "And what about you? Are you ever going to have time for love in your life?"

"I don't know. I either need the kind of woman who will sit at home waiting for the time we can spend together, or the type of woman who wants to be on the move as much as I do and we can grab time whenever we can."

Meaning it sincerely, she offered, "I can visualize both for you and maybe one will turn up."

He laughed. "And just how do you visualize? I've never asked you that before."

"Lots of ways. Promise not to laugh."

"I won't," he swore solemnly.

"Nana believes strongly in saying the Rosary. It's a great meditative tool. I keep one by my bedside and fall asleep some nights saying Hail Marys. Other times, I say the Rosary, but on each decade I imagine a picture of the person I'm saying it for and wish the best for them."

"I would never laugh at that." He reached over and patted her hand. "You're a special woman, Caprice De Luca. I hope Grant appreciates what he has. If he doesn't, call me and I'll give him what for."

"I guess this is the last time I'll see you for maybe years." That thought made her a little sad.

"Face-to-face, anyway. And that's probably the way it should be."

"I'm glad you called me to catch up." It was good to see him again. Finally, she felt as if the "Seth" part of her life had come to a satisfying conclusion.

The waitress brought their orders then. While they ate, they talked about Seth's work and a few of the houses she'd staged. A half hour later, he was standing to leave. She gave him another quick hug and then watched him walk out of the restaurant.

She didn't go to her room, however; she sat back down in the booth and pulled out her cell phone. She wasn't going to wait another second to tell Grant about this meeting.

To her disappointment, she reached his voice

mail. Her conscience needed purging, so she left him a message.

I just wanted to tell you I had coffee and a sandwich with Seth. He called me because he wanted to catch up. He's leaving for Chicago soon. I wish I had told you before I had coffee and a sandwich. Nothing to worry about. We said good-bye. I hope I'll see you here for the final results. I'll text you the address again. I've missed you.

She wanted to tell him she loved him, but not in a voice mail. So she ended the call. She just hoped he'd understand why she'd had to see Seth, why catching up and putting a final dot on their relationship had been good for them both.

Until Friday night rolled around, Caprice was more nervous than she ever thought she could be. She wasn't nervous about whether she'd won or lost. She was concerned about what Grant was thinking. She'd gotten a text this morning around seven a.m. just as she'd gotten to the model home and into the thrust of the final taping instructions. His text had said: Didn't know charge was out on phone. Got your message this morning. Will talk tonight.

Grant wasn't the type to add a heart or smiley face, so she had no idea what he was feeling or thinking. A live segment with all three completed homes in The Model Home Challenge had been shown last night. The TV population had voted until midnight. This evening at seven, they'd all receive the results of those votes. The model homes would be spotlighted again as the winner was announced.

Would Grant be here? Would he come with her family? He said they would talk. Maybe he meant after she got home. Maybe he was seriously upset about her late supper with Seth.

Caprice remembered her own advice to Bella when she'd made a coffee date with an old flame and hadn't told Joe. The thing was, Bella's marriage had been in trouble and the coffee date had been a way to let steam out of the pressure cooker. Bella had intended to flirt and have a good time. Caprice hadn't flirted with Seth. She'd just enjoyed his company. Their situations were very different.

But would Grant see them differently?

Whether Caprice won or not, her house would be seen by scads of people, not only on TV tonight, but at an open house this weekend. With all the publicity and advertising, house hunters might line up to tour the homes. A sale could be imminent for any one of them or all of them.

Since the night weather had turned chilly, she'd brought along a dark turquoise Jacqueline Kennedy–style dress, a sheath with a matching coat trimmed in black with black frog fasteners. Keeping in style with the coat, she wore a pillbox hat also in turquoise with black trim. She knew her sister Bella would say that she looked like an escapee from the sixties. She believed you could sometimes look fashion forward by going back. Her black kitten heels would make it easy for her to do interviews and walk quickly from here to there. But her hands were shaking a little as she waited to get started.

When she checked her watch, she saw that it was six-fifty. At seven o'clock, the live show began. Crossing to her mark at the black tape in front of the model home she'd decorated, she was almost blinded by the floodlights. She couldn't see far beyond them.

Then out of that duskiness beyond the lights she heard a familiar voice yell, "You go, Caprice. You're going to win this."

She had to laugh. That was her sister Bella's voice. She'd know it anywhere.

"You bring home that trophy, sis." That was Nikki. Her clear, clean voice could cut through a crowd.

Then she heard guys cheer. "Go, Caprice, go." She couldn't separate out the voices, but she thought they belonged to Vince, her dad, and maybe Grant? She so hoped Grant had come along.

At the opening of the segment, the cameras followed the first competitor, June Walters, into the first house as June took them on a quick tour and explained about her decorating scheme. As the cameras disappeared into that house, Caprice caught a glimpse of her family just beyond the crowd-control barricade. Grant *was* with them. But he was too far away to make eye contact and she couldn't tell if he was smiling.

Finally it was her turn for the tour with the cameras. She explained about her "Flair for Wood" theme, how the cherrywood cupboards in the kitchen had led to her bringing in a cherry table for the breakfast nook, and a bench to accompany it. The banquette along the windows was covered by a flowered cushion in reds, greens, blues, and oranges. It was the pop of color for that room and coordinated with the place settings of multicolored china on the table. The chandelier overhead was cherry along with wrought iron and worked beautifully with the rest.

Pointing to the crown molding that finished off the space, she mentioned the granite countertops and chef-quality stainless-steel appliances would make any homeowner happy to cook in that kitchen. The kitchen flowed into the dining room with its glossy mahogany table. A green table runner embroidered with baskets of flowers was reminiscent of the flowered cushion in the breakfast nook. A similar scarf runner lay across the mahogany buffet under a double-tiered soup tureen. The walls had been painted a light sage and the crown molding was the same green as the table runner. A framed photo of peonies in a garden basket hung above the buffet while metal sculptures of cat tails graced another wall. Sheer curtains on the French doors lent privacy, and an Aubusson-style rug added rich elegance to the space.

Caprice's wood theme continued in the master suite with polished oak. The four-poster bed was fit for a king. Instead of painting the wall behind the bed, she'd hung a huge quilt in taupe and blue. It gave the room the warmth a bedroom should have. She'd carried the same color scheme through the bedspread and draperies in more muted tones. Huge white and blue poppy throw pillows danced across the bed and adorned the love seat in one corner. The oak armoire that almost reached the ceiling was a striking piece itself trimmed in black like the dresser and the bed. It made a statement that the couple who slept here had impeccable taste.

In the second bedroom, with its simpler maple bed and accompanying pieces, she'd achieved a look that could be for male or female. In this room, she'd added a chestnut rolltop desk to the mix and it picked up the rich orange tones of the maple. She'd taken a chance on a landscape with a wide chestnut frame that depicted a cozy glen where two horses grazed near a white wooden fence. The bedspread was the palest yellow with intricate brown embroidery. The draperies were the same pale yellow, but the valances carried the embroidery across their swag. The black wrought-iron rods balanced the lightness of the draperies, making the room both masculine and feminine.

Caprice had lucked out and found a stark white washbowl light that went perfectly on one nightstand. The other nightstand held a taller wrought-iron light with an octagonal taupe shade.

Finally the tour ended in the living room where Caprice had combined woods from all the rooms to coordinate and pull the theme of the house together. She'd hung the flat-screen TV on the wall, but around it she'd decorated with inlaid wood designs that were 3-D in nature so the wall wouldn't look so flat. A cranberry-colored sectional sofa brought a pop to the room. Across from the TV with its many cushions and chaise lounge, it offered comfortable seating but was also an eye-catching piece. The low, rectangular coffee table with a mosaic top in the same colors as the floral cushions in the kitchen gave TV watchers a place to set drinks or food. There was another conversational corner with chairs facing the fireplace. The room was bright with its cranberry, yellow, orange, red, and sage green. It tied all the other rooms together.

Caprice knew she'd done her best and now all she could do was wait.

The live tour of each house took ten minutes, but it seemed much longer as Caprice waited for the results.

Suddenly the doorbell to her model home rang. The emcee of the show, the one who had started all of this, Roland Vaughn himself, stood there, a broad smile on his face and balloons in his hand. Her heart practically stopped. Was he going to tell her she'd won or lost? After a few moments that seemed like an eternity, he said, "You've won my Model Home Challenge, Caprice De Luca. What do you have to say?"

She was speechless, not like her at all. But she did remember to smile, and she remembered to point outside the door. "I owe everything to the support of my family and my friends. I can't tell you how much this means to win. Thank you for appreciating my decorating designs."

Fortunately they were already out of time. Roland had to wrap things up. All three designers were brought out in front of her house until he made closing remarks and signed off.

As soon as the producer shut down the taping, Caprice asked, "Can I go?"

Roland looked surprised that she'd want to. "There's paperwork to sign, contracts for me to give you so your lawyer can go over them."

"I just need a minute to see my family. They're right over there."

"Sure, go see them. But then come back here. You're going to have a few interviews to do."

Interviews. She needed to talk to Grant. That was as important as any interview.

Her family closed around her in a group hug, and she could hardly breathe as her hat almost fell off. She heard: "Congratulations," "Way to go," "We knew you could do it, honey." Her nana kissed her on the cheek and said, "Grant's waiting to talk to you."

Grant didn't hesitate to envelop her in a big bear hug. "Good job, Caprice. Now, before I let jealousy turn me into a green-eyed monster, tell me if coffee with Seth was just coffee."

"Actually, it was coffee and a turkey club."

Grant's eyes narrowed.

"I should have told you. I don't want you to think I was sneaking behind your back. I just didn't want to worry you."

"Or have me disapprove and say you couldn't go? Did you really think I would do that? I will *never* make your decisions for you, Caprice. I'll weigh in, but I won't make them." His gray eyes were steady on hers, filled with conviction.

"You really mean that, don't you?"

"I do. Tell me you and Seth have doused the romantic flames and I'll believe you."

"They're doused," she assured him. "We know we're not right for each other. We'll probably be exchanging Christmas cards. Will you do that with Naomi?"

"Yes, I probably will."

She asked, "So we're both good?"

Grant's smile was slow in coming, but it came. Then he took her in his arms again and kissed her soundly. That kiss could get her through any interview. That kiss could get her through life.

Chapter Thirteen

The De Luca family dinners occurred one Sunday a month unless something special happened—a surprise birthday party, a congratulations event, an impromptu get-together. When Caprice and her brother and sisters were growing up, they took turns inviting friends. Her mother and father invited friends too. It was always a celebration with lively conversation, catch-up chatter, and the best food on the planet. As the family matured, these dinners became their way of connecting in a busy world, the one time when they pulled together as a family and remembered the bonds among them.

Everyone contributed something to the dinner. Although Caprice, her mother and Nikki, Nana and Bella made most of the food, her dad sometimes did too. Vince was their wine connoisseur who enjoyed wine tasting at area wineries. He chose the wines to go along with the meal. Since Roz had been dating Vince and attending the dinners, she usually brought a table arrangement. She was good at that. Grant contributed fruit or imported chocolates, depending on the season.

Patches, Lady, and Dylan scurried into the living room with Bella's kids as Grant carried a basket of apples through the foyer and into the dining room. He positioned it on the credenza.

Nana winked at him. "Are you hinting you'd like me to make an apple pie?"

"Your pies are the best, so is your apple cobbler."

Nana laughed. "At least you're honest."

Caprice's mom poured water from a pitcher into the tumblers on the table. "I hear you're swamped since the TV show. How many new projects did you get?"

"Enough to keep her busy for the next six months," Grant said. He gave Caprice a hug and whispered in her ear, "I'm going to find your dad. I have something I want to discuss with him."

"Anything important?" Grant hadn't mentioned this before.

"Just guy stuff," Grant responded, gave her a smile, and headed for the living room.

"I think he's in the library," Fran called after him. "He was looking for his copy of Treasure Island for Timmy."

Guy stuff. What did that mean? The latest sports predictions?

"What's your next house staging?" Nana asked, as she took one of the apples from the basket and examined it. It was a Golden Delicious.

Caprice took a stack of napkins from the sideboard and began arranging them at each place setting, folding them as she went. "I'm scurrying to get it done. It's in West York at one of the newer developments."

"What's the theme?" Fran asked.

"Americana Retreat. Juan worked on it while I was gone. I put finishing touches on it yesterday. We can videotape tomorrow morning and the open house is on Wednesday. Denise is moving away from weekend open houses. She feels we'll only get serious house hunters during the week when people aren't just looking for something to do. Since I can use lots of antiques, Isaac helped us put this one together. I don't know what I'd do without him."

The door from the side porch into the foyer opened. The only person missing was Uncle Dom. But Uncle Dom didn't walk through the door, Dulcina did!

Caprice rushed over to her. "Hi. This is a surprise."

Uncle Dom stepped in behind her.

Dulcina was smiling from ear to ear. She was dressed in chocolate brown slacks and a burnt orange blouse. She'd even curled her hair. "Your uncle invited me to join him today."

Well, well, well, Caprice thought. *Somebody's moving along.* She exchanged a look with her uncle and then gave him a hug. This was going to be one of those unforgettable family dinners. She could just tell.

Caprice had brought homemade bread. Along with that, they passed around the table her mom's baked ziti and meatballs, Nikki's feta olive tomato salad, Bella's cheesy cauliflower casserole, and Nana's cannoli for dessert. Caprice could hardly keep up with the conversation swirling around the huge table. Supervising Megan and Timmy, Bella handed off Benny to Joe. He held him in one arm and ate with the other. Soon, however, Nana took the baby and then passed him to Caprice's mom, who walked and talked to him in between bites of food.

Caprice glanced around the table and felt a little misty-eyed.

Grant took her hand. "What's up?"

"Just appreciating what I have," she told him honestly.

He interlaced his fingers with hers.

Caprice's mother was sitting next to her. "I heard that you're involved in the Newcomb murder investigation."

"Who told you I was involved?" Caprice asked.

"Bella has a cat from the Wyatt estate! That in itself was a huge clue."

She never could keep anything from her mom. Now that her mom knew Caprice was involved, Caprice asked, "Did you know Leona Wyatt or Wendy?"

"I saw Wendy at church now and then when I went to early Mass. And Leona—at one time she was involved with some of the charities in Kismet. She often brought donations to the thrift store or our annual clothing drive. But there was always an aura of reserve about her, a distance she put between herself and other people."

"Do you know why?"

Fran sighed. "We suspected."

"We?"

"Friends. Volunteers at the thrift store. Leona sent her children to a private school in York rather than the public school or the Catholic school here. I had another friend whose children were in that same school. She said Leona never attended the meetings. She conferenced with the teachers by phone."

"And the reason?"

"Bruises she didn't want anyone to see. I caught sight of a few on her arm one time when she donated clothes to St. Francis's Thanksgiving collection. She saw that I noticed them and made some flimsy excuse about bumping against a cupboard door. But it didn't look like that. The bruises circled her arm as if someone had grabbed her—hard. After her husband died, I thought she might become more social, but she didn't. She kept to a secluded lifestyle as if habits from years of hiding kept her hiding even then."

"Do you think her children knew what was going on?"

"Children always know what's going on, even if it happens behind closed doors. Domestic violence affects everyone in the family, even relatives who only suspect it from a distance. They feel helpless."

"But Leona got close to Wendy."

"In small towns there's always gossip. I think when Leona got sick, she finally realized how much she needed a good friend. Wendy was in a position to be the kind of friend she needed because she would have understood what Leona had gone through. I can see how a bond formed very easily."

That was probably true. Someone who had gone through the same experience would understand the best.

Suddenly the doorbell chimed. Caprice's gaze immediately went to Nana's. Nana's eyes twinkled.

This time, it wasn't her mom or Nana who stood up from the table but rather Nikki. She was slightly flushed as she excused herself and went to the door.

Caprice heard a male voice and she recognized that voice. It belonged to Brett Carstead.

Fran explained, "Nikki said she invited him, but he didn't know if he could get here and take the time away from work."

Caprice was glad he'd decided he might want a relationship as well as a dedicated career.

And another thought quickly followed. Maybe she could find out more about his investigation.

* * *

It was a little after noon on Monday when Caprice found herself in Scott and Darby Wyatt's home after a morning of videotaping her Americana Retreat. Darby had called her this morning because Scott had seen Caprice on the local televised news last night in replays of her win in Baltimore. He'd told Darby he thought it would be prestigious for Caprice to decorate their living room.

Caprice wasn't too keen on the prestigious part. She'd rather Scott Wyatt call her because he liked her style. But a client was a client, she supposed. She'd received about twenty calls to set up meetings within the next three weeks with TV viewers who'd watched the Baltimore cable show. Her escapade into TV fame had definitely brought in business. But the way Scott Wyatt looked at her, she didn't know if she wanted his. There was just something sleazy about him.

There was nothing sleazy about the house, though. It was a Georgian about 3,500 square feet. The living room was long and spacious, probably about twenty-five feet by twelve. She could see why Darby wasn't entranced with it. The sofa belonged to the nineties with its gray background, cranberry and green geometric shapes. A wing chair in a darker cranberry didn't fit in with other modern pieces like the black entertainment center that took up one wall and occasional pieces that matched that. The pale gray carpeting wasn't necessarily worn but didn't look fresh either.

Sitting across from her now, Scott handed her a printout. "That's my budget," he said. "Do you think you can stay within that amount?"

Caprice could juggle any budget. She could always repurpose furniture and ask for Isaac's help finding unique pieces. The wholesale furniture outlet she dealt with sold escalating levels of quality in tables, lamps, and accent pieces. The budget wouldn't be a problem.

"I can work within your budget. I'm concerned more about what kind of style you enjoy and what your favorite colors are."

"You know," he said with a wave of his hand, "I don't care about all of that. My only condition—I'd like a big comfortable recliner for me. Darby can pick out whatever else she wants as long as it comes in under budget."

He gave Darby a look that said she better not go one penny over either. Caprice would be absolutely mindful of that.

Scott stood and gave her another one of those looks that made her skin crawl, a look that told her she wouldn't want to be alone with him in a dark corner.

"I have to be getting back to work. I'm looking at a piece of property to develop into condos."

"In Kismet?" Caprice asked.

"Oh, no, over near Wrightsville. You and Darby have a good planning session." He gave Darby a penetrating look. "I'll want to hear all about it when I get back."

Scott went over to Darby and gave her a quick kiss. His hand ran down her back and patted her fanny. Then he was gone, out the front door with his car keys jangling.

Was it Caprice's imagination or did Darby breathe a huge sigh of relief? His wife didn't speak until Scott had started his car and was backing out of their driveway.

Caprice took out her electronic tablet. She had a

form on there that she filled out for clients. She could take notes and list everything they talked about.

Darby stared out the front window as if making sure Scott was truly gone. "I used to work from home," she mused.

"You did? What did you do?"

"I designed Web sites before Scott married me. I have an associate's degree in graphic design. But after we married, he didn't and still doesn't want me to work."

"He wants you to have a life of leisure?" Caprice joked, knowing this opportunity to probe around in Darby's life was an unexpected gift.

"Not exactly," she said shyly, turning around. She crossed to the sofa and sat down beside Caprice. "I think it's because he doesn't want me to deal with clients. He gets jealous very easily, not only of other men, but of my time. You know, if he wants me for some reason and I'm busy doing something else."

Isolating a spouse was a sign of abuse. Did Scott Wyatt not want Darby to have contact with anyone outside of him? If not, why?

"Do you have family living around here?" Caprice asked.

Darby shook her head. "They're in West Virginia. I haven't seen them since I married Scott two years ago. When we're supposed to visit, something always comes up."

"Life can get crazy," Caprice empathized.

"I suppose, but sometimes I think Scott puts up roadblocks on purpose." She said this quickly as if the thought had passed through her own mind many times and she'd never said it aloud. But as soon as she had said it aloud, she looked a little scared and she grabbed one of the sample books that Caprice had brought along and started paging through fabrics, telling Caprice which ones she liked and which ones she didn't.

They talked about styles of sofas—those with roll backs or wood trim or cushy throw pillows that created the back support. Did she want a sofa long enough to stretch out and take a nap? Or maybe a sleeper. After they'd nailed down the fact that Darby wanted something comfortable without pretense, Caprice had a handle on the style of furniture she should look at.

Then out of the blue, as Caprice was making notes on her tablet, Darby revealed, "I spoke with Wendy Newcomb before she died."

Darby's soft words seemed to echo in the large living room, but Caprice wasn't going to let them fade away.

"Spoke to her about what?"

"I met Scott at a bar. A couple of girlfriends and I had stopped at Susie Q's for Happy Hour one Friday afternoon after work. Since I worked from my apartment, I made a point of getting together with friends a couple of times a week so work didn't take over my life."

"I can understand that," Caprice said. Anyone who worked from home knew work was there twenty-four hours a day, always ready to grab your attention.

"My two friends had nine-to-five jobs and needed to unwind. Friday was our standard girl's night out."

"But Scott was at Susie Q's?"

Susie Q's was a combination sports bar and singles hangout located downtown near the community center. Caprice didn't frequent the establishment, but she knew Vince and Nikki stopped in at Happy Hour now and then.

"I think he just had a business meeting with another fellow in a suit. I think it's the suit that grabbed my attention. You rarely see men in suits anymore unless you're in an office building."

Grant wore a suit for court dates and client meetings. He looked good in a suit. But then she was probably prejudiced.

"I thought Scott was charming and sophisticated that night. For the next couple of months, he courted me like I was somebody special. But then we got married and he became all possessive. I love him and I don't want my marriage to end, but I do want it to change. That's what I talked to Wendy about."

"How did you meet Wendy?"

"I didn't meet her per se. I picked up one of the pamphlets from Sunrise Tomorrow in the Sunflower Diner."

Caprice had seen the rack there that held pamphlets from area businesses and services.

"So you called Sunrise?" she asked.

"Yes, the receptionist put me through to Wendy. We met and had lunch, and Wendy suggested a counseling program through Sunrise Tomorrow. But when I told Scott about it, he blew a gasket and broke an expensive vase."

"This vase. How did he break it?"

"He threw it but just missed me. He was so sorry afterward that I just let it go. We got along fine for a week or so, but then his words got really cutting and hurtful. He corrects me and criticizes me, not only when we're alone, but when we're with others. And he won't let me have any friends. I never meet up with the girls at Susie Q's anymore. He's never hit me, but I think I'm becoming afraid he might. I'm anxious all the time. I can't sleep. I'm losing weight. I just feel so trapped."

Apparently Darby didn't have anyone she could talk to, and this opportunity to meet with Caprice to decorate the house was a chance to unload.

"I think you need more than a friend," Caprice suggested. "You need someone who knows about situations like yours. I know Wendy's gone now. I suggest you call Lizbeth Diviney, who's the acting head of Sunrise Tomorrow now. She can match you up with a counselor advocate."

"I can't get away without Scott seeing where I go. He watches the mileage on the car. I think he even has one of those apps on my cell phone that tells him where I am."

Caprice wanted to shout that none of that was okay . . . that Darby needed to free herself from the web Scott had wound about her. But she couldn't say that. She couldn't give that kind of advice. All she could do was try to get Darby help.

"Maybe I can help you with that. If we're decorating the living room, we can make up an excuse to meet at a furniture store. If you talk to Lizbeth, maybe you could meet your counselor there. I'm sure something could be worked out."

Darby seemed to think about it, to weigh the pros and cons, and maybe the consequences. She stared at the wall across the room, then out the window. In a low voice, she said, "I heard Scott talking to Doris one time about how badly their father treated their mother. Apparently Doris didn't know about one particular incident. Scott's father hit Leona in the head. It was years later that Leona revealed to Scott that after that day, she went to a gun store and learned to shoot. She admitted that if her husband hadn't died in a car accident, she might have killed him. So there was a good reason she wanted her money to go to Sunrise Tomorrow and not to Doris and Scott. She understood how Sunrise Tomorrow could have changed her life and the lives of her children. I can't imagine having kids with Scott with him like this. I can't even imagine five years from now. But I can't imagine leaving either, and I need to know what to do. He has a temper and—"

The way Darby said that made Caprice's insides lurch, and she had to ask the question: "Darby, do you think Scott could have killed Wendy?"

Yesterday Brett was closemouthed about the investigation as well as quiet with her family. Overwhelmed maybe by how outgoing everyone had been? Yet she had gotten the feeling that he was frustrated and stymied by a lack of progress in the case. Maybe Scott Wyatt was another direction to pursue.

Caprice watched Darby blink away tears; then she gave a slow nod. "I think it's possible, and that's what really scares me."

Caprice pulled her purse from the coffee table, took out a small notepad, and tore off a slip of paper. She opened her phone, found Lizbeth's number in her contacts, and wrote it down. She handed the paper to Darby. "Call Lizbeth. Get help. And if you need an excuse to meet someone someplace, call me and let me know. I'll set it up."

A half hour later, after having a cup of tea with Darby and encouraging her again to get help, Caprice headed for home and all the calls she had to return because of the house decorating competition. After giving some love to her two felines, brushing them and telling both Sophia and Mirabelle how beautiful they were, she pulled out Lady's leash. She just wasn't ready to sit and make phone calls, not to talk about house stagings or redecorating.

Capturing Lady's leash from the antique oak mirrored bench in her foyer, she wiggled it at her. "How about if we go for a walk? It's gotten chilly, and the breeze will sweep out my brain. What do you think?"

Lady ran around Caprice's legs twice and then sat at her feet looking up expectantly.

"I thought that would appeal to you."

She attached the leash and off they went.

Although the October day was sunny, the yellowing leaves splashing color against the bright blue sky, the sense of summer's end lingering in the air, she couldn't get her conversation with Darby out of her head. No, she couldn't sit and make phone calls to clients right now. Yet she knew she had to call someone else—Brett Carstead. If he wasn't there, she'd leave a message. But at least she would get some of the burden off her mind.

Instead of the station's number, she called his cell phone directly. Since he'd told her he'd appreciate any information she discovered, she felt she had the right to do that. He answered on the second ring.

"Who did you talk to?" he asked, not wasting any time. He'd obviously seen her number on his caller ID.

She told him where she'd been this afternoon and what she'd learned, not only about Darby's marriage to Scott, but about Leona Wyatt's marriage and the abuse she must have taken.

He was silent for a few seconds. "I appreciate your telling me this. It certainly gives us another direction in many ways. But, Caprice, you've put yourself in the middle of it again." He didn't sound angry as much as frustrated.

"I only put myself in the middle with Darby. That's why I called you. It's out of my hands now."

"Not exactly. Not if you help Darby meet up with a counselor. If Scott Wyatt learns of your help and if he's the killer, you're in danger."

"I'm in danger anyway if he finds out Darby told me what she did. He wants her in isolation."

She heard Brett blow out a breath. "Look," he said patiently. "I'm glad for the information, but not about what you're going to do. If Darby needs help, you have to let the professionals handle it. Wendy Newcomb didn't always follow protocol, especially if she hit a wall. That's probably what got her killed. I don't want to see that happen to you. You should never, ever go into a situation with someone like Scott Wyatt alone."

"I promise I won't. Grant has my back. If I'm ever unsure of a conversation with someone, I phone him and leave the line open. I'm not as naïve as I used to be."

"That's debatable," Carstead said. Then he relented. "You're a smart woman. I just want you to act smart."

"I will, and I want you to act smart too. Are you going to be seeing Nikki again? Or did our family scare you off?" Okay, she hadn't intended to ask that, but someone had to talk sense to him.

"I'm in the middle of—"

"A murder investigation," she finished for him. "I understand that, and I know you're at the police station twenty-four hours a day probably, catching a few winks on your sofa at night, right? You're eating stale donuts in the break room and drinking that coffee that has to be burning a hole in your stomach. Nikki's schedule is flexible. Ask her to meet you for an ice cream cone at Cherry on the Top. That's all. Unless you're not interested in her. Unless you don't care if you ever have a family and kids and a house of your own. Unless the De Lucas are too much for you to handle."

She must have caught him off guard because he didn't have a comeback. They'd had a conversation not so long ago when he'd talked about wanting more than work 24/7.

"Nikki's a busy woman. Catered Capers is taking off," he said.

"That's true, but she's not too busy for friendship or a little conversation."

"She wouldn't be insulted if I said I could meet her for twenty minutes to gobble down a scoop of Rocky Road ice cream?"

"No, she wouldn't be insulted. I think she'd be delighted."

"So in order for you to take my advice, I have to take yours?"

"Something like that."

He chuckled. "I'll think about it, and you think about what I said."

When Caprice ended the call, she had the feeling they'd both take each other's advice. She crossed the street with Lady, heading back to her home. Now she was ready to make those calls. Now she was ready to get down to work. She wanted to finish all of it before yoga class tonight.

Chapter Fourteen

Caprice and Denise Langford, the luxury real estate broker who often worked with Caprice, always had a crowd who wanted to see a property as well as partake in Nikki's food.

Americana country cooking had inspired Nikki in the dishes she chose to prepare for today's open house. She'd taken down-home recipes and turned them into mouthwatering masterpieces. What could be more American than chicken soup? Nikki added corn and sliced hard-boiled eggs, the way the soup was often served in firehouse social halls across the state.

Accompanying the soup were cornbread muffins. Main dish recipes included meatloaf with brown gravy, roasted chicken, and a rich stew that was best served on a cold day. For dessert, Nikki had topped chocolate cake with fluffy white frosting and decorated the apple pies with spun sugar. The Boston crème pie was layered with a rich, creamy vanilla pudding and accented by chocolate icing.

Yep, only good food served here.

The house with its cathedral ceiling and open beams was made unique with its foot-wide window ledges, its stonework floor-to-ceiling fireplace. No open concept here as the living room led through an archway into a full dining room. Through another arch, house hunters would find a family-style kitchen. The quartz counters and white appliances invited good times, as did the long pedestal oak table with rustic stoneware dinner settings and Mason jar glasses. Caprice had carried the Americana theme throughout with rustic handcrafted wood sculptures, hand-painted window-sill decorations, and red, white, and blue ribbon adding a celebratory air to floral arrangements, vases, and wrought-iron accent pieces.

Between the eat-in counter, the pedestal table, and the whitewashed table in the dining room, at least thirty guests were enjoying Nikki's food. Caprice was about to congratulate Nikki on another fabulous feast when she felt a tap on her shoulder. Turning around, she found Denise dressed in a red two-piece suit today, black pumps, her hair swept up on top of her head. She was smiling.

"We have two couples ready to make an offer. This open house is going over well. Maybe you should use this theme more often."

Caprice tried to make each open house unique, never using the same theme twice. Denise should know that. But instead of becoming defensive, she said, "Americana just seemed to fit this property. It was a no-brainer. Wood, red, white, and blue, and lots of pillowy furniture."

Denise waved toward the living room. "We still have guests filing in, and we only have an hour to go. More offers could drive the price up. Spectacular."

The price going up didn't affect Caprice's bottom line because she charged a set fee for staging. However, driving the price up could help her reputation and earn her more business. Houses that had sold because of her staging efforts generated chatter about her abilities.

But when she looked toward the new flow of people entering the dining room, she froze, catching sight of someone she didn't want to see—Scott Wyatt. She didn't intend to have a confrontation here. Yet she wouldn't run from him either. Yesterday, she'd set up a meeting with Darby at a furniture store where a counselor Lizbeth sent could meet with her. She'd left after the two women connected. Last night, Scott Wyatt had left a message for her that she was supposed to call him immediately. It had been late after she'd gotten in from seeing a movie with Grant and she'd ignored the call, intending to deal with it today after the open house. Apparently he wasn't willing to wait until she called him back.

"Are you looking for a new house?" she asked him politely.

His face flushed red as he said, "You know I'm not in the market for a new house or a marriage counselor."

"Mr. Wyatt, this isn't the place—" she began, noticing how other guests had looked their way because Scott had raised his voice.

"You didn't call me back."

"I was going to call you later today after I was home. I'm working."

He looked around with disdain. "As if you could call this working. What you're doing is interfering."

"I'm helping your wife redecorate your living room."

"So her little meeting at Woodruff's furniture store yesterday was about redecorating?"

Before the counselor had arrived, she and Darby

had looked around at the furniture, choosing a sofa and armchair that would accompany the new décor.

"Didn't you see the order your wife placed?"

He waved away Caprice's words. "That order means nothing. Nothing. Mr. Woodruff and I go way back. We're golfing buddies. He let me take a look at the security tapes. You left Darby there all right, but not until after you introduced her to that counselor from Sunrise Tomorrow."

Just how had he known that woman was from Sunrise? His expression took on a smug look. "You think I don't know about facial recognition software? You think I don't have access to the best computer money can buy? Everyone has a profile somewhere now—Google, LinkedIn, professional Web sites."

Caprice knew that was true. Any business or profession was all about networking now. Those networks were online and created digital footprints anyone could find if they knew where to look or even half look. Apparently Scott Wyatt did.

"Darby has a free will even though she's married to you. If you squelch it, she'll find some other way around your control. So why not help her by learning to communicate with her, let her tell you what the counselor had to say without bullying her." Caprice knew she should watch her words more carefully, but men like Scott Wyatt caused a fury in her she didn't know she was capable of. And it came out in the honest truth.

"Let me tell you something, Miss De Luca. You'd better watch yourself or you'll get what Wendy got if you don't stay away from my wife."

After that threat, which almost left Caprice's mouth agape, he spun around on his heels and left.

Nikki came running over to her. "I heard everything and so did everybody here. You need to call Brett."

"Do you think Wyatt killed Wendy?" Caprice asked.

"I don't know, but I don't think you should take any chances. Please, call Brett."

Did Caprice really want to raise a stink? Did she want to put Brett Carstead on Scott Wyatt's trail again? Wouldn't that just cause more trouble?

But Nikki was having none of her hesitation. She took out her own phone, tapped her contacts list, and pressed a number.

An hour later, the last few guests were finishing up taste-testing and taking a tour of the house when Brett Carstead entered. Caprice was straightening the throw pillows and looked up to see him in the foyer. Nikki, who had been watching for him, came to join them.

He didn't smile at Nikki, but the look he gave her said he was interested in her. Caprice could tell by the way Nikki looked back that she was attracted to him. Yep, if these two found time for each other, they'd be a couple. That's if Brett's career didn't interfere.

"So what happened?" he asked Caprice.

"Nikki shouldn't have called you. It wasn't that serious."

"Anything can be serious in a murder investigation. If Nikki called, she had good reason. She said Wyatt threatened you."

Caprice told him about the conversation as well as she could remember it, with Nikki adding a phrase or two here and there.

He looked from one of them to the other.

"As I said before, this is a messy investigation. It's a messy list of suspects. We're on top of it . . . at least trying to be," he admitted. "But when something like this happens, it poses another curveball, and I don't like where it puts the two of you."

"He didn't threaten *me*," Nikki assured him, raising her hands as if she were completely innocent.

"Maybe you have more common sense than your sister. Caprice, I'd advise you not to have any more contact with Darby. Forget about redecorating her living room."

"You want me to dump a client?"

"I want you to dump the situation. I think you should consider getting a restraining order against Scott Wyatt."

"And just what good is that restraining order going to do me? If he decides he wants to come after me, the police can't do anything until he hurts me, right? I know how this works, Brett."

He shook his head in frustration. "If you get a restraining order—a protective order—you've scored the first point. He knows we're all on alert. He knows you mean business."

"With a man like him, it's also going to fuel his anger." She saw Brett was about to protest, so she added, "But I'll talk it over with Grant. If he thinks I should get the protective order, then I will. I had to connect Darby with Sunrise for her own safety and well-being. You can't tell me you wouldn't have done the same thing."

"I'm a man with a gun. You're a woman with a color chart."

"Don't condescend to me."

Nikki stepped between the two of them. "Okay, you've made your major points. We did our civic duty and reported what happened."

Brett sighed and stuffed his little notebook inside his jacket pocket. He took a look around the house.

"This one's kind of nice. On a smaller scale, I could live here."

"Do you want me to let you know if I happen to see something on a smaller scale?" Caprice asked sweetly.

"I can always take a look," he responded, surprising her. "There comes a time in a man's life when a bachelor pad is just a bachelor pad, and he wants to think about having more." This time his gaze shifted to Nikki. Then he added, "But cops have a high divorce rate, and girlfriends don't seem to last."

"Then maybe they're not the right girlfriends," Caprice suggested.

Nikki's face turned a little pink. "I'll see you out," she said to Brett.

Caprice wondered if they'd have a little tête-à-tête on the porch . . . if they'd make arrangements to see each other soon. She hoped so. She'd rather think about that than discussing a restraining order with Grant.

The following morning Caprice had scheduled a meeting with Lizbeth at Sunrise Tomorrow. There were so many rooms in the Wyatt mansion to furnish and Caprice wanted to make sure Lizbeth was on board with the designs and the styles. She found face-to-face meetings accomplished a lot more than sending a client an e-mail with links and photos. They just didn't read them, and Caprice didn't want to come to the end of this project and have Lizbeth shake her head if the trim or the molding or a wing chair with a particular fabric didn't meet her approval. Wendy had wanted to be included in every detail. Caprice had to figure out where Lizbeth stood on that matter.

As she rang the buzzer at Sunrise, she thought

about her conversation with Grant the night before. They both had decided it might be best to hold off on the restraining order. Grant agreed it wouldn't do much good if Wyatt actually wanted to do her harm. On the other hand, if he made another threat, a little power play might not hurt.

After they'd finished discussing Wyatt, Grant relayed the fact that he'd talked to Ace, and Ace wanted them both to come to his estate for dinner tonight. Since he was touring, she hadn't seen the rock legend for a while, and it would be great to catch up. So she'd agreed to meet Grant there at seven.

Rena opened the door to Sunrise and looked as made up and poised as ever. She motioned to Lizbeth's office. "She's waiting for you." And in an aside, Rena said, "I don't think she's into this decorating stuff like Wendy was, so you'll probably only have half of her attention."

"Half is good as long as she remembers she gave it to me," Caprice said seriously. She wanted Lizbeth to remember everything they discussed.

"She knows how to multitask," Rena assured Caprice. "I don't know how she does it, but she does."

The door to Lizbeth's office was open and Caprice stepped inside. Lizbeth was searching through her file cabinet for something, or rather Wendy's file cabinet. This had been Wendy's office. But now Caprice saw that Wendy's things had been removed. Lizbeth had added new art on the wall. It was a modern print by a famous contemporary artist. She'd also brought in a shelving unit from her office and hung the shelf on the wall that held a jar with seashells, a trinket box, and a framed photo of an older couple who Caprice assumed was Lizbeth's parents.

As usual, Lizbeth seemed a bit frazzled as she

closed the file drawer, sorted through some papers on her desk, and came up with a legal pad. "I'm ready," she said. "But I've got to tell you, I trust your taste. If Wendy hired you, she did, too, so we don't have to check out everything together, do we?"

"I know this seems inconsequential to the other work you do here," Caprice assured her. "But the choices you make now for the mansion will be there for years to come. The women who have a group session in a counseling room, the women who take refuge in the bedrooms, the reception area that welcomes everyone when they walk in—all that matters. It sets an atmosphere, and I want to make sure that you know what that atmosphere is, and that you approve of it."

"All right," Lizbeth agreed, sitting at her desk now. She ran her hand through her short hair. "Sometimes I don't feel like I know what I'm doing. I dreamed of being director someday, but not like this. Wendy kept so much to herself that it's hard for me to sort everything out."

"You mean about the women here?"

"Not only that. For instance, I have no idea why Wendy suddenly decided to end Evelyn Miller's contract."

"I overheard a conversation that led me to believe Evelyn wants to branch out with her own facility."

"That's possibly true. But there's nothing in Wendy's notes to indicate that. When I asked Evelyn about it, all she would say is that she and Wendy decided to part ways after her contract is finished this month. She'll be working at Green Tea full-time."

That was an interesting observation. Had Evelyn decided to leave on her own? Or had Wendy fired her? If so, why?

"I have something else to tell you, too, before we get started on the house. It's about Scott Wyatt," Caprice explained.

"I'm not supposed to have anything to do with him."

"That may be true, but you might not have much choice. He came to my open house yesterday, furious that I put Darby in touch with you and the counselor. I don't know if he might try to warn you off too. I just want you to be prepared."

Lizbeth's eyes misted a little. "I'm not prepared. As assistant director, yes, I handled crises, but mostly they came one at a time. Now as director, I have crises bumping into each other."

"Rena told me you're good at multitasking."

"I'm surprised she has anything good to say about me," Lizbeth mumbled. But then right away, she jumped into something else before Caprice could comment. "I saw you talking to Wendy's dad at the reception at Sebastian's house."

"I did for a little while. Why?"

"He was a huge help in relocating some of our clients. Did he say whether he intends to stay involved now that Wendy's gone?"

"He talked about her work as if he believed in it. Why don't you set up a meeting with him?"

"I will, but I don't have time to drive to Delaware now, and I don't know if he'd want to drive back so soon after the memorial service."

"You won't know unless you call him. If he's important to the work here, you have no choice."

"No, I guess I don't," she admitted. "Unless I find somebody else who helped out the way he did. But that's not so easy. There was someone else Wendy used in New York City."

"For new ID packets?" Caprice guessed.

"Her father told you?"

"It's not so difficult to figure out, but yes, he did."

Lizbeth nodded. "If I could just find that number. It's not the kind of thing Wendy kept in her regular Rolodex."

"And Sebastian doesn't know?"

"No, he thinks she might have kept it with all that other information that we talked about before. I just wish she'd been more open . . . about everything."

"Maybe she didn't feel she could keep confidences as well that way."

"That's true. Still, I feel like I'm on a scavenger hunt every time I have to look for information. It isn't just plain background or forms we have to keep on file."

"You'll sort it out. I know you will."

Lizbeth wasn't usually this rattled. She was overwhelmed by the position and new responsibilities. That was easy to understand.

Lizbeth pointed to Caprice's briefcase. "Come on, let's talk about furniture, then maybe I can go back to everything else I need to do with a fresh eye."

Caprice just hoped Lizbeth could handle her new responsibilities at Sunrise Tomorrow. Because if she didn't, or couldn't, just what would the foundation do?

Caprice drove up to Ace's estate and thought that something looked different. She wasn't sure exactly what. A floodlight shone down on the tall iron security gates. She stopped before them, reached out of the car, and punched in the code. Ace changed it once a month but made sure his housekeeper always texted her the code. He'd needed her to get in on more than one occasion and he trusted her. She drove through the gates and up the long driveway.

She'd figured out what was different at that point. When Ace was home, almost every light in the house blazed, whether he was upstairs or down, inside or out. That probably came from his being in the spotlight so much of the time. Tonight, however, only the first-floor lights were lit, and not even all of those. Odd, really. If she hadn't parked beside Grant's car and known he was here, she might hesitate to go up to the house. But Grant was here and so was Ace, and probably Ace's housekeeper. So she didn't hesitate to walk to the entrance.

She expected Mrs. Wannamaker to open the door and show her into the den where Grant and Ace were probably having a before-dinner aperitif—a liqueur that Ace had chosen because it was imported and impressive.

Again she was surprised when Grant opened the door.

"Mrs. Wannamaker is on vacation?" she asked with a smile.

"She does have the night off, at Ace's and my request."

Caprice suddenly noticed that Grant was wearing a suit and a tie. It even had one of those classy tie pins on it. Who else might Ace have invited to require that kind of outfit for Grant to wear for dinner?

Caprice herself had dressed up a bit, wanting to look good, not only for her own image, but for Grant too. She was wearing a turquoise V-neck long-sleeve loose dress that just went over her head with no fasteners or buttons or zippers. Since it was a sweater dress, even though it was loose, it clung here and there as she moved. She thought it would be something different from her usual Katharine Hepburn–style pants, her Audrey Hepburn–style dresses, her Stevie Nicks–style tops. After all, they were her favorite fashions, but as she'd determined, she wanted to look good for Grant and wear something a little different. Her shoes had closed toes and a closed back but were open on the sides with a heel not worth mentioning. She'd swung a fuchsia shawl around her shoulders hoping she'd be warm enough if they took a stroll around Ace's pool or even sat out back to talk.

Grant was wearing a smile as he studied her outfit. "You look gorgeous."

"You look pretty good yourself. I didn't expect to see you in a suit."

For a moment, just a moment, Grant looked unsure. Then he revealed, "We have Ace's place to ourselves tonight. No animals. No other people around. Just us." He reached out and took her hand. "Follow me, will you?"

She followed him, but she had lots of questions. "You mean Ace isn't here?"

"No, he thought he'd give us some privacy. I was looking for a nice place to have you alone to myself and he offered."

Caprice was even more puzzled when Grant picked up two blankets to carry outside. They went through the sliding glass doors from Ace's dining room that led onto the patio and pool area. Then he guided her to the right, a newly renovated space that Ace had finished earlier in the spring. There was a fire pit with seating around it, tiki torches that weren't lit by oil but rather by electricity. Tonight the fire pit was burning brightly under an almost-full moon. Suddenly Caprice realized there was more than a fire pit blazing. Twinkle lights decorated the trees and flameless candles circled the rim of the fire pit. The whole space looked so very . . . romantic.

She turned to Grant, but he just put his finger on her lips.

"You'll understand shortly. Come here. I have something for you." He took her to one of the most comfortable chairs and sat her down. Then from a nearby table, he presented her with a colorful bouquet of fall flowers.

Caprice was absolutely speechless. And when Grant got down on one knee before her, produced a box from his pocket, and looked her in her eyes, her heart started thumping so loud the whole town could probably hear. Her mouth went completely dry. She couldn't get a word out. In fact, she could hardly breathe.

Grant opened the box and she'd never seen a ring more beautiful. A heart-shaped pink diamond was set in a band of alternating channel set pink sapphires and diamonds. It was gorgeous!

"Oh, Grant."

But even more than the ring, she realized the sentiment behind it. She all at once realized what he intended to do.

He began with, "I love you, Caprice. I want to build a life with you. I spoke with your dad last weekend because I wanted his blessing. He gave it. We're going to have some complications to work through, but first, I just want to ask you the important question. Caprice De Luca, will you marry me?"

Tears came to her eyes and she swiped them away quickly with one hand because she didn't want anything marring her vision of Grant. There was no hesitation at all as she answered him quickly. "I love you too. Yes, I'll marry you."

At that he rose to his feet again, pulled her up with him, and slipped the ring onto her finger. It fit perfectly. Taking her in his arms, he lifted her chin, gazed at her lovingly, then took a kiss that held promises and passion and so much more.

When they finally broke away, he said, "Dinner is in the oven and dessert's in the refrigerator—double chocolate cheesecake. We can have the place to ourselves all night if we want it. But I told Ace I was sure you'd want to get back to your animals."

This time she put *her* finger on *his* lips and she kissed him.

When they came up for air, Grant wrapped one of the blankets around her, then asked, "Can we talk before we eat?"

"Of course, we can. What do you want to talk about first?"

They nestled beside each other on a chair big enough for two, Grant's arm around her and the blanket. She kept looking at the ring, the light from the fire pit making it sparkle.

"This is so beautiful, Grant."

"As beautiful as you are. Wait until you see the facets in the daylight. It's just like you, all heart with so many unique qualities I'll never be able to count them all."

She leaned into him and snuggled against him in the night chill.

"I don't know exactly how to say this next part except to say it. So hear me out, okay?"

She'd hear out anything he had to say.

After she nodded, he continued. "I know your faith is important to you. Mine has come to be important to me again, too, with time passing . . . and because of you. After Sally died, I was so angry I couldn't even think of a God let alone pray to one. But that's eased up now. I see your faith, your family's faith, and I know it means a lot to you. So does being able to receive Communion. I talked to your nana about this."

"Grant."

"I needed some input, Caprice, that's all. Everything we decide will be between the two of us. We can't get married in the Catholic church unless I get an annulment."

"I know."

"I've done some research and I have grounds. Naomi and I were dating, but we weren't in love. She became pregnant and I wanted to do the right thing. We were never a real true love match. I went into that marriage with reservations. An annulment doesn't mean we were never married. What it would mean was that the sacrament of marriage wasn't present when we were married, when we said our vows, because our minds weren't at the right place. More important, our hearts weren't. Besides that, after Sally died, when each of us was feeling so alone, Naomi had an affair. So the grounds for an annulment will be fairly cut-and-dried. The Pope recently simplified the annulment proceedings. I'm willing to go through them for you, for us, and for your family's sake. I know they would want you to, and I think the way Naomi and I have left things, she would help me out with this. She has to be part of it with interviews and questionnaires to answer."

"You really think she'd cooperate?"

"I do. After she visited last summer, we both wished each other happiness. I would do this for her if she asked, but that's another thing that will make this a little easier. She's not Catholic and we were married before a justice of the peace. With the new guidelines, I could have the annulment in a few months.

"I want you to know upfront that I'd marry you tomorrow if I could and we'd be sharing everything, including our beds. But, I rushed into marriage once before. I want to make sure I know everything about you and you know everything about me. I want this to be totally right, Caprice."

"You'd be willing to wait to get married . . . to have sex?" There, she'd said it.

"I would see this engagement as a very special time for us. The two of us would make a vow to hold back physically, but not in any other way. We'd get to know each other on levels couples only dream about. And when the time for our marriage comes, we'll have no doubts. We'll be prepared for a partnership that will last a lifetime."

She gently ran her finger down his cheek. "You'd do all of this for me?"

"I'd do this for *us*."

"You've put a lot of thought into it."

"I have. And now I want you to think about it too. We'll make this decision together."

As Grant took Caprice in his arms again, she knew they'd make all their decisions together from now on.

Chapter Fifteen

Caprice felt as if she were floating on a cloud the next morning as she ran errands. She kept touching the ring on her finger, holding it up to the light, admiring its beauty and the meaning behind it. Over and over, she thought about Grant's proposal and the future ahead of them. She couldn't be any happier. Maybe she could be happier if they were getting married tomorrow, but good things come to those who wait, right?

She thought about the decision they'd come to—wait to get married, to physically connect in that most intimate way. They could do it, she was sure. They could make this engagement one of discovery and adventure and the anticipation that would culminate in the very best way—in a church, before all their friends and family, with vows that would last forever.

Speaking of family . . . Grant had called his parents last night to tell them the news. To his surprise, they'd agreed to fly to Kismet for a visit. His father would be calling the airline today to book their seats. It was exciting and a little scary to think about meeting Diane and Samuel Weatherford.

She'd called her mom first thing this morning before her mother left for school. Ecstatic herself, her parents had been excited too. She'd even talked to her dad and heard how much he admired Grant for asking for his blessing. She loved Grant even more for that, if that was possible, for including her family. That meant so much. She'd called Nana next, then Nikki and Bella and Vince and Roz. She couldn't wait to see them all and share her joy in person. But all of her conversations had left her grateful for her family and friends. Her sisters and Roz wanted to see the ring as soon as possible. Her mom and dad had already seen it because Grant had shown it to them.

Trying to keep her mind on her errands, she mentally went over the list in her head of the items she needed from Grocery Fresh. Grant would be coming over for dinner tonight.

Once inside the market, Caprice thought of the roast that was cooking in her slow cooker. She'd pick up red-skin potatoes to make parsley potatoes and fresh green beans. She'd also buy enough Stayman apples for apple crisp. They were an old-time apple and not many farm markets carried them anymore. But Grocery Fresh stocked them and they were the best-tasting apple for cobbler and pies. It was a meal she knew Grant would enjoy.

She was choosing apples carefully and pushing them into a plastic bag when a woman drew her basket up next to Caprice's.

"Miss De Luca, isn't it?"

It was Penny Claussen, Sebastian's neighbor. "Hi, Penny. Please, call me Caprice."

Penny nodded as if she'd be glad to. "I see we're both apple shopping," she said conversationally, as she too started choosing Stayman apples.

"I'm making apple cobbler tonight, how about you?"

"Actually, I'll be stirring up applesauce. Our family likes homemade, so does Carly and her daughter."

"I was just wondering, do you share your meals?"

"As often as we can. The girls are involved in different activities, so sometimes it's tough. But the neighborhood as a whole believes sit-down meals are the best way to communicate and share the day."

"My family always believed in that concept too. If my mom could pull us together for family dinner, she did. We still get together once a month."

"If more families did that, maybe none of us would have as many problems. More talk and sharing and less TV and video games."

Caprice was about to turn away and go on her way when Penny stopped her with a lowered voice and the question, "Are you still looking for information concerning Wendy?"

Caprice glanced around and no one was in their immediate vicinity. "Yes, I am. Have you heard something you think is important?"

Keeping her voice lowered, Penny said, "I was wrong about Wendy seeing someone. At least I think I was. I should have known she wouldn't do that to Sebastian."

"Why do you think you were wrong?"

"Because word around the neighborhood is that Sebastian is seeing someone already."

"Any inkling who that someone is?"

"Yes, and I'm absolutely aghast. It's Lizbeth Diviney."

Caprice didn't know if she was aghast, but she was a little shocked. "Do you believe this is more than gossip?"

"First of all, I don't think anyone would gossip

about something like this—about Sebastian so soon after Wendy's death. Pierson Raychek is quite conservative and doesn't gossip at all. He claims he saw Sebastian and Lizbeth in the parking lot at the Purple Iris Bed and Breakfast. Their compromising embrace and kiss gave him the impression this wasn't the first time. Poor Wendy. No wonder she was staying so late or overnight at Sunrise Tomorrow. If she knew what Sebastian was up to, she probably couldn't stand sharing a bed with him. Who would blame her?"

"This is still conjecture," Caprice reminded her.

"Maybe so, but the truth will come out. It always does."

That was most likely the case. Caprice thought about Lizbeth, the way she seemed overwhelmed when she was a multitasker and high energy at heart. She thought about Sebastian and his show of grief. Were either of them capable of murder, either alone or together? Had Lizbeth asked her to look into Wendy's murder to throw her off her scent? Was it possible Wendy had been seeing someone new too? Or, as Penny suspected, had Wendy been spending nights at the shelter because she and Sebastian weren't as close as they once were?

So many questions, so many suspects. She was glad Penny had told her what she had. Caprice would be on the lookout for clues and signs that what she said was true. And if it was true, then maybe Brett Carstead should know. After thanking Penny again for the information and wishing her a good day, Caprice went to the register to check out. Were couples ever what they seemed?

She knew they could be. After all, she'd witnessed her mom and dad's marriage since she'd been born.

Her mom often told the story about how they'd met, how Nick De Luca was fixing the flashing on her parents' chimney when she'd been home from college. He'd been shirtless and oh, so masculine, standing on that roof with his black hair blowing in the wind. Her parents had their ups and downs like any couple, but they were affectionate, best friends, partners, and still happy they were married to each other. She'd witnessed the same kind of bond with Nana and Papa Tony. Her grandfather's barber shop had done well enough to support his family. He'd loved Nana with all his heart and that was so obvious whenever they were together. He'd been old school in many ways— both his parents and Nana's parents had come to America as immigrants. He'd believed Nana shouldn't work and should take care of their two sons and daughter. But Nana had opened his eyes to the fact that women could be equal partners. She'd helped him with bookwork for the shop and organized their personal finances. Nana was never one to take a backseat, although Papa Tony had believed he was the one in charge. Nana had been the heart of their family and he'd known it. After he died, they'd all worried about Nana. When she'd moved in with Caprice's parents, it had been a good decision for everyone.

Yes, couples could marry and last. They could overcome problems like Bella and Joe had. She had to remember all this when she became anxious about marrying and joining two very different lives.

For the rest of the day, Caprice concentrated on her next house staging, Tuscan Dreams. She wore a smile bigger than she'd ever worn before when she'd shown her ring to Dulcina, Isaac, her family, and anyone else who wanted to see it. She also thought about Wendy's murder . . . a lot.

* * *

On Saturday morning she received a call from Grant. His parents had booked a flight because they'd found an economical last-minute deal. They were flying in on Tuesday! That was sooner than she'd expected. Grant too. To calm restlessness at the idea of getting along with in-laws, she spent her morning at Ralph's Rentals choosing furniture she felt would go along with rustic Tuscan flavor. Ralph assured her everything could be delivered to the property on Monday. She'd found a console with mirrored doors in distressed pale green, a kitchen island in that same green with posts, a shelf, and a butcher block surface. She'd chosen a double pedestal table with bulb legs and a beautiful walnut top as well as Solvie armchairs with acorn finial accents. She'd even stumbled across barstools with rush seats, an armoire with antique brass hardware, and a locking cabinet that would be perfect in one of the bedrooms. Side tables in pale yellow, a lingerie chest, and a secretary desk painted with grapes and vines along with a Palladian open bookcase suggested visions of vineyards.

She intended to replace the chandelier in the main hall with one that looked like a globe in a metal design. Four candle-style lights burned within the globe. Checking her list of necessities, she picked out buffet lights as well as a marble table lamp with a square parchment shade.

She'd done well this morning, and she was sure Juan would approve of everything she'd rented. While she'd selected furnishings, he'd driven to her storage unit with a second list, pulling out items to transport to the house. They'd meet up there Monday to consult. Although the house had embellishments and dormers reminiscent of a Cupertino castle, Caprice hoped to create a welcoming interior that was warm and inviting and could wrap around a family.

Pleased with what she'd accomplished, she headed for Perky Paws. She'd bring home treats for Lady and Patches, and organic catnip for her felines. Thinking about Grant coming over for dinner again tonight gave her that anticipatory thrill that made her heart beat faster. At some point they'd have to start making specific plans. Maybe when his parents arrived on Tuesday, they'd talk over plans with them too. Even though she was anxious about it, she looked forward to all of it.

On a Saturday, Perky Paws was busy all day. Folks were lined up at the cashier's desk. Gretta and her part-time help had their hands full, so Caprice wandered to the back of the store to pick up the catnip first. She was passing the dog food row when she caught sight of Sebastian's son Kevin.

"Hi there," Caprice said.

Kevin's dog came right over to her, sat at her feet, and looked up at her. Caprice laughed, petted Dover's neck, and scratched around his ears. Everything Penny had related about Sebastian came roaring back, and she wondered if any of it was true. Just gossip, or had he been having an affair before Wendy was killed?

A bag of dog food in his arms, Kevin crossed to her.

"How are you?" she asked him.

He gave her one of those teenage, one-shoulder shrugs. "Okay. Dad had to go to the hardware store so he dropped me here so I could pick up dog food."

"I've been thinking about your family. Is there anything you need?"

Kevin's eyes glistened a little and he shook his

head. "Nope, we're just trying to pretend everything's okay when it's not."

"I'm sorry. Can you talk about how you feel with your brother and your dad?"

"Not so much because they feel bad too."

"Is there anyone else you can talk to?"

"Yeah, Penny understands. She's been bringing over lots of casseroles."

He set the bag of dog food down on the floor. "I was thinking about you yesterday."

"Uh oh," Caprice joked. "Was that good or bad?"

That brought a weak smile. "Good, I guess. I lost my password list that I keep on a sticky note."

"You know that's not the safest place to keep them, right?"

This time he gave her a wry grin. "Yeah, Cody and Dad warned me about that. Anyway, I couldn't find it, and it's really important. I have a different password for each game I play and other sites I'm in and out of. So I was really stuck. Even Dad and Cody looked all over for the sticky note and they couldn't find it either. I thought maybe Dover ate it."

"That's been known to happen," Caprice said, understanding.

"Anyway, I rode my bike to that shrine I told you about on the Wyatt estate, and I prayed to Saint Anthony. Last night, I found the sticky note attached to one of my sweatshirts. Praying to Saint Anthony works!"

"I'm glad. Now you don't have to make up new passwords for all those sites."

He nodded and looked as if he wanted to say something else, so Caprice just stood there and waited. While his dog wagged his tail on Caprice's foot, Kevin finally admitted, "I know something and I don't know if I should tell Dad."

"What do you mean you know something?"

"About Wendy."

Caprice hoped with all her heart that Kevin hadn't discovered Wendy was having an affair. She didn't want his ideals shattered this early.

"Do you want to tell me?"

He nodded again. "The night before Wendy was found murdered, I was riding my bike to the Wyatt estate and I stopped in to see if she was there."

Caprice gave Kevin her full attention now. This could be vitally important to the investigation. "Did you find her?"

"After I went inside, I overheard her and Rena arguing. You know, Rena from Sunrise Tomorrow?"

"I've met her," Caprice said.

Now that he'd started telling her, it seemed that he wanted to get it all out. "They were shouting at each other."

"Did you hear any of the conversation?"

He stuffed his hands in his jeans pockets. "The only thing I really heard that I could understand was the word *embezzlement.*"

Embezzlement. That had nothing to do with an affair or even blackmail. Or did it?

"I didn't tell my dad because I didn't think much of it until the next day when I learned Wendy was dead. Since she and Rena were fighting, I just left and she never knew I was there."

Deciding exactly what she should do, and what Kevin should do, she advised the teenager, "You have to tell your dad. I'll call Detective Carstead and tell him you have information that could be important to the investigation. But he'll contact your dad to talk to you. So you have to tell him."

"Are you sure it's going to be Detective Carstead and not Detective Jones? He was a grouch."

"I've been interviewed by both of them and I know what you mean. I'll make sure Detective Carstead talks to you. I have his number and he usually listens to what I have to say." *At least lately,* she mentally added.

"Thanks for telling me this, Kevin. It could be really important."

"I'll talk to Dad as soon as he comes in."

She nodded and impulsively gave the teenager a hug. "You take care of yourself."

He mumbled, "I will," into her shoulder.

As Caprice left him gathering up the dog food, she thought about what he'd said. If Rena had embezzled money from the foundation and was found out, could she have killed Wendy?

On Sunday morning, Caprice woke up groggily, thinking about the kiss Grant had given her before he'd left the night before. Could they really wait a few months? It might even be six months until the annulment came through and they could plan the wedding.

Lady climbed out of her bed on the floor and stretched, then put her paws up on the bed. Mirabelle had arranged herself across Caprice's lap on top of the covers like a furry pillow. Sophia's meow came from atop the chest where she looked down at Caprice with chastisement in her gaze.

You slept later than usual, it seemed to say. *Don't you realize we're on a schedule?*

Caprice gave a little laugh, moved Mirabelle to the side gently, and swung her legs over the side of the bed. Lady sat on her foot for a few rubs of her own. Caprice was bending down to her when her cell phone on the bedside table played the Beatles' "If I Fell." Picking it up, she saw Sunrise Tomorrow's ID. How odd for someone to call from there this early on a Sunday morning.

"Hello?" she asked, not knowing what to expect.

"Caprice, it's Lizbeth." There was panic in the woman's voice.

"Hi, Lizbeth. What's going on?"

"The police took Rena in for questioning. She was supposed to be here manning the desk this morning, and she called me to tell me she couldn't take her shift. I don't know what's going on. She wouldn't say why they took her in."

Caprice knew why they'd taken her in for questioning. That phone call to Brett had started the ball rolling.

"Do you know what's going on?" Lizbeth asked.

"I might, but I shouldn't say."

"Caprice, I have to know what the situation is. She's here every day, and if I have to find someone to replace her—"

"Maybe the questioning won't go on for long and she'll be back."

"That's possible, and I'm going to try to get someone to cover, just in case she doesn't get back. But I'm completely in the dark and I don't like it."

How much could Caprice tell her, and what should she tell her? If she had a chat with her, however, maybe she'd find out if Lizbeth was seeing Sebastian and how that fit into the whole situation.

"I have to take care of my animals and then I'm going to Mass. I'll stop in at Sunrise afterward and we can talk. All right?"

"All right," Lizbeth said with a sigh. "Maybe by then I'll hear something. I'll see you around eleven?"

Mass was at ten and eleven should work. "Around eleven."

Since Mass ran a little long, it was five after eleven when Caprice rang the buzzer at Sunrise Tomorrow. Lizbeth came to the door immediately to let her in. She nodded to the reception desk where a brunette sat working on a computer.

"Ariel came in to take Rena's place. She said she can stay until four, so I'm good until then. I might just have to stay until midnight."

The buzzer at the door buzzed again. Lizbeth checked the monitor on the receptionist's desk.

"It's Rena. She's back." Lizbeth rushed to answer the door.

When Rena came in, she looked anything but happy and ready to take her place at her desk. "I want to know what you two have to do with my being pulled into the police station."

Caprice remained silent, but Lizbeth protested, "I had nothing to do with it. What did they want?"

Rena gave Caprice a long look, but Caprice didn't flinch. She wasn't going to admit to anything . . . or get Kevin into trouble.

"They treated me like a criminal. Me. I've been by Wendy's side since the beginning." Now Rena turned her wrath on Lizbeth. "But she gave you the assistant directorship."

Now Lizbeth's hackles rose, too, and she defensively stated, "Apparently I was the better candidate for the position. I deserved it."

"Deserved it? I don't think so. Half the time you run around here like a chicken with her head cut off. I needed that extra money from the position to live on."

"So what happened at the police station?" Caprice asked, cutting off the argument before it turned nastier. "Did the police have something specific in mind to ask you?"

"Yes, they did. They had a search warrant for my bank records. My guess is, they're going to come in here and take the computers too. So I might as well just pack up my things now."

Some of Lizbeth's defensiveness deflated and she looked puzzled. "I don't understand. Why are you packing up your things?"

"For an assistant director and a director now, you're pretty slow. As I said, I didn't have enough money to live on. What do you think I did? That big foundation pot is just sitting there, doing nothing. When the Wyatt money came in, it was like a pot of gold. I needed some of that gold. Do you understand now?"

"So you've been embezzling from the foundation?" Caprice asked.

"What else was I supposed to do? I was going to stop when Wendy gave me the directorship of the new facility. But she found out about the money I was taking and she wouldn't give me the position. She just wouldn't understand."

"She gave it to me because I deserved it," Lizbeth muttered.

"That's the problem, Lizbeth, you think you deserve it all, including Sebastian. Maybe the police should be pulling you in for questioning. I didn't let it slip you're seeing him. I know about the concept of loyalty, but it won't take long till somebody tells them."

Lizbeth had gone white.

From the state Rena was in, Caprice might get the truth out of her. Maybe. "So Wendy found out you embezzled funds? Were you angry enough to hurt her?"

"You sound like that Detective Jones. No, I didn't hurt her. I did not kill Wendy Newcomb." After that statement, Rena stalked over to the desk where Ariel was sitting, picked up a photograph of her and her sister, a small Buddha statue, and then made Ariel back up in her wheeled chair so she could fish in the top drawer. She pulled out a notebook and a gold pen, stuffing them into her purse.

"I hope that you people get what you all deserve, and the police make your life miserable like they just made mine."

As she strode for the door, she suddenly stopped, turned, and shook her finger at Caprice. "And you'd better watch out. If you get people in trouble, they're not going to like it one bit."

After she went to the door, opened it, exited it, and let it slam behind her, Lizbeth faced Caprice, looking pale and shaken.

Caprice asked her, "Are you seeing Sebastian?"

Lizbeth gave a small nod.

"Did it start before Wendy died?"

Lizbeth gave another nod.

"The police will find out. Maybe you should tell them yourself."

Lizbeth drew in a breath, went to her office, and slunk down into her desk chair, looking like a limp rag doll.

Unknowingly, Kevin might have just stepped up this whole investigation.

Rena's words echoed in Caprice's mind. *You'd better watch out.*

She was going to step back from this investigation now. That was the safest thing to do.

Chapter Sixteen

Caprice had two reasons to stop at her sister Bella's on Monday. First, Bella wanted to see her engagement ring in person even though Caprice had taken a phone pic and texted it to her. And second, Caprice wanted to see how Sunnybud was getting along and if Bella wanted to keep him. If she didn't, Caprice would have to find another home for him.

Not knowing what to expect when she walked into Bella's house, she walked straight into the kitchen where Bella was cooking. "Something smells good."

"Beef stew. Do you want to stay for supper? Or do you have a hot date?"

"I can stay for supper. I'm meeting Dulcina for a yoga class at seven-thirty, but that gives us plenty of time."

Glancing around, wondering if Sunnybud was hiding somewhere, she peered into the family room. To her surprise, Sunnybud was sitting on Joe's recliner, his paws tucked under him. As she watched, he rolled over, stretched out, front paws reaching for one arm, back paws reaching for the other, his belly exposed. That was the picture of a contented cat.

"I haven't made beef stew for a while," Bella confessed. "With the weather getting colder, it might be a meal Grant would like."

"He would. I see Sunnybud is taking over Joe's chair. You're allowing him on the furniture?"

Bella gave Caprice a sideways glance as she tore up lettuce for the salad. "It seems we have a pet. He actually drapes himself over Joe's arm when Joe sits there. And the kids? When the kids pet him, they seem to calm down. It's not like when they play with Lady and get all excited. I think he's good for them."

Caprice was finding it hard not to smile. "And what about you? Are you going to mind yellow and white cat hair on your black slacks?"

Bella chose a carrot to scrape. "It's like this. When I had Benny, who I didn't expect, I had to accept the fact that the house wasn't going to be as clean as I'd like, and baby drool and spit-up were going to stain my blouses. The world didn't cave in. I don't know how to explain it, but Sunnybud just seems to go with this house. He wanders upstairs after the kids into their rooms. He sleeps on the foot of Joe's and my bed. It's like he became part of the family overnight. When I look into those green eyes of his, I can't give him up."

"Pets are good for people," Caprice said without an I-told-you-so attitude.

"I guess I can see that now. I'm not saying I want a dog to go along with the cat, or that I want any more cats, but this one—he just seems special."

"He needed a home."

"I suppose. We have an appointment to get him snipped this week. I'll make sure I don't have to work the next day so I can take care of him. Now, enough talk about our new furry member of the family. Let me see your ring."

Caprice held up her hand.

Bella squealed. "It's beautiful. Now tell me all about it again. Did he really get down on one knee?"

"He did. And he made me feel so special, arranging all that at Ace's, having the fire going, bringing me flowers. I'll never forget it, Bella. Never."

"That's the way the memories of a loved one should be."

Caprice picked up a cucumber, washed it, and began peeling it for the salad. "Is there a secret to making a marriage work? You were married young, so were Mom and Nana. Grant and I . . . I guess we're more set in our ways."

"That shouldn't have anything to do with it." Bella sliced her carrot into the salad. "Sure, when you're young you kind of grow up together. But when you're young, you also don't know what the world and its problems hold for you. Experience is a good teacher, and you and Grant will be bringing experience to your marriage."

"You and Joe have changed."

"Yes, we have. Counseling did a lot of that. We learned to communicate better, and I learned to say exactly what I need. Men really aren't mind readers, not even after years of marriage."

"I didn't think a man could change."

"You mean you didn't think *Joe* could change? And really, he didn't change. He always had a good heart. I'm not sure he knew how to show it. I'm not sure he understood how I felt about everything, or if I knew how he felt about everything. Getting pregnant with Benny really changed us both. By the way, he's napping." She nodded to the monitor on the counter. "He should be waking up any time."

Bella went on. "For what's it worth, I think Grant has a good heart too."

Caprice liked the fact that her family thought Grant was right for her. That was important.

One thing Bella was—always bluntly honest. So Caprice had a question for her. "Do you think we're doing the right thing, waiting for the annulment to come through? Grant already spoke to Naomi about it. He talked to Father Gregory, too, and the whole process is in the works."

"Do you want to get married in the church for Mom and Dad or Nana, or do you want to get married in the church for yourself?"

Caprice knew what Bella meant. Her family had a deep faith, and they would want Caprice to be able to partake in everything the Catholic Church had to offer. But this was about more than family approval. It was about Caprice and Grant, and the promise of faith they wanted for their lives. If their marriage was rooted in their faith, that would carry over for their children too.

"I want to do it for me," she answered Bella. "Grant and I both feel it's the right thing to do. But it's going to be hard to wait to . . . you know."

Bella gave her a wicked grin. "Oh, yes, I know. But I think you're making a smart choice."

"Grant's parents are flying in tomorrow. They got a really good price on last-minute seating so they decided not to wait to come. I'm nervous."

"Why?"

"Because Grant seems anxious. He's warned me that they're not outgoing like Mom and Dad."

"And the rest of the De Lucas," Bella said with a

grin. "Just go with the flow like you always do. You'll be fine."

They finished with the salad and Bella covered it with plastic wrap to set it inside the refrigerator. "There's something else we need to talk about," Bella said.

"What?"

"Nana's birthday's coming up. We have to figure out what to give her. Do we want to plan a party?"

"I found table scarves at the Harvest Festival she should like. Do you think she'd want a party?"

"Maybe not a surprise party. I don't think she'd be too keen on that. But we can plan a get-together, tell her we're giving her a party and the date. Then we can invite whoever she'd like to be there. How does that sound?"

"That sounds like you've given it some thought. We can run it by Nikki and Vince."

Sounds began to come from the monitor.

Caprice gestured toward it. "Good, I'll have play-time with my nephew."

"The kids will be home any minute, and Joe not long after that. Maybe while you're playing with Benny, we can come up with some ideas for presents for Nana."

After Bella got Benny up, Caprice held him, walked him, and played with him in his activity saucer. At nine months, he was developing his own personality. He was a happy baby, gurgling and laughing a lot.

Supper was noisy and fun, and Caprice watched Joe and Bella interact, trying to study the aspects of their marriage. Joe kept Benny occupied in his high chair while Bella went to the refrigerator for the chocolate cream pie she'd made for dessert.

"It's only a graham cracker crust," she claimed. "I didn't have time to roll pie shells."

Joe looked at the pie and the spritz can of whipped cream. "It will taste delicious, honey. This is a great meal."

As Caprice appreciated the fact that there were good marriages in the world, as well as abusive ones, her cell phone played.

Bella waved at her pocket. "Go ahead and take it. I'll make coffee."

Caprice saw it was Isaac's number. That was unusual. He didn't have much cause to call her. Maybe he'd unearthed great finds at a public sale.

She rose from her chair and walked into the living room where Sunnybud blinked at her and crossed one paw over the other. She went to him and petted him around the ears. He purred.

"Hi, Isaac," she said.

"I've got news. Did you hear about the break-in?"

"What break-in?"

"You really need a police scanner."

"It would only distract me. What break-in?"

"Sebastian Thompson's house was broken into."

"Is everyone okay? Were they there when it happened?"

"Only the police were called to the scene, not the rescue unit. My guess is that Thompson came home and found it. But I thought you'd want to know."

She *did* want to know. And because she did, tomorrow she was going to visit Sebastian and his boys and find out what happened.

The following morning, Caprice was driving to Sebastian's house when Grant called her. Putting her phone on speaker, she said, "Good morning."

"I hope it's going to be a good morning," he said.

"What about the afternoon?" She knew he'd be picking up his parents. Their flight got in at three.

"We'll see how that goes after Mom and Dad arrive."

"I should come along with you to pick them up."

"No, we're going to do this as we discussed. I'm going to pick them up alone."

"Do you want me to cook dinner?"

"No, I booked them a room at the Purple Iris. Can you meet us there for dinner? I'll text you when I'm on the way back from the airport. I imagine it will be around five."

"We shouldn't need reservations midweek," she decided.

"How did dinner go at Bella's?"

"I had a good time, but Isaac called to tell me that Sebastian Thompson's place was broken into. I'm on my way there now."

Grant went quiet.

"I'm just going to see if he's home. My guess is he and the boys might have stayed somewhere else last night if the police considered it a crime scene and attempted to lift prints. If he's not there, I have a lot to do to finish a house for staging."

"And the theme?"

"Tuscan Dreams."

"I've always wanted to go to Tuscany. That could be a destination for a terrific honeymoon."

"We'll have to talk about it."

"Yes, we will. Stay safe. I'll see you tonight."

After Caprice returned with, "See you tonight," she ended the call. A few minutes later she was glad to spot Sebastian's SUV sitting in the carport at his house. She also took note that there wasn't any crime scene tape wrapped around the property. She did see a forgotten stake in the ground, however, that told her it might have just recently been taken down.

After she exited her car, she went up the drive to the kitchen door instead of to the front and rang the bell.

A disheveled-looking Sebastian answered the door. He had beard stubble, a rumpled shirt, and looked as if he'd been up all night.

"I heard what happened," she said, not standing on pretense.

"The police left about a half hour ago. I'm trying to figure out what to do for cleanup."

"Fingerprint dust?" she asked.

He nodded. "Nothing gets that stuff up."

"There's a special cleaner that cuts right through it."

"One of the officers told me to sweep up as much of it dry as I can. He said a tile cleaner can work too."

"The hardware store carries a couple of products. But there's a professional cleaning service you might want to call." She pulled a card from her wallet and gave it to him. "They sell the best products because they know they work."

"It's not just the fingerprint dust," he grumbled. "You should see the place. I want to right as much of it as I can before the boys get home from school."

"Do you need help?"

"Are you serious?"

"Sure."

"Then come on in. I haven't even started. Penny came over when the police were here last night. She said she'd help. But I hated to ask."

"I thought this neighborhood was all about helping each other? Why do you hesitate to ask?"

Sebastian looked embarrassed. "Because she's a single mom, and she's looking at me as if . . . as if she might be interested. She's brought so many casseroles we can't eat them all."

"And you're not interested in her."

"No, not that way. She was a friend to me and Wendy. That's it."

Caprice wondered if Penny was bitter because Sebastian wasn't interested and that was why she'd revealed the gossip she'd heard to Caprice.

"And how about Lizbeth?"

At that question, Sebastian's cheeks under his beard grew ruddy. "So you know."

"The word is out. Haven't you talked to Lizbeth?"

"Not in the past few days."

"You don't know about Rena and the police?"

"Rena from Sunrise Tomorrow?"

"Yes."

"Tell me," he said wearily.

So while Caprice helped Sebastian close cupboard doors, as they put cushions back on furniture and books back on the shelves, she told him what had happened with Rena and Lizbeth.

"So Lizbeth was actually going to go to the police and tell them we were having an affair?"

"I think she was. Maybe you should do the same."

"Kevin started all this, didn't he, with the conversation he overheard?"

"Yes, but I'm sure it would have all eventually come out. He just helped hurry the investigation along."

"Do you think that was the impetus for this break-in? I mean, just look at the place. Even the cushions are slashed. Whoever came in here was motivated and it wasn't for robbery. They were looking for something."

"Like Wendy's journal or her thumb drive."

"Exactly. And what would have happened if we were here?"

"My guess is that whoever did this either knew you and the boys would be gone, or was watching your house and they were sure you were gone."

"You mean someone is stalking us?"

"Think of it more as surveillance."

Sebastian ran his hand through his hair. "The police don't have enough manpower to put a patrol car here. Maybe I should hire security."

"If whoever broke in made a thorough search, they might realize by now that you and the boys don't have the journal or the thumb drive. I mean, let's face it. If you or the boys found it, you'd turn it over to the police. As soon as you did, there'd be a flurry of activity in the department and a lot more suspects brought in for questioning."

"Then why did they bother to break in?"

"To be sure . . . to see if what you couldn't find, they could."

"What if they found it? What if the journal or thumb drive was here and we didn't know?"

"If they found it, then it could be a long while until they're caught."

"If ever." He sighed.

Not one to hold back, Caprice asked, "So you and Wendy were having problems?"

"Not problems exactly."

She looked Sebastian straight in the eye. "What exactly?"

"I didn't kill her if that's what you're thinking. She didn't even know who I was having the affair with."

"But she knew you were having an affair?"

"Not explicitly. But I think women just know. She was spending more time at Sunrise Tomorrow. And, really, that had been the whole problem from the start. She'd gotten so wrapped up in her work there, we hardly had a life together."

"Lizbeth is wrapped up in her work there."

"Yeah, but Lizbeth wasn't a permanent thing. I knew it would never be a permanent thing. She was just an outlet because I was so frustrated with Wendy."

An outlet. Caprice was sure Lizbeth would be really pleased to know that. Men. Were men really from Mars and women from Venus? No. Grant had confided Naomi had had an affair, too . . . because of grief and loneliness. The bottom line was simply communication, becoming bogged down, stilted, closed. She and Grant had to make sure that never happened with them.

And they'd start with dinner with his parents tonight. She wanted everything out in the open. She couldn't wait to meet them, but for some reason, Grant was anxious about the whole thing.

She'd soon find out exactly why.

Caprice smelled trouble with a capital T. Her palms were sweaty and now she was doubly anxious about having dinner with Grant and his parents. She'd been keeping those nervous quivers at bay until she received Grant's phone call a half hour ago.

He'd said, "My parents are settled in at the Purple Iris, but they think their room's too fancy and they don't want to have dinner downstairs at the hoity-toity restaurant. So how about if you meet us at the Sunflower Diner in about half an hour? Unless you'd like to run in the other direction and then I might be tempted to run with you."

The last had been said with an attempt at humor, but she could hear the dismay in his voice.

"It's going to be okay, Grant. The Sunflower Diner is fine. If they're more comfortable there, so be it."

"Why can't they just accept what I want to give them?"

"I don't know. Your dad probably has a lot of pride and he wants to stay and eat at a place he can afford. Maybe after I meet them, I'll be able to understand them."

"Don't think you're going to psychoanalyze them. It won't do any good."

"Anything I should know before I show up?"

"No, just be yourself. And I'll try to be myself, which is always more difficult when I'm in their company. See you in half an hour."

Caprice hadn't been sure what to wear, but he'd told her to be herself. She wore an outfit she'd found at Secrets of the Past by a new designer who concentrated on the mid-century look. It was something Twiggy might wear. The dress had a cream and black geometric design. Pleats ran around the lower part of the hem. What made the outfit, in Caprice's estimation, was the cream jacket that had a double row of buttons down both sides that didn't altogether meet in the middle. She decided the weather was cool enough for black leather boots that came up to her knees just under the hem. She thought about changing into red bell-bottoms, Beatles T-shirt, and fringed vest. That would have been more casual and definitely "her." But she felt she wanted to get a little dressed up for this encounter simply for added confidence.

When Caprice walked into the Sunflower Diner, she spotted Grant and an older couple in a back booth. He stood and waved, though he didn't have to.

Her Grant-radar could find him anywhere. His mother and father sat in the booth with their backs to her.

She said hello to the hostess who knew her and pointed to the back to Grant. Then she made a bee-line toward him.

When she arrived by his side, he hesitated only a moment; then he wrapped his arm around her. "Mom and Dad, meet my fiancée, Caprice De Luca. Caprice, these are my parents, Diane and Samuel Weatherford."

Caprice didn't hesitate to extend her hand and first shake Samuel's and then Diane's. "It's good to meet you."

Grant's parents were older than hers, maybe by about five years. In her sixties, Diane's straight gray hair was cut in a bowl shape around her face. It was soft and cottony and shiny. At five-three with a rounded figure and a frown, she didn't look at all comfortable. Caprice hoped she was just tired from her trip.

Grant's dad was tall, maybe five-eleven or six foot. He had black hair like Grant's, laced with gray. It was parted to the side and thinning just a bit, but not much. He had a hard jaw, high cheekbones, and a well-proportioned nose. It was easy to see what Grant would look like thirty years from now. His father wore jeans and a light flannel shirt. His mother wore navy slacks, a white Oxford blouse, and a navy windbreaker lay on the seat beside her. Caprice wanted to step into the conversation gap, but she wasn't sure where to go. That was unusual for her.

Finally, Mr. Weatherford said, "This was quite a surprise—your engagement, I mean."

Caprice stole a look at Grant. He gave a little what-can-I-say shrug, which probably meant he hadn't talked to his parents very much over the past year or told them about their involvement.

Because she couldn't think of anything else to say, she came up with, "Grant and I have known each other for a long time, since he and my brother went to college together."

This time Diane and Samuel exchanged a look. "He knew you before Naomi?"

Now Caprice turned to Grant, and he stepped into the gap. "I did. Remember, I told you Caprice's brother, Vince, was my roommate at college."

"And when you came home with him, you saw her," Samuel clarified.

"It wasn't like that back then. Caprice was younger, still in her teens."

"But I had a crush on him," Caprice admitted, wanting to be honest with them.

Now Diane spoke. "I see. So you started practicing law in Pittsburgh and met Naomi."

"Yes," Grant responded.

"So now you're going to say you never really loved her even though you had a child together."

"Mom, I really don't want to get into that," Grant said. "It's between Caprice, me, Naomi, and the church."

Samuel's eyebrows arched as if he wasn't used to Grant standing his ground.

Fortunately, the waitress came to take their orders. Caprice didn't even have a menu, but she quickly borrowed Grant's, chose something easy and non-messy to eat, and realized the rest of dinner could be as much of an ordeal as the beginning of dinner.

After the waitress left, Caprice clutched at something Grant had told her about his mom. "Grant said you have a vegetable garden. What do you raise?"

"A little bit of everything," Diane answered, perking

up a bit. "We have broccoli and zucchini, kale, Brussels sprouts, and of course, tomatoes."

"My mother raises heirloom tomatoes from seed. I plant them in my yard too."

"What kinds?" Diane asked.

"Marianna's Peace, Anna Russian, and Amish Paste."

"It's unusual for someone your age to be interested in planting heirloom tomatoes."

Grant patted her knee under the table as if she'd made a point. Good for her.

Gardening and farming were the topics until their orders arrived. But then the conversation went downhill again. His father asked Grant, "So you're still working from home?"

"I'm working both places, my home and downtown. Patches is learning how to behave at the office so I can take him along. When I have a court date, my neighbor takes care of him."

"I can't see that working from home is a good thing when you have clients to see. It's just not professional, and I really think it's a stupid idea to do it all because of a dog."

Unable to hold her tongue, Caprice backed up Grant. "I have two cats and a dog. Lady goes with me lots of places, just as Patches goes with Grant. Our fur babies are family. I believe loving them teaches us how to love people better. We also learn how to receive unconditional love in return."

Grant's father looked at her as if she were crazy, but Grant's mother studied her speculatively. "That's a very interesting philosophy."

In case that topic wouldn't bring out the best in his father, Grant asked about a few people they knew back in Vermont. While he and his dad had a quiet conversation, Caprice showed his mom her ring, exclaiming how much she loved it, and how great Grant's taste was.

"A heart diamond," Diane mused. "I never would have thought Grant would be so sentimental.

Somehow they finished dinner. No one wanted dessert. Grant's father insisted on paying the check, and Grant let him, maybe remembering what Caprice had said earlier about his dad having pride.

Once outside, Caprice walked with them to Grant's SUV. She said, "I'm so happy you came to Kismet. I'd like you to meet my parents. You're staying through the weekend, right? Maybe you could come to dinner on Sunday night."

Samuel cut a glance at his wife. "We'll talk it over and let you know."

After Grant's parents were seated in his car, Grant took her by the arm and led her to the blind spot where they weren't in plain sight. "Do you still want to marry me?"

She couldn't help but smile. "I do, even more than before."

He shook his head and kissed her. "I'll try to convince them to have dinner with you and your parents, but don't hold your breath."

"I wouldn't think of it," she teased, then headed for her Camaro.

If her parents and his parents did have dinner together, the occasion could be quite entertaining.

Chapter Seventeen

Caprice sat across from her nana the following afternoon. While they shared a cup of tea and nibbled on biscotti, Lady chased Nana's kitten Valentine up the cat condo. The animals stared at each other until finally Lady sat and Valentine, a gray tabby Caprice had found in her backyard last February, curled in a nap position.

Nana liked to keep up to date on Caprice's decorating schemes and she told her all about the Tuscan Dream house.

"It sounds lovely."

"I hope it will be. Grant says maybe Tuscany would be a good place to take a honeymoon."

"Aha," Nana said, pointing her biscotti at Caprice. "Now that's a topic I think we should discuss. How did dinner go last night? No one in the family seems to know anything about it. That means you didn't call us afterward, and that means, maybe it didn't go so well?"

"His parents are . . . are . . ." Caprice wanted to put

this in the most positive of terms. "They're not as supportive and accepting as you and Mom and Dad."

"I see. You mean they criticized Grant, though I don't see what there is to criticize."

Caprice smiled. "I don't either. I'm not sure they approve of the annulment. I'm not sure they approve of me. But I asked them to come to dinner on Sunday night with you and Mom and Dad. Are you game?"

"I'm always game for a good conversational rumble."

"I'll let you know what they decide. Grant is trying to convince them it would be a good idea to have our families meet."

"It will work out," Nana proclaimed, patting Caprice's hand. "Tell me something, though, do Grant's parents know you're involved in a murder investigation?"

"I'm not really involved—"

Nana gave her a knowing look.

"No, I don't think they know anything about me being involved with murder investigations. Maybe it's better we keep it that way."

Nana held up one finger. "The truth always . . ."

"Comes out," Caprice said along with her. "I know. But we've got to get past the introductions stage first."

"And what about the murder investigation? Have you figured out who killed Wendy?"

"You're kidding, right? This one's a tough one."

"So go over it with me. You know how it works. Maybe an idea will pop out of you when we talk about it."

She hadn't really discussed the suspect list with anyone, and now she did, from Warren Shaeffer to Wendy's ex-husband to Lizbeth and Sebastian, and even Rena.

"You do have quite a mixture there. What's your gut feeling telling you?"

"Maybe this time I can't see clearly because I can't get past Wendy's death. I just feel so bad for Sebastian's boys, especially Kevin. He seems to be really connected to her. He told me about the bike rides they took to the old Wyatt estate. There's a Saint Anthony shrine there and Wendy believed Saint Anthony could help find lost things. When I saw Kevin the last time, he told me he'd prayed to Saint Anthony to find his password list, and he did. I think he's finally a believer." She took a sip of tea, then admitted, "The break-in that happened at Sebastian's worries me. Sebastian's talking about hiring security until the murderer is caught."

"That could be quite expensive."

"I know. But it's either that or take the boys and go stay somewhere else for a while."

"So you don't think Sebastian is the murderer."

"I really don't. I don't think he'd do that to his boys, even if he and Wendy were having problems."

"And you have no idea what the intruder was looking for?"

"Oh, we do. We think he or she was looking for a journal and or a thumb drive that Wendy kept somewhere and nobody knows where."

Nana looked thoughtful for a moment. "I suppose the talk about Saint Anthony came up between Wendy and Kevin because of the shrine?"

"Yes."

"Have you ever seen it?"

"No, I've never been to the back of the property. I've only been inside the house."

"If I remember correctly, that shrine is closed in and protected. It's huge."

Suddenly Caprice remembered that Wendy had told Kevin if he ever lost something, he should go to the shrine to pray to Saint Anthony and he would help him find it. Caprice snapped her fingers. "Maybe Wendy left us a clue. She told Kevin if ever he lost something, he should go to the shrine and pray to Saint Anthony. I just wonder—"

"Wonder if something could be hidden there?"

"Yes, I think I'm going to make a pilgrimage to visit Saint Anthony."

"Are you going to take someone with you?"

"Grant's entertaining his parents today. He's going to drive them to Gettysburg to see the Battlefield and the Peace Light. And truthfully, I don't know how much I trust anyone else. I'd ask Sebastian to go along, but I've been wrong about suspects before."

"What about your uncle Dom? He might be game."

"Yes, he might. I'll take Lady home and go out for a good play session with her. Then I'll give him a call. But if he's not available, I'm going to go myself. This can't wait any longer, especially if something's hidden there."

"If you do go alone, you have your cell phone in one hand and your mace gun in the other. Understood?"

"Got it, Nana."

Then Nana solemnly said, "May all the saints protect you."

Caprice parked her van to the rear of the Wyatt estate just outside the gate. When she'd called her Uncle Dom, she'd heard his voice mail message. She'd waited fifteen minutes and tried again. When he still didn't answer, she figured he was on a pet-sitting assignment. Instead of waiting or trying to call again, she decided to take Lady with her. What could it hurt? When she took her pup along, she had to use her van with Lady's crate in the back. It was the safest way for Lady to travel.

Mid-October dusk was starting to settle in and she knew she had to make this excursion quick. As she'd promised Nana, she kept her cell phone in her hand. Her mace gun was in her pocket. She opened the door to the van and unfastened the latch on Lady's crate. Lady came out and sat.

"Good girl," she praised her. Lady always responded well to praise and treats, so Caprice used both. Lady was a lower pack dog who was content to stay close to Caprice and to please her as much as she could, giving unconditional love all the while.

Caprice waited until Lady jumped down from the van and then they started off toward the obvious gap in the tall wrought-iron gates. They looked as if a good wind could knock them over, though that was probably an illusion. But something had separated them, whether a storm or years or a vehicle running into them. Caprice could see easily how Kevin and Wendy could ride their bikes right through the gap into the back acreage and ride out again.

Lady snuffled at all the fallen leaves as if she were searching for buried treasure . . . or maybe she smelled the route Wendy and Kevin had taken. After all, Caprice didn't think anyone had been back here for a long time. The whole yard was weed filled with grass growing up between the stone path pavers. There were gravel paths, too, becoming overgrown, but not so much so that a bike couldn't pass through.

Caprice wasn't sure which way to go.

"I should have asked Nana where the Saint Anthony

shrine was. I could call her, but it might be good if we explore a bit, don't you think?"

Lady gazed up at Caprice, waiting for direction.

Caprice peered in between the tall tree trunks and thought she saw a couple of structures to the east. She said to her pup, "Let's go this way first and see what we find."

Lady gave a little yip as if she agreed.

As they shuffled through the leaves, Caprice got a chill up her back. From the breeze that blew through? Maybe. She looked over her shoulder toward the gate but couldn't see any movement nor hear any vehicles. She was just jumpy. Was she trespassing? She could have gotten Lizbeth's permission to be on the property, but she didn't want to tip her off. Lizbeth could be the killer, or Rena, or Warren, or Doris or Scott Wyatt. All had motives.

Lady stopped at an area that must have been very pretty at one time. What was obviously once a pond had dried up. It was full of leaves now and the pump that used to operate the waterfall was still. Had a gardener once tended to these flower beds? To the rose bushes in a circle around a birdbath? A burning bush was noticeable from twenty feet away. Caprice had always wanted one of those in her yard but had never planted one.

She and Lady walked toward it now, seeing the structure shadowing it. It was brick, about six feet tall and four feet wide. The base was solid, but a statue of Saint Anthony sat on the shelf. Caprice knew her saints and how they were depicted. This robed saint with his round face, holding baby Jesus, lilies sculpted down his robe, was Saint Anthony of Padua.

The silence surrounding the shrine, as well as the dusk falling, unsettled Caprice. Lady rustled leaves at

the base of the statue as she snuffled around. Caprice
studied the brickwork and then—

Was that a noise? Somewhere to her right?

She was crazy for being here. Crazy. She fingered
the cell phone in her left hand and whispered to
Lady, "Quiet, girl."

That wasn't a command Caprice often used, but obviously hearing something in Caprice's voice, Lady sat
and looked up at her, brown eyes shining.

Silence again. She needed to look around and
leave.

She took her phone in hand and pressed the flashlight app. The brickwork behind the statue looked the
same as the rest of the brick in age and wear. Some of
the mortar was loose here and there. Her dad would
have a fit if he saw it, and he'd want to fix it. As she
kept studying the bricks, she saw one that looked a
little different. Not the brick itself, but the mortar
around it. It was evenly cracked, a little of it missing.
About three bricks from the bottom, to the left of the
base shelf, Caprice poked it with her fingers. There
seemed to be a notch in the top and the bottom of the
brick. That was odd that notches were in both places,
as if they would make fingerholds.

Apparently tired of sitting quietly, Lady stood and
swished leaves again. Caprice paid no mind as her dog
went around behind the shrine. She managed to poke
her thumb into the little cleft at the top of the brick
and another finger at the bottom of the brick. Then
she pulled. The brick came out.

Giving a little cry of success, she laid it aside next to
the statue. Shining her flashlight into the cavity as well
as she could, she saw something there! Excited now,
she wrapped her fingers around the small journal and
took it out, laying it on the shelf. Feeling around, she

thought she felt a stone, but it was too smooth for a stone. It was a thumb drive.

Pay dirt.

"I found it, Lady. We got what we came for."

Quickly, she slipped the thumb drive into her deep cargo slacks pocket so she couldn't lose it; then she picked up her phone.

"Detective Carstead has to know about this." She doubted if he could lift fingerprints from the bricks, but who knew these days. She'd better not touch anything else.

She'd no sooner pressed Brett's number, heard his voice mail message, and started to say, "Brett, I'm at the Wyatt—" when she heard real rustling now, and it wasn't Lady. Because the noise was shoulder high. She began to turn . . .

Caprice felt jarred . . . bumped . . . lifted. She was strapped down—on a gurney. She couldn't move her head because it was in a fixed position. There was sound all around—voices, barking, and more barking. That was Lady.

She opened her eyes and almost closed them again, but she had to make sure Lady was okay. The lights almost blinded her, at least that's what it felt like. Suddenly, whatever she was lying on was shoved into a vehicle.

She called, "Lady."

She could dimly see a figure standing outside the vehicle as a man beside her wearing a blue shirt with an ID badge took her blood pressure and then shone a flashlight into her eyes. Just what she needed when she had a raging headache.

From outside the vehicle she heard, "Caprice, it's

Brett. I'll make sure one of the officers takes Lady to Nikki. She's fine. I checked her over. I'll talk to you at the hospital."

She wiggled her arms under the seat-belt-like strap that held her. She didn't know where her phone was, but she managed to reach into her pocket. There was the thumb drive.

"Brett," she called. "Call Grant. Please."

"Got you," the detective shouted back. And she was glad he had. The call must have gone through and he'd come to find her. Bless him. Or bless the saints that Nana had sent to protect her.

With no hospital in Kismet, Caprice was transported to York. At the hospital there, she was registered and examined, thanks to Brett Carstead vouching for her identity. Her purse was in her van back at the estate.

Once she'd been sent to an ER cubicle, Brett had appeared and she'd told him exactly what had happened, given him the thumb drive, and asked him about the journal.

The journal was gone.

Apparently whoever had hit her thought that was all she'd found.

Brett had done his usual scolding, then left. But before he'd gone, he'd given her a thumbs-up sign.

She was taken for a CT scan and by the time they returned her to the ER cubicle, Grant was there pacing.

When he saw her, he rushed toward her. "Carstead called me. What did you do?"

"It wasn't what I did," she said indignantly. "Someone hit me on the head."

Grant stared at her, speechless for a moment. Then he gave her a huge hug and kissed her. Afterward he asked, "Did that hurt?"

"It made my head spin, but my head was already spinning," she teased. "So it was hard to tell which spinning was from the bump on the head and which was from the kiss."

He gave her a weak smile. "Honest to goodness, Caprice. That gave me such a scare when he called me. He said you were conscious but the doctors had to determine the damage."

"I have an awful headache and a lump on the back of my head," she said, gingerly touching it. "We'll know if anything's really wrong after the radiologist reads the CT scan."

He squeezed her hand and she squeezed back. She told him exactly what had happened. Then she asked, "Were you with your parents?"

"We'd just gotten back to the bed and breakfast. They're worried too."

"I didn't tell Brett to call my parents for that reason. After we talk to the doctor, I'll call them."

It wasn't long before a doctor who looked to be a few years older than they were came into the room. He introduced himself as Dr. Pettis and brought a rolling stool to sit beside Caprice's bed.

"You're very lucky, Miss De Luca. No skull fracture. A concussion. You might have headaches for a while, but they should diminish day by day. You need someone with you for the next twenty-four hours, forty-eight would be even better. Whoever's with you should wake you up every few hours and ask you questions to make sure your faculties are clear."

"I'll be with her," Grant said, squeezing her hand again.

The doctor nodded. "Ask her the year, who's president, her name, her age, her address, anything that will let you know she's in the present and understands what you're saying. Do you have any questions?"

"You want me to rest for forty-eight hours?" Caprice asked.

The doctor stood. "I'd advise it, but my patients don't always listen to what I advise. Your brain is bruised. You need to treat it with respect. No exercise or any activity that will shake it up more. Do you understand?"

"What about driving?"

"Rest for forty-eight hours," he said again. He looked at Grant. "If she's nauseous, dizzy, or anything like that, you bring her back in here."

"You didn't give me a yes or no on the driving," Caprice reminded him.

Grant capped her shoulder. "If you need to go anywhere, I'll take you. I'm staying with you for forty-eight hours. That means no walking Lady, no running around the yard stooping to clean up after her, no unnecessary excitement."

"He's got it," the doctor said with a smile.

Caprice crossed her arms over her chest. "In other words, I'm going to be a prisoner."

"In other words," Grant contradicted, "you're going to be pampered."

"Listen to your fiancé," the doctor said. "And let him pamper you. After all, who knows how long that will last. I'll send someone in with your discharge papers and written instructions." With a lift of his brow, he left.

She looked up at Grant. "Sitting around for two days. Seriously?"

"Do you know what being pampered means?" Grant asked, brows arched.

"Yes, but I think you're going to explain it further."

"That means you're going to sit on the sofa, and I'm going to massage your feet. It means I'll bring you coffee or tea or a sandwich. It means you're going to stay quiet with Mirabelle on your lap and heal."

"But your parents are in town."

"Yes, they are, and they rented a car. Tomorrow they're going to take a tour of Lancaster and the Amish country. They don't know what they're doing the day after that, but I'm sure they'll think of something."

"We're having a dinner party with my parents on Sunday," she said adamantly.

He sighed. "They'll probably agree to come just because they feel bad you were hurt. But don't think you're going to do all the work. And we're only having the dinner party if you're one hundred percent. This is your fiancé talking. Are you listening?"

"You're being awfully bossy," she muttered. "Are you going to bring Lady home?"

"I talked to Nikki. She and Lady are going to visit you tomorrow. By then, if you're feeling okay, you can sit outside on the back porch while Lady romps in the yard. Deal?"

Caprice knew even though Grant was giving her dictates, he was restraining his protective streak. She had the feeling he'd keep her confined in her bed if he could—with him in the next room, of course.

For a few months.

"I'll listen," she said, meaning it; then his arms were around her and he was kissing her again.

Chapter Eighteen

Caprice had to admit that resting for two days wasn't as bad as she thought it might be. Grant took good care of her. On Friday when her mom and dad and Nana visited, she'd convinced him to spend time with his parents. After all, that's why they'd come to Kismet—to see their son. Although the bump on her head was still sore, the headache had diminished by Saturday. She could look into the sunlight and move around without her head throbbing.

After Grant had brought in takeout for supper, she'd announced that she wanted to see Sebastian and the boys to tell him about the stolen journal, if not the thumb drive, and to see his reaction. She wanted to figure out if he could have been the one who had knocked her out.

She admired Grant's diplomacy when he said, "I'd feel better if you let me drive you, especially since it's getting dark. If you want to talk to Sebastian alone, I'll busy myself in conversation with one of his kids."

"You're going to have to trust that I'm feeling good enough to take care of myself at some point."

"I'm already trusting that you're feeling good

enough to have my parents and yours and Nana over for dinner tomorrow."

"It's my last chance to spend some time with your parents before they go back to Vermont. I won't overdo it, I promise. Mom and Nana are helping."

"I'll give in if you'll give in."

"Such a negotiator," she teased, but then closed the carton of Chinese to stow it in the refrigerator. "Okay, it's a deal. Do you think Lady and Patches will nap while we're gone?" Both dogs were sitting under the table, their tails wagging as they waited for any scraps.

"Patches has his kibble ball. If we fill a ball for each of them, that should keep them busy enough until we get back. I don't expect this will be a long visit, do you?"

"Probably not." She checked her watch. "The Cupcake House will still be open. Let's stop there to pick up a dozen cupcakes to take along. I know the boys will appreciate them."

"How's your head?"

"My head is fine, but I'll let you drive so we don't have to argue about it."

He smiled. "Smart girl."

When Grant and Caprice pulled into the driveway at Sebastian's and neared the carport, a motion detector light went on. It was a huge floodlight and Caprice could tell Sebastian had made some changes. One of those changes was a little sign that stood in his front yard, proclaiming the name of a security company. He'd had an alarm system installed.

When she pointed that out to Grant, he nodded. "Who can blame him."

She'd done the same thing after someone had broken into her home.

After Sebastian answered the door, he seemed

pleased to see her. He'd heard what had happened and was solicitous. "I'm so sorry you were hurt. Do you have any idea who did it?"

Caprice studied his face. Was he fishing? Trying to find out if she could identify him?

"No, I was too absorbed in what I was doing, I guess, to notice anything. One minute I was holding Wendy's journal in my hand, the next everything went black."

Kevin said, "A secret compartment. Wow. Just like in the movies. Was it there all along or did Wendy make it?"

That same question had occurred to Caprice. "It was there all along. The bricks just formed a front on the cavity so there was plenty of room behind them to hide something. I just wonder how Wendy found it in the first place."

"It's possible Leona knew about it and told her," Sebastian concluded. "They got really close. Who knows? Leona might have hidden things there herself and if Wendy told her about the journal, the hiding place might have been her suggestion."

Caprice studied Kevin. "I'm glad you told me what you did, or I never would have thought of looking there." She lifted the box of cupcakes. "I brought you chocolate with chocolate icing. Interested?"

"Always," Cody said with a wide smile. "Can we have them, Dad?"

Sebastian smiled. "I'll brew the coffee."

As they enjoyed coffee and cupcakes at the kitchen table, Caprice decided Sebastian didn't seem like a man who had anything to hide, at least not anymore. He told them he'd looked into hiring a security guard, but then decided a state-of-the-art alarm system would be a better investment. The front door camera even recorded who came and went.

The boys downed the cupcakes as if they hadn't seen a sweet before.

When Dover came over and laid his head on Caprice's lap, she stroked it. "I guess you're too friendly to be a guard dog."

Sebastian frowned. "I don't know what would have happened if he had been here the night of the break-in. I'm glad he was with us. I wouldn't have wanted to see him hurt."

"I know exactly what you mean. I had Lady along at the Wyatt estate. Fortunately my attacker didn't bother with her, just took the journal."

"Do you think the person followed you everywhere you went?"

"The police found a GPS tracker on my van and one on my car."

"Could they trace it to someone's phone?" Kevin asked.

"It was sold from a company online, paid for with one of those prepaid Visa cards that you can pick up at any convenience store."

"You can download phone apps for those trackers," Cody explained. "Somebody probably had a burner phone and that couldn't be traced."

"I can't believe how up to date you kids are on this stuff," Grant said.

"The whole thing is scary," Caprice agreed.

Sebastian looked worried. "Maybe I'd better check over my SUV."

"I can do it, Dad," Cody offered. "I know what to look for."

"We can do it together," Sebastian told his son.

After a few more minutes of catching up, Grant

and Caprice exchanged a look and decided to leave. She knew Grant was thinking he didn't want her to become overtired. She felt fine, but she didn't want the headache to come back either. After all, she had a dinner to get ready for tomorrow.

Sebastian, Kevin, and Cody all walked Grant and Caprice outside. It was a beautiful autumn night with a bright moon. The motion detector light came on as soon as they walked to the edge of the carport. Grant's SUV was parked a few yards away. Caprice didn't know if it was the moonlight or the motion detector light, but she caught a glimpse of something shiny in the driveway. It could be a nickel. It could be the tab off a soda can.

She went toward it, stooped down, and picked it up. "I think someone lost a necklace, or at least part of one," she said, coming back into the light where everyone was standing.

"We don't wear necklaces," Cody mumbled.

"It could be off a key ring, I suppose." She looked at Sebastian.

"I use my car remote for my key ring."

She turned the coin—that's what it looked like—over in her fingers. She could see now it was decorated with a purple butterfly emblem. A hole was drilled in it as if it once hung on a chain.

She held it out to everyone. "Have you seen this before?"

Cody and Kevin shrugged, and Sebastian shook his head.

"Could it have belonged to Wendy?" Caprice asked. After all, it could have been lying in the gravel drive for a while.

"I never saw her wear anything like that," Sebastian said. "I don't suppose that means anything."

Grant went to the area where Caprice had found the necklace. He crouched down, pushed the stones aside here and there, and came up with a chain. He brought it to where the others were standing.

"Broken links," he disclosed.

"I know Wendy didn't have a necklace like that," Kevin said. "I would have noticed a purple butterfly."

"You had a lot of people coming in and going with the reception and condolence calls," Caprice pointed out. "I suppose it could belong to anyone. But I also wonder . . ." She stopped. "It could have belonged to the person who broke in. It wasn't very deep in the gravel, and you haven't had as many cars here since the break-in."

"I should probably give Detective Carstead a call," Sebastian decided. "He said the smallest thing could make a difference. Maybe this is that smallest thing."

That and the thumb drive, Caprice thought.

"You call Detective Carstead, but I'll see what I can find out in the meantime. I know just the person to consult—Isaac Hobbs. He sees all kinds of jewelry in his shop, at estate sales, and at public auctions." She examined the disc again. "That could be a one-of-a-kind pendant, but it looks to me like a coin that might be given out at a meeting or something like that. I don't know. Let's get into some really good light and I'll take a photo of it with my phone. I'll e-mail that to Isaac and see what he thinks."

"You have a good eye," Sebastian said. "I never would have seen that."

"Maybe I'm just a sucker for moonlight," she kidded, and looked over at Grant.

He gave her a slow smile.

Once in the car, Grant turned to her. "A sucker for moonlight, huh?"

"It seems to me the moon was glowing when you proposed."

He leaned over and kissed her.

As Grant drove her back to her house, she e-mailed Isaac from her phone and attached the photo.

Grant had no sooner parked in her driveway and gone inside the house with her—to the delight of Patches, Lady, and two sleepy felines—when her phone dinged. She checked her e-mail.

"Isaac says he has seen the coin before. He has a few in a box at his jewelry counter. They're given out at a national support group meeting that gathers for weight control. He says a branch of it meets at the library. If I talk to the head librarian, she should be able to tell me more."

Caprice texted back a quick thank you to Isaac; then she glanced at Grant. "I can't get into trouble at a library."

He just groaned because he knew she could get into trouble anywhere.

Standing in her dining room the following evening, Caprice looked over her dining room table with a critical eye. The fifties-style mahogany table wore a few scratches. Yet covered with a white tablecloth with a flower design, no one would see them. She'd used a lint brush on the needlepoint covers on the chairs. That didn't mean a cat wouldn't climb on one before the guests arrived, but she'd given it a shot.

As she took her good china from a hutch—Nana had passed it down to her when she'd gone to live with Caprice's parents—she studied the yellow and pink roses that decorated the plates. Her everyday dishes came in assorted colors of lime green, fuchsia, turquoise, and yellow and could be jarring to someone who didn't understand her tastes. These plates were classic. The stainless-steel flatware she'd found at Isaac's when she'd moved in here was a shadowed rose pattern and went beautifully with the dishes, as did the Princess House tumblers from the seventies that had been hand-blown and delicately etched. She suddenly wondered if Grant's parents would find all of this a little hoity-toity, too, but it was too late to worry about that. The chicken was roasting in the oven and the minestrone simmered on the stove.

Patches and Lady sat by the door, eager for another run outside. Grant had dropped Patches off earlier, thinking that if the two dogs had some playtime together before company arrived, then they'd settle down. Wishful thinking? They were both still pups, and who knew what could happen.

As Caprice gave the soup another stir, she considered her meeting with the head librarian that afternoon. Caprice had known Willa Renquist since she was a teenager, wandering the shelves at the Kismet library for good research material as well as novels to read. Willa, with her tightly rolled gray perm and her tortoiseshell glasses, had been forthright when Caprice had shown her the picture of the coin on her phone.

"The group's called Wings," she'd explained quickly. "They meet here once a week, have weigh-ins and pep talks. I actually belonged for a while," the librarian admitted, patting her rounded hips.

Willa had always been about thirty to forty pounds overweight and Caprice could see why she would try to lose weight.

"But I just couldn't give up sugar and flour," Willa

admitted. "And you have to do that to belong to that group. I know it would have benefited me, especially as I grow older." Then she laughed. "I guess I am growing older. But for now, I just want to enjoy the kinds of foods I like." She pointed to the photo on Caprice's phone. "That particular coin with the silver background and purple butterfly is given out as a milestone reward for fifty pounds lost. If someone loses a hundred pounds, they receive a gold coin with a purple butterfly.

"So it's just a coin, not a necklace."

"Just a coin. But that coin means a lot. So I could see why someone would have a hole drilled into it and put a chain on it so they could wear it daily. It's like a reminder to stay on course."

Caprice was still considering what Willa had said when her doorbell rang. Her mom, Nana, and dad arrived first, hugging her and fussing over her to make sure she was recovering. Nana tested the potatoes to see if they were ready to mash. Her mom tasted the soup, gave her a wink and a thumbs-up.

When the Weatherfords arrived, they looked uncomfortable throughout introductions. Then Grant explained, "Caprice's dad is a mason and her mom teaches high school English." During the next quarter hour or so, the men went outside with the dogs. Caprice didn't know how that was going to go over since Grant's father didn't seem to be a huge animal lover. His mother asked how she could help in the kitchen. Caprice asked her to watch the green beans so they didn't boil over and maybe test them for tenderness.

A half hour later when everyone finally sat around the table, Caprice's dad asked, "Do you mind if we say grace?"

Diane murmured, "That would be nice."

Her father kept it short, thanking the Lord for the food and the company. Caprice ladled out the soup, dish by dish, while the rest of the meal was kept warm and covered on the stove.

Grant's father asked, "What's that green stuff floating in the soup?"

Nana explained, "This is my recipe. That's endive. Caprice knows just when to put it in so it's still a little crisp."

"I've never had salad in my soup before," Sam muttered. "And I have a dog sitting on my foot."

Grant peered under the table. "That's Patches. He likes you, Dad."

His father gave a grunt.

Conversation limped through the soup course until her mom and Caprice whisked the dishes away. They brought out the chicken, mashed potatoes, green beans, and gravy and Grant's father's eyes lit up. "This is like Thanksgiving."

Caprice had asked Grant if his parents enjoyed wine. When he said they didn't drink, she'd decided not to serve it.

Nana still didn't seem to be over Grant's dad's soup comment. She explained, "The De Lucas have a meal like this once a month to bring the family together."

"You go to all this trouble then?" Diane asked.

"Oh, it's not trouble," Nana said. "In an Italian family, food is love. We show our love to each other by what we make. Everyone brings something. It's quite a party atmosphere unless there's a squabble or two, and that happens."

"Have you been to these dinners?" Grant's father asked him.

"Since I was Vince's roommate. This isn't a new thing.

The De Lucas have always done it. It's like a family reunion once a month and guests are invited too."

"Grant fits right in," Caprice's mom said. "He's always seemed like a member of the family."

Grant's father looked from him to Caprice, then back to Grant again, and said, "I see." That "I see" made Caprice wonder what was going on in his mind. Did he think Caprice was the reason Grant hadn't fallen head over heels for Naomi when they were involved? That couldn't be. She and Grant had never intended to reconnect with Grant practicing law in Pittsburgh and her opening her decorating business in Kismet. Yet she had to admit, she'd never forgotten him or her crush on him.

Finally, Diane and her mom began talking about gardens. Sam and her dad seemed to find common ground talking about small-town living, traffic, and the difference in the weather between Vermont and Pennsylvania. Nana had made cannoli shells and her mom had mixed the cream. While Grant served coffee, Caprice filled the cannoli shells, then decorated them with a few mini-chocolate chips and colorful sprinkles and brought them to the table. She'd considered making an apple pie, but the cannoli were often part of their family dinners. Grant's parents needed a taste of what the De Lucas were all about.

After she'd sifted powdered sugar on top of the cannoli, she carried the crystal dish to the table.

Diane said, "They look like they came from a bakery."

"We don't buy cannoli at a bakery," Nana protested. "Fran used real whipped cream and ricotta in the filling."

Grant's father didn't look as if cannoli were on the list of desserts he'd like to try. But Grant offered the serving plate to him and he took one, maybe deciding it was the diplomatic thing to do since he'd criticized the soup.

After a taste and a swig from his cup of coffee, Sam smiled. "That's really something."

Score one for their side, Caprice thought.

After dinner, the men found a football game on TV with Lady and Patches settled at their feet. Caprice's felines had gone upstairs for a little privacy and she supposed that was best. She didn't think either Sam or Diane would appreciate Mirabelle jumping on their laps.

As her mom and Nana stacked the dishes on the table, Diane came up beside her at the counter. "Can I ask you something?"

"Sure," Caprice responded.

"Because of what happened the other night, Grant told us you get involved in murder investigations. Why do you do that?"

"I never intended to," she said honestly. "But I had a good friend from high school, and her husband was murdered. That's how it started. The police suspected her, and I wanted to help clear her name. With Wendy, the woman who was murdered recently . . ." Caprice shook her head. "She was a good woman. She saved other women from abusive situations. So many people were affected by her death, and the assistant director at the women's shelter asked me to gather information too. That's all I intended to do."

Diane lowered her voice. "And you found something useful to the police, Grant told us."

"I hope it's useful. I hope it helps them find the murderer."

Diane nodded, then she asked, "What do you like most about my son?"

That question made Caprice smile. "If I had to pick

one quality, I'd pick Grant's ability to care. I love that about him as well as everything else."

Diane seemed satisfied with that answer. After she gave a little smile, she went to help Caprice's nana and mom. Diane might not be the hugging type, but her smile said she approved. Maybe Caprice would be able to have a relationship with her in-laws after all. She'd just have to work harder on Grant's dad.

Chapter Nineteen

Caprice parked in the lot at Green Tea Spa on Monday evening just as the first pings of sleet hit her windshield. The weather had been rainy and unusually cold all day with the prediction of ice later tonight followed by rain later. She'd hoped it would hold off until she was home from yoga. When she'd spoken to Dulcina earlier today, her friend had told her she couldn't attend the class tonight because she had emergency transcriptions to finish.

Caprice figured the class might be short with the weather so terrible. Soon she'd be back home curled up with her pets.

She'd just turned off the ignition when her cell phone played. Taking it from her pocket in her knit turquoise pants, she saw the caller was Grant.

"How was your parents' flight?" she asked, knowing why he was calling.

"They're home and tucked in. We're supposed to get the bad weather before they are. I'm glad they had smooth sailing. Maybe they won't think it's such a big deal to fly down here again."

"So how do you think the visit went. Really?"

"I think it went as well as can be expected. You and your family did a great job welcoming them."

"But then there's the big question. Did they approve of me?"

"I approve of you. It doesn't matter what they think. But, honestly, I think they liked you. I'm pretty sure Mom did. Dad's hard to read."

"So he's grumpy about everything?"

Grant laughed. "Most of the time. It's just his way. You can't take it personally. He did say you're a good cook."

"That's something," she agreed. She checked her watch. "I really should be going into yoga. Class starts in five minutes."

"You could turn around and go home before the roads get bad. It's sleeting, Caprice. Haven't you noticed?"

"It started after I arrived."

"I can pick you up if it gets too slippery. My SUV is better than your van."

"I'll be fine," she assured him again. "I'll call you after I get home."

"Dulcina's not with you?" he asked.

"She had work to do tonight. Don't fret. I'll take my time."

"It's not you I'm worried about, it's the other drivers."

"I'll talk to you later," she said, reminding him she had a class to go to.

He sighed. "Later," he agreed, and ended the call.

Caprice ran inside Green Tea Spa and brushed the sleet from her hair. She nodded to the receptionist and smiled. "It's nasty out there."

"So I heard," the blonde said. "I'll be leaving while you're in class. Evelyn knows how to lock up."

Caprice thought about Grant and his offer to pick

her up. She probably should have let him. But it wasn't that far to her house, and hopefully, the mayor would have called out trucks with chemicals to melt the ice. The problem was, sometimes during the first storm, especially an unexpected one, the town just wasn't as prepared as it should be with inclement weather services.

As she made her way to the room designated for the yoga class, she thought about Grant's parents back in Vermont. She was glad they'd gotten home safely.

Entering the yoga room, she saw Evelyn was seated at the desk in front. Only two other women were present and they were involved in a conversation in the back of the room where the mats were located.

Caprice stopped at Evelyn's desk. "Are you going to go ahead with class?"

"The three of you came out in this messy weather. The least I can do is try to relax you. But I'll shorten the session." Eyeing Caprice studiously, Evelyn said, "Word around town has it something happened at the Wyatt estate and you were taken to the hospital. Are you okay?"

"A concussion," Caprice admitted.

Evelyn studied her again as if looking for signs of injury. "I won't do anything too strenuous. You take a break from poses we do where your head would be lower than your shoulders. No point in increasing blood flow to the brain and starting a headache."

That sounded like a good idea to Caprice.

"Have you talked to Sebastian lately?" Evelyn asked. "The word is out about him and Lizbeth and I wondered how he's handling it."

"He and his boys are coping as well as can be expected. I stopped in on Saturday. He'll feel better once the police catch the killer."

"I can't imagine someone breaking into my place," Evelyn said. "Sebastian and the boys must feel so . . . invaded."

"Exactly. But the intruder might have left a clue behind. Sebastian was going to call Detective Carstead and talk to him about it."

The other two women brought their mats up to the front of the room, and Caprice went to find one of her own. Minutes later, lying on her back on her mat, she followed Evelyn's instruction to align her neck, spine, and legs and relax her arms at her sides for an abdominal breathing exercise. For the next few minutes, she concentrated on her belly and her breaths. Her headaches had tensed up her neck and shoulder muscles. Her job was to relax them or tease them into relaxation by giving them more oxygen. The next exercise—Butterfly Breathing—aided her to that end. She felt Evelyn had inserted that exercise just for her.

After the breathing exercises, Evelyn brought them to a standing position and began with the Mountain Pose.

The sleet that had been pinging gently against the windows now took on a different rhythm. The sound was harsher, louder, more of a *rat-tat-tat*. The two women who had been there before Caprice glanced at each other. Mary and Janet were probably in their fifties.

After they exchanged a look and nodded toward the door, Mary spoke up. "Evelyn, we hate to cut the class short, but I don't like driving in this. Janet and I came together, and I have to take her home. So I think we'd better leave."

"All right," Evelyn agreed amiably. "I certainly understand. But please, when you step outside, take about ten deep breaths and try to remain calm. If you tense up behind the wheel, you're more likely to have less control. And remember, if the road's too slippery, pull over and wait until a truck comes along to treat the road."

Mary and Janet stepped off their mats, rolled them up, and placed them in the back of the room. Then they took their coats from the rack and waved their good-byes.

Evelyn looked at Caprice. "What about you? Do you want to finish?"

"The way I see it, the roads could be worse now than if I wait a little bit. The weatherman says this precipitation could turn to rain. If it does that, the roads will be safer then. If it doesn't, and it's a sheet of ice out there, I'll call my fiancé."

"Good thinking," Evelyn agreed with a nod. "How about if we do stretches specifically for neck and shoulders. I imagine with headaches, the base of your neck would be all tense, right?"

"It's tight," Caprice admitted.

"Okay, we'll loosen it up and then maybe your fiancé can give you a massage."

The idea of Grant massaging her shoulders made Caprice tingly all over. The idea of it also made her long to be at home in front of the fire with Grant and their pets.

Evelyn was wearing a semi-fitted, short white crop top with sleeves. Her tan yoga pants settled at her waist. Her yoga socks had individual toes. "So many of the poses to stretch the neck and shoulders are done on the floor, but I think it's better if you stand in an upright position. So just follow my movements, okay?"

Caprice did just that. She stretched out her arms perpendicular to her body, palms down, as Evelyn did. Evelyn advised her on an exhalation to clasp her hands and turn her head to the left, then breathe in, do the same, and turn her head to the right.

"How does that feel?" she asked.

"It feels good," Caprice said.

Evelyn then had her take three relaxing breaths and push her shoulder blades together while clasping her hands behind her. She held the pose and breathed smoothly for about forty-five seconds, then released her hands and dropped her arms to her sides. Next, she wrapped her right arm around herself to the left and the left arm around herself to the right. Instructing her, Evelyn suggested she crawl her fingers as far as she could across her back until she felt the stretch in both arms. Again she was to hold the pose for thirty to forty-five seconds and imagine each inhale of breath bringing fresh energy to every part of her body, especially her neck and shoulders. With each exhalation, she stretched more into the pose.

Next Evelyn had Caprice reach above her head as high as she could and Evelyn did the same. As Evelyn reached up, Caprice gave a small gasp.

There was a tattoo on Evelyn's left side at the waist—a purple butterfly. It was the same purple butterfly that was on the coin Caprice had found in Sebastian's driveway.

Evelyn's gaze met Caprice's.

Caprice said, "That muscle is more sore than I thought." She deluded herself into believing the yoga teacher bought her explanation for her gasp until Caprice's phone played from her pocket.

Evelyn's gaze again met hers.

For the session, Caprice was supposed to have left her phone in her car. Thank goodness, she'd forgotten to do that. She said, "Grant's probably worried about me. I'd better get it."

As she reached for the phone, she saw the caller wasn't Grant. It was Brett. She quickly took the call, keeping her face neutral.

Brett said, "I've seen a report about the thumb drive. Evelyn Miller was charged with domestic abuse before she came to Kismet. I know you're taking yoga. You need to stay away from her."

"I'm at Green Tea now. Sure, I'd love it if you pick me up."

As soon as the words were out of her mouth, Evelyn pounced on her and Caprice fell to the mat on the floor with a thump. Caprice tried to push her off, but Evelyn was strong and her hands aimed for Caprice's neck.

This is ironic, Caprice thought, *when Evelyn had just helped her stretch it.*

"I can strangle you and leave before anybody gets here. Wendy got in my way, and I won't let you do the same."

Caprice struggled to break free . . . batted at Evelyn's hands . . . trying to push them away from her collarbone.

"The police are on to you," she gasped. "They know you were charged with domestic abuse before you came to Kismet."

Evelyn's hands surrounded her neck now, but Caprice kept moving from side to side, turning her head, keeping some space there.

"Did Wendy find out about it?" Caprice asked, guessing, trying to keep Evelyn distracted so she could break away.

"She did," Evelyn grunted. "And she ended my contract. She did a background check on me when I asked her to invest in the yoga studio. She was going to ruin me."

Evelyn was sitting on Caprice's chest now, pressing down. "But I was going to blackmail her by telling how she interfered in a custody case, helping a mother and her child disappear. I know where they are."

There was something in the way Evelyn spoke that told Caprice the woman thought she had the upper hand. Maybe she was on top, but not for long.

Remembering a self-defense maneuver she'd been taught, Caprice brought her knees up and Evelyn lunged forward. When she did, her hold broke a little. Caprice used her elbow to jab Evelyn in the kidney . . . hard.

Suddenly Grant burst in the door.

Sirens blared outside now.

Grant didn't ask any questions, just tackled Evelyn as if she were a football player in the wrong place at the wrong time. He managed to push her onto the floor on her stomach and yanked her arms behind her.

Two officers rushed in then, along with Brett Carstead. As the three of them subdued Evelyn, who was spitting mad, cursing, and trying to break free, Grant rushed to Caprice and knelt down beside her. He took her into his arms and she threw hers around his neck.

"Are you okay?" he asked, leaning away to look at her. He gently touched the red marks on her throat.

"I'm fine," she said a little hoarsely. "But now my neck and shoulders are really going to be tensed up."

"I was worried about you driving in the sleet. I came to pick you up and get you out of here before the streets became a sheet of ice. Did you call the police?"

"No, Brett called me to tell me to stay away from Evelyn, and I told him it was too late . . . that I was here."

Brett Carstead was reading Evelyn Miller her rights.

Grant held on to Caprice tightly, then proclaimed, "I guess I'll have to take up yoga and whatever other hobbies you like in order to keep you safe."

"For a start, you could just give me a massage," she said weakly.

Instead of giving her a massage, he hugged her close.

Epilogue

The De Luca family dinner the following weekend was another celebration of Caprice and Grant's engagement. Her parents' house was definitely full. Besides Bella, Joe, and the kids, as well as Vince and Roz, Nikki had invited Brett, Uncle Dom had invited Dulcina, and Caprice's dad had invited Chief Powalski since his wife was out of town.

Caprice had pulled the lasagna from the oven and was letting it rest when Grant circled her shoulders with his arm. "Come with me to the library for a few minutes. Brett and the chief want to give you the lowdown on everything they learned about Evelyn Miller."

All had been quiet after Evelyn's arrest and Caprice had tons of questions. But she knew better than to ask them. Evelyn had been arraigned and was awaiting trial, but that's all that Caprice knew.

When she and Grant stepped into the library, Mack Powalski shook his finger at her. "You were one lucky lady."

"I've been told that," she said, glancing at Grant.

"But because I've always been like a favorite uncle

to you, because I pushed you on the swing when you were in pigtails, and because you played a large part in solving this case, I thought we should fill you in. Evelyn confessed and has been charged with second-degree murder, as well as aggravated assault and criminal attempt homicide for her attacks on you." Then Mack nodded to Brett.

Somberly Brett warned her, "One thing you have to learn about investigating is to keep information to yourself. You never should have told Evelyn that the police now had a clue as to who broke into Sebastian's house. That could have been a fatal mistake."

"I know," Caprice admitted. "I never suspected her because she was so Zen, at least on the outside. I should have had an inkling, though, from that phone conversation I overheard." Caprice had told the police all about that when they'd interviewed her after Evelyn had tried to kill her.

"The blanks on Miller's history are filled in now," Mack told her. "Evelyn was the abuser in her marriage. She'd had a history of being overweight and overbearing. The night she assaulted you, we got a mug shot from New Jersey from seven years before."

Brett elaborated. "Friends of hers in New Jersey told us that, after she was divorced, she joined the weight-loss group Wings and shed seventy-five pounds. She became healthy, started taking yoga, progressed from being a student of it to teaching it, and she changed her life. But apparently she'd been bullied as a child and she still had anger issues that were never really resolved. They emerged full-blown again when Wendy thwarted her. She wouldn't invest in Evelyn's plans for the future because of what she'd found out, and then she ended Evelyn's contract with Sunrise Tomorrow.

What else could Wendy do? She ran a women's shelter, and Evelyn had been an abuser."

"Along with the window shade Evelyn used to whack Wendy, we found Wendy's journal in Evelyn's apartment too," Mack explained. "And on the thumb drive you gave us, we read private investigator's reports on clients and employees. They included Evelyn's arrest record and a P.I.'s report on her."

"I don't understand something," Caprice said. "When Wendy hired Evelyn, didn't she do a background check then? Why did this just come to light now?"

"Because Wendy didn't really hire Evelyn. When Evelyn started with Sunrise, she volunteered her services just to help the other women feel better. When Wendy found the yoga classes were worthwhile, she contracted with Evelyn for her services. Wendy wasn't Evelyn's employer per se. Evelyn was self-employed. So I guess Wendy didn't think it was necessary to run a background check then. It was only when Evelyn wanted her to invest in a yoga studio with her that Wendy took that precaution. But it was a precaution that ended her life. Sometimes too much information is worse than not enough."

"I'm glad it's over," Caprice said with relief. "I spoke with Lizbeth yesterday. She and Sebastian broke up, no surprise there. Starting this week, I'll be moving furniture into the mansion. Sunrise Tomorrow—Residential could be ready before Christmas."

The living room had gone quiet and Caprice could see Bella and the kids and everyone else were moving into the dining room for dinner.

Nikki peeked in the door. "The lasagna's ready to serve." She wandered over to Brett and smiled up at him. "Are you talking shop again?"

"Not for the rest of the night," he assured her, and gave her sister a smile.

Caprice could see the chemistry between the two of them and she suspected they were heading into couple's territory. Mack capped Grant's shoulder. "I don't think I congratulated the two of you on your engagement. When's the big day?"

"We haven't set the date yet," Grant told him. "But we're planning on spring."

Nikki whispered to Grant, "Caprice has been looking at vintage wedding gowns online." She addressed Caprice. "Are you going to show him what you found?"

"Absolutely not," Caprice protested. "He's not going to see my gown until I walk down the aisle."

Grant wrapped his arm around her, hugged her, and whispered in her ear, "I can't wait."

As Brett, Mack, and Nikki filed out of the library to follow everyone else into the dining room, Caprice gave Grant a kiss that said she couldn't either.

Original Recipes

✳

Caprice's Shredded Potato, Ground Beef-Sausage Bake

1 pound ground beef
½ pound loose sausage meat (I use tomato basil if available.)
¼ cup chopped onion
⅛ teaspoon pepper
¼ teaspoon salt
1 ½ cups spaghetti sauce

Preheat oven to 350 degrees.

Brown ground beef and sausage with onion, adding ⅛ teaspoon pepper and ¼ teaspoon salt while the meat is browning. When no pink is showing, add tomato sauce and let simmer while you prepare the topping.

1 ½ pounds shredded hash brown potatoes (thawed)
1 can cream of celery soup
2 cups shredded cheddar cheese
½ teaspoon salt
¼ teaspoon pepper

While the meat mixture is simmering, mix thawed shredded hash brown potatoes, the can of cream of celery soup, and the shredded cheddar in a large bowl. Stir in ½ teaspoon salt and ¼ teaspoon pepper.

Pour ground beef-sausage mixture into a lasagna pan and then spread the potato mixture on top. Bake covered (I use foil) for 30 minutes, then remove foil and bake an additional 20 minutes or until potatoes are browned.

Serves six to eight.

Nikki's Feta Olive Tomato Salad

½ cup pitted and halved Kalamata olives (I buy
from the olive bar already marinated, but you
can use jarred olives.)
½ cup chopped fennel from the heart or bulb
(I cut off the bulb, separate the upper stalks,
wash and dry well, then chop and slice the
bulb for recipe.)
1 pint (2–3 cups) cherry tomatoes (Measure
whole, then halve.)
1 tablespoon oregano
¼ teaspoon salt
⅛ teaspoon pepper
¼ teaspoon garlic powder
3 tablespoons balsamic white vinegar
2 tablespoons sesame oil
½ cup Feta cheese (crumbled)

Sprinkle halved olives, fennel, and halved tomatoes
with oregano, salt, pepper, and garlic powder. Stir in
vinegar mixed with oil. Fold in Feta cheese.

Makes four to six servings. Refrigerate leftovers.

Bella's Old-fashioned Coconut Cake

½ cup solid coconut oil
1 ¾ cups granulated sugar
5 egg whites
1 whole egg
1 teaspoon salt
3 teaspoons baking powder
1 teaspoon baking soda
1 ½ teaspoons vanilla
1 cup unsweetened coconut milk (I use
    Silk Coconutmilk.)
2 ½ cups all-purpose flour

Preheat oven to 375 degrees. In electric mixer, cream
the solid coconut oil with the sugar. Add egg whites
and whole egg slowly and mix until batter is smooth.
Add salt, baking powder, and baking soda. Mix until
blended. Add vanilla and coconut milk and mix
just until blended. Add flour ½ cup at a time, mixing
2 minutes or until batter is smooth.

Pour evenly into a 9 × 13 inch greased and floured
pan. Bake at 375 degrees for 25 to 30 minutes or until
toothpick comes out clean.

FROSTING

1 stick (½ cup) margarine (softened)
½ cup Crisco shortening
1 cup granulated sugar
3 tablespoons flour
2/3 cup coconut milk (This should be tepid
    temperature and added slowly. I use
    Silk Coconutmilk.)
½ teaspoon vanilla
Flake coconut

Cream together the softened margarine and Crisco. To this mixture, add sugar, flour (one tablespoon at a time), coconut milk (add slowly), and vanilla. Beat 8 to 10 minutes at high speed until frosting is smooth. Spread over the cake and sprinkle the top with flake coconut.

Please turn the page for an exciting sneak peek of
Karen Rose Smith's next
Caprice De Luca Homestaging Mystery

SLAY BELLS RING

coming soon wherever print and e-books are sold!

Chapter One

"Your Christmas Delight theme for staging this house is perfect," Sara Merriweather told Caprice De Luca on the Sunday before Thanksgiving. Yet Sara's voice held forced cheerfulness and her eyes were troubled.

Caprice was enchanted with the nineteen-eighteen historic Colonial on a side street in the oldest neighborhood in Kismet, Pennsylvania. But ever since she'd been putting the finishing touches on staging the house to sell, her client had looked worried.

Part of her job as house stager was to set up a house to sell quickly. The other part? Listening to homeowners' concerns, helping them declutter and teaching them to show off the home in the best possible light. However, listening was her best asset.

"What do you have doubts about?" she asked Sara.

Her client glanced around the grand entry, the beautiful heart pine floors under the Oriental rugs, the wide entrance to the living room on the right, a hall leading back to the kitchen along the stairway as well as the spacious parlor to the left.

"This house has been nothing but a delight for all

the years we've lived here," Sara explained. "Chris is so sure about selling it, about moving us into a condo in a retirement village so I don't have steps to do and we have less to maintain. But he's acting like we're eighty years old instead of sixty-six. I love this house, especially now with the way you've decorated it for Christmas. I just don't understand why he's pushing to sell so fast."

"Maybe now that he's made the decision, he just wants to do it. He doesn't want to linger over the memories here as you do."

Sara shook her head as if she just couldn't understand her husband's thought process or lack of attachment. "Our children love this house too."

Caprice had used her red and white theme throughout the colonial in addition to lots of brass. She'd chosen to keep the pine antiques in place as well as the huge sleigh bed in the master bedroom. This time of year, especially, with the house on the historic home town tour, it could sell quickly. Still, she heard all of the doubts in Sara Merriweather's voice—none of the doubts that she'd heard from Christopher Merriweather when the couple had signed the contract to stage the home.

Pushing her straight long brown hair over her shoulder, she focused her attention on Sara and asked, "Do you want to have a cup of tea and talk about it?"

"Do you have time?"

Caprice made time for anything important to her. The Merriweathers weren't simply her clients. Christopher Merriweather was her dad's poker buddy. She knew her father was especially fond of Blitz, Chris's white Malamute, who usually attended the poker games too. As a favor to her dad, Caprice had spoken to Chris about staging the house to sell it more quickly, and he'd convinced Sara. Now Caprice wondered if that had been the best idea.

Sara led Caprice back the hall to the state-of-the art chef's kitchen with its black granite eat-at counter, its custom crafted walnut-finished cabinets, its high-end appliances. The terrazzo floor extended into a dining area where Caprice knew Sara and Chris had enjoyed many dinners with their children. The Merriweathers were proud of their family just as the De Lucas were.

Sara filled the copper teapot from the filtered water spigot and set it on the burner. She turned on the stove and looked around the kitchen.

Chris's hobby was crafting toys in the workshop out back. Some of those toys Caprice had scattered behind the decorative spindle railing along the top of the cupboards. They were interspersed with sparkling flameless candles on timers. She'd switched them on to see how they'd look and she liked the effect. The wooden toy train, the horse pull toy and the assorted blocks accompanied the old-fashioned look of most of the house.

Sara motioned to the table, its gleaming polish reflecting the crystal vase that held pine boughs, white mums, red roses, and red Christmas balls. "You've really done a beautiful job with this staging, Caprice. When you suggested we take a storage unit for the extras, I never thought we'd fill it, but we did. You've eliminated furniture that just wasn't necessary to make what *is* here really stand out."

Taking a seat at the eat-at counter, Caprice brushed the cuffs of her Bohemian top's flowing sleeves above her wrists. Her retro fashion sense was at work even over the holidays. Her hunter green bell bottoms matched the swirls in her red and green blouse. She responded to Sara's statement with a smile. "That's what staging a house is all about. Nikki has a wonderful buffet planned. We'll go over it before the open house." Caprice's sister, who ran a catering business, helped make each open house a success with her layout of tempting dishes.

When the economy had hit a downturn and decorating houses and Caprice's design degree hadn't been in demand, she'd transformed her business into that of a home staging company. Her reputation for coming up with unique themes for high-end clients had made the rounds of the surrounding area, even leading her to a win a competition for designing a house on a cable TV show. That had garnered her even more clients.

Over the past few years, she'd learned the ins and outs of the business the hard way by trial and error. She kept up with trends, but mostly went with the feel of the house. The idea of doing this colonial, and a historic one at that, with the theme of Christmas Delight had been a no-brainer. After all, Chris Merriweather even played Santa Claus!

The tea kettle whistled and Sara switched off the burner. Her thoughts apparently running in the same direction as Caprice's, she said, "They moved the Santa cabin into the community park."

"I imagine Chris is looking forward to starting his Santa role after the parade next Sunday."

Children came from the surrounding areas to see Santa or drop off their letters to him. The downtown area would extend store hours between Thanksgiving and Christmas, and the park would be lit up with twinkle lights especially along Santa Lane, the path leading to the cabin-like structure.

"He looks forward to meeting with the children

and reading their letters every year. I'm hoping his Santa duties a few evenings a week and on Saturdays will bring up his energy."

"He's been tired lately?"

"He's been taking shorter walks with Blitz. Ever since his yearly trip to DC with his friends, he's been quieter than usual yet he won't slow down. This time of year business really revs up at the craft shop and Chris always feels as if he has to be on top of everything. Sometimes I think he needs to sell the business and retire. My memory isn't as great as it once was and neither is his. He keeps all the facts and figures in his head for inventory sheets and payroll. I finally convinced him to hire help. Marty enters all the receipts into the computer and can keep records as well as Chris. But, of course, Chris always feels he has to go back and check everything that Marty does."

Merriweather Crafts had been in business for at least the past twenty years. It was a craft shop that had changed with the times and done well. Caprice knew Sara helped out when they were busy, but she spent most of her time teaching scrapbooking and tole painting classes as well as helping to keep the office in order.

"Is Chris at the craft store now?"

"Yes. He's getting ready for a rush on Christmas crafts when we open in the morning."

"Is Blitz with him?" Caprice missed the friendly presence of the Malamute.

"They're together. They're inseparable. And I suppose that's a good thing. We all need a friend who loves us unconditionally. That's what Blitz does for Chris."

After Sara had pulled a beautiful decorative tin from a cupboard and opened it, Caprice chose an orange cinnamon teabag and dipped it into the hot water in her porcelain teacup. Sara chose chamomile tea, and Caprice could see that she was stressed by the whole idea of selling the house. Maybe they should clarify something now.

As Sara sat with her and they let their tea cool a bit, Caprice said, "You're contracted with me to stage the house, and you're listed with Denise Langford to sell." Denise was a luxury real estate broker who handled many of Caprice's clients. "But maybe you should talk to Chris again about this. We can still cancel Saturday's open house and you can back out of the listing."

Sara shook her head. "I hate to say it, but I think the only thing Chris is going to miss about this house is his workshop in the carriage house. There is nothing to talk about."

Except Sara's feelings, Caprice thought ruefully. "Is he going to continue to make hand-crafted toys if you sell?"

"He insists he can rent a space if he wants to continue. He seems to have everything worked out yet I don't understand his thinking at all. Most of all, he doesn't seem happy."

A Vietnam veteran, Chris Merriweather was the jovial Santa-type at Christmas. Other times . . . Oh, he was always pleasant and very kind, but even Caprice had seen shadows in his eyes of the time he had spent in Vietnam that he could probably never forget.

Caprice said, "I have a few finishing touches to make then I'll be out of your hair—at least for now. I'd like to hang a heritage wreath on the spare room door upstairs and add the spruce and pomegranate sachets to the bedrooms."

"That sounds nice. Those crystal compotes you

found in my hutch to display them are perfect for all of the bedrooms. Yes, I want you to go ahead with it. Do you really think this house will sell fast?"

"Oh, I do. It has the square footage and the polish and the charm. If it doesn't sell from the open house, think about how many people will be coming through for the historic house tour. There's no way to know for sure, but I would expect you to have a contract by the New Year."

"This is really happening." Sara sank against the shiny wood of the chair back. At sixty-six, she looked closer to sixty. Her ash blond hair was permed in sort of a pompadour, then trimmed snuggly to fit against her neck and around her ears. Her blue eyes were usually full of excitement and smiles. However, today, even dressed in a beautiful red, two-piece suit with a holly pin on the collar, she looked a bit weary. Maybe Chris wasn't the only one who was tired of working and juggling life.

Suddenly, a loud *bang-bang-bang* on the front door startled them both.

"Are you expecting someone?" Caprice asked. "Someone who doesn't know you have a beautiful sounding doorbell?"

"Not expecting anyone. I'd better answer it before whoever it is breaks the door down."

Caprice could see down the hall to the front door as Sara hurried to open it. When she did, she faced a male who was about six-two with gelled black hair that wasn't exactly a Mohawk but could have been. He was wearing a leather jacket but Caprice spotted tattoos rounding his neck. They were probably down his arms too. Caprice caught a glimpse of the man's face as he shifted from one booted foot to the other.

Sara remained calm, however, in the face of his

scowl. "Can I help you, Boyd?" she asked politely, obviously knowing the younger man.

"You certainly *can* help me. I received a phone call from the chief of police last night. Chief Powalski told me that if my band doesn't find another place to practice at night, we'll all be charged with disorderly conduct. I can't make a living if I can't practice."

Sara suggested, "Can't you practice at another band member's house?"

"No, we can't. I have the equipment and I'm not lugging it all over town. If your husband knows what's good for him, he'll lay off calls to the cops or he'll be sorry."

Whew! Caprice thought. She wouldn't want that guy who was obviously a neighbor coming to her door.

When Sara returned to the kitchen, Caprice asked, "Who was that?"

"His name is Boyd Arkoff and he lives next door. Chris has enough trouble sleeping at night. I don't know if this band has Christmas gigs or what, but they've been practicing nightly right back there in Boyd's garage." She motioned toward the rear of their yard. "We have a wide property with the carriage house and the garage, so you can imagine how loud Boyd's band has to be for us to hear it in winter with the windows shut and furnace running. Chris couldn't take the noise any more and he asked Mack to make the call."

The chief of police, Mack Powalski, had been like a favorite uncle when Caprice and her siblings were growing up. He was a good friend of her dad's and he was a friend of Chris' too. In fact, she remembered that he'd served in Vietnam with Chris. It only made sense that Chris might have asked Mack to do him a favor. Yet this one might have backfired.

"Do you know what Boyd means when he says Chris will be sorry?"

"Oh, just that he'll just turn up the volume and play even more at night. I don't think he has the best attitude. I heard he dropped out of high school, got a GED, and has been playing music trying to become famous ever since. But his band mostly ends up in low-end lounges in Baltimore, DC, Lancaster, York— wherever they can get a gig."

Sara sighed. "I don't know where my manners are," she said dismissing the subject. "I have some of that apple cinnamon loaf you gave me the recipe for. Would you like a slice?"

Caprice wondered if Sara really wanted a snack, or if she wanted to prolong their talk. Caprice checked her watch. She was fine on time.

Sara sliced each of them a piece of the apple cinnamon loaf and they enjoyed that while they talked about the neighbors in the area. When a house cost this much, four to five hundred thousand dollars— and Denise believed that's what it would go for— Caprice liked to be filled in on the neighbors. That was important information to have at the open house when interested parties wanted to know who they'd be living close to.

"If Boyd practices often, that's something we'll have to reveal," Caprice explained to Sara. "You don't want somebody putting a down payment on the house, living here a week, and deciding you didn't disclose something they can't live with."

"I know," Sara responded with a resigned expression. "That's why I hope we can get it worked out. Maybe Chris and Mack can visit Boyd together and help him see reason."

Caprice wasn't sure Boyd was in any mood to see reason.

They were eating their apple loaf and drinking tea, talking about festivities planned in the upcoming weeks for the holidays when a musical noise came from Sara's pocket. She slipped her phone out, took a look at the screen, and then said to Caprice, "I'd better take this. It's my son-in-law."

But instead of staying at the table and having a genial conversation, Sara stood with a frown creasing her brow and walked into the hall. She wasn't gone long, maybe five minutes, but when she returned Caprice could see she was upset.

"Is something wrong?"

"You know I promote a sense of family. I try to never say anything negative about one family member to another. But sometimes . . ." Her voice shook a little.

"Sometimes I imagine you need to vent."

"Yes. I just can't vent to the wrong person."

Caprice waited.

"You could be objective," Sara decided.

"I can try to be."

"You know my daughter Maura."

"I do, though not well. She was older than me so we didn't run into each other in school very much. How is she?"

"She married late in life, and I'll admit Chris and I didn't approve of her choice. Reed Fisk is a car salesman and that's fine. But he's been married twice before. We've tried to be supportive but Reed borrowed money to meet bills that got out of hand. Now Maura is pregnant and Reed is asking us for money again to move to a bigger place. He wants us to help with the down payment. Chris has told him no, but Reed wants me to convince him otherwise. I told him I can't. The whole thing is upsetting, especially this time of year when I want peace and harmony around the table . . . when I just want to enjoy the idea of becoming a grandmother."

Caprice felt for Sara and she certainly understood. Her own family had had its ups and downs. Her uncle had been separated from them for a dozen years, although recently he had reunited with them and that was a good thing. But when daughters-in-laws and sons-in-laws were involved and parents didn't like them, that could be very sticky.

She looked down at her engagement ring. Simply glancing at it made her smile. The diamond was a pink heart-shape with pink sapphires and diamonds alternating in a channel setting along both sides. It was the most beautiful ring she had ever seen and Grant Weatherford, her brother's law partner, had picked it out all on his own.

Sara must have seen her looking at the ring. "When are you and Grant getting married?"

"We're not sure. We're waiting for Grant's annulment from his marriage to come through, but we're thinking spring."

"It's a good thing the Pope refined the rules or you could have been waiting a lot longer. Is the annulment process as complicated as before?"

"The complications arise in uprooting all the emotions and asking his ex-wife to fill out a questionnaire too. Grant's ex is willing. Thank goodness, they have an amicable relationship now or this could be much harder."

"I admire you standing up for what you believe in."

"Grant and I decided together that waiting for the annulment is what we want to do. Our faith is important to us and we want to be married in the church."

"Chris and I were once active at St. Francis of Assisi. But that was before he went into the service. After he came back, he wouldn't even go to church. I kept going. Still, the past few years I've felt it's more important to spend time with him than to sit in a pew and listen to a sermon that's not much help in my daily life."

Caprice empathized that some sermons were helpful and others weren't. But she needed the spiritual connection Mass offered with or without a meaningful homily. She said truthfully, "Grant had been away from the church ever since he lost his daughter. But he's slowly come to realize he still needs faith in his life," Caprice admitted.

"We all need faith, hope, and love, especially this time of year," Sara agreed.